The Last Lullaby

CARIN GERHARDSEN

PENGUIN BOOKS

PENGUIN BOOKS

UK | USA | Canada | Ireland | Australia
India | New Zealand | South Africa

Penguin Books is part of the Penguin Random House group of companies
whose addresses can be found at global.penguinrandomhouse.com.

First published in Sweden as *Vyssan lull* 2010
This translation first published in Great Britain in Penguin Books 2015

001

Text copyright © Carin Gerhardsen, 2010
This translation copyright © Paul Norlén, 2014

The moral right of the author and translator has been asserted

Set in 12.5/14.75 pt Garamond MT Std
Typeset by Jouve (UK), Milton Keynes
Printed in Great Britain by Clays Ltd, St Ives plc

A CIP catalogue record for this book is available from the British Library

ISBN: 978-1-405-91409-3

The Last Lullaby

Carin Gerhardsen was born in 1962 in Katrineholm, Sweden. Originally a mathematician, she enjoyed a successful career as an IT consultant before turning her hand to writing crime fiction. *The Last Lullaby* is the third title in the Hammarby series, novels following Detective Inspector Conny Sjöberg and his murder investigation team. Carin now lives in Stockholm with her husband and their two children.

March 2008, Late Saturday Night

For a moment it sounded like the cawing of a bird, then there was silence. The body was heavy in his arms and in the bathroom mirror he could see how her head fell backwards towards his chest. Leaning back unnaturally, with closed eyes and mouth wide open – she could have fallen asleep like that on the bus. Perhaps the uncomfortable position would make her jerk awake and then she would fall asleep again, wake up, fall asleep, wake up . . . But no, the gaping cut across her throat and the blood pumping more and more slowly out of it bore witness to something else. This woman would never wake up again.

He wiped off the blade of the hunting knife on his jeans and set it on the sink. Then, with minimal exertion, he tossed her up into his arms, his right arm under her knees and the left behind her shoulders and neck. He carried the dainty body through the bathroom door and into the bedroom, where he carefully set her down on the double bed beside the two sleeping children. With quiet, deliberate steps he returned to the bathroom to retrieve his weapon. The girl, lying between her mother and her older brother, was disturbed by the movement in the bed, whimpered and started groping for her mouth with her thumb.

Just as it reached its target he was back with the hunting knife, and without a moment's hesitation he cut the girl's slender throat with a single motion. She did not let out a sound; her big brother's calm breathing was all that could be heard in the room. He himself was hardly breathing at all. He stood quietly for several seconds and watched the blood running out of the little body. Then he quickly made his way around to the other side of the bed and leaned over the soundly sleeping boy, before ending that young life too with a single cut across the throat.

Tuesday Morning

At first sight Detective Inspector Conny Sjöberg thought they looked like they were asleep – the little girl enchantingly sweet with her thumb in her mouth, and the boy close beside her, completely relaxed on his back. But the unnatural position of their heads in relation to the bodies quickly undeceived him. And as his eyes grew used to the darkness he could make out the large quantities of blood that had now dried into the sheets and on the three bodies. The slit throats were actually more than he could take, but Sjöberg forced himself to observe the macabre scene for almost a minute before he turned his eyes away. The boy could be about five, like his own Maja, the girl a year or two younger, perhaps the same age as his twin sons. Jens Sandén came to stand beside him, with his back towards the dead bodies. He spoke quietly, leaning forward a little, with his mouth so close to Sjöberg's ear that he could feel the words against his skin.

'They get to be together anyway.'

'What kind of person could –'

'We have to see it that way,' Sandén interrupted. 'Mother and children got to die together.'

'It must have happened quickly,' Sjöberg mumbled. 'It looks like the children didn't even wake up.'

There was a clatter as Petra Westman managed to get the blind to go up. Grey March light streamed in and the scene was suddenly starkly clear. Sandén glanced towards the bed. Neither of the children was under the covers. Both had pyjamas on; the boy's were red with a black spiderweb on the trousers and a picture of Spider-Man on the chest, the girl's light blue with little teddy bears. The woman was dressed in jeans and a white, close-fitting tunic shirt with a vest underneath. Her feet were bare, with transparent polish on the toenails.

'There's a lot of blood in the bathroom,' said Sandén, gesturing towards the open door. 'And on the floor all the way from there and up to the bed.'

'He killed the woman first,' Sjöberg commented. 'While the children were sleeping in her bed. Then he carried her body here. I see no signs of a struggle. But why did he kill the children too, if they hadn't seen anything?'

'Maybe they *knew* something,' Sandén mused.

'Crime of passion or a relationship drama perhaps. Is there a man in the family?'

'Well, it says "Larsson" on the door . . .'

'And they don't look like their name is Larsson,' Sjöberg filled in.

They turned at the same time towards the bed. The black, glistening hair and, despite the lifelessness, beautifully chiselled Asian features on all three of them suggested they had originally come from somewhere very far away.

'Thailand maybe?' Sandén suggested.

'Maybe so.'

On the bedside table was an open book of English nursery rhymes:

What are little boys made of?
What are little boys made of?
Snips and snails, and puppy dogs' tails,
That's what little boys are made of.

What are little girls made of?
What are little girls made of?
Sugar and spice, and everything nice,
That's what little girls are made of.

'She may have been adopted,' interjected the thirty-year-old detective assistant Jamal Hamad, who was crouched outside the bathroom studying what might be a print from a shoe on the outer edge of a dried pool of blood.

He stood up and looked at his superiors.

'There's a handbag hanging on the coat rack in the hall,' he continued. 'Should I take a careful look and see if we can identify the woman, so Einar has something to work with until Bella is finished?'

Gabriella Hansson and her technicians had not arrived yet, but Sjöberg knew they were on their way. He relied on his instincts and always wanted both himself and his crew to get an impression of the crime scene before the technicians took complete possession of it.

'Do that,' he answered, without further instructions. He had great confidence in Hamad and did not think he needed to explain to him how to behave at a crime scene. 'Where is Einar, by the way?' he asked.

Sandén shrugged.

'Don't know,' Hamad replied, already on his way into the hall.

Sjöberg stepped cautiously out of the bedroom, careful, despite the protective covers over his shoes, not to set his feet in inappropriate places. He made his way through the hall and into the kitchen, where Westman stood with her back turned towards the window, surveying the kitchen.

'What do you see, Petra?'

'Mainly I see children that have come to grief,' she said dejectedly. 'Again.'

He presumed that she was thinking of the little boy she had found in the bushes about six months ago. Sjöberg's own thoughts stopped with a girl in a bathtub.

'I see a lonely woman,' Westman continued. 'A lost woman, short of money.'

'In a luxury flat in Norra Hammarbyhamnen? The apartments here cost millions.'

'Yes, I know; it doesn't add up. But otherwise there is no excess. The fridge and the pantry contain only the bare essentials. Everything here is cheap: clothes, furniture, household utensils, toiletries. Sparsely furnished, you might say. Almost no decorative objects. It doesn't look finished. You see that too, don't you, Conny?'

'Why do you think she was lonely?'

'For just that reason. Because it's so impersonal. She didn't want to be here. She belonged somewhere else.'

When the technicians showed up, with Gabriella Hansson in the lead, Sjöberg had left the apartment at Trålgränd 5 and was down in the courtyard.

'Hi, Bella,' said Sjöberg.

'You look tired.'

She did not stop but simply reduced her speed as she passed the police officers.

'It's children. Blood everywhere,' Sjöberg warned her.

'Accident?'

'Not a chance.'

She speeded up again and hurried purposefully ahead, slightly bent under the weight of the big bags she was carrying, one in each hand. Sjöberg turned and jogged back to the building entrance, and while he held the door open for her he ventured a cautious appeal.

'We need everything we can get that will tell us something about her. ID documents, addresses, bills –'

'Photographs, receipts, correspondence and so on,' Hansson filled in. 'You'll have it on your desk by four.'

The medical examiner Kaj Zetterström and one of his associates also managed to slip in before Sjöberg let go of the door behind them and turned his steps towards the Hammarby canal and the footpath that led to the police building a few blocks away. He was in no hurry to catch up with his colleagues, whose backs he glimpsed through the pouring rain a hundred or so metres ahead of him. He wanted to be alone with his thoughts for a while, at least during the four minutes it took him to reach Östgötagatan 100.

Tuesday Afternoon

A few hours later Conny Sjöberg, Jens Sandén, Petra Westman, Jamal Hamad and the lanky prosecutor Hadar Rosén – dressed as usual in grey suit, white shirt and tie – were at the table in the blue oval room. Also present at the meeting, to Sjöberg's surprise, was the deputy police commissioner, Gunnar Malmberg, who wanted to form an impression of how the work would be organized in this sensational case. Malmberg greeted each of them, attempting to smile while keeping his face as sombre as the circumstances demanded, and Sjöberg noted with relief that even Westman seemed relaxed with him here. He could not recall having seen them in the same room since the unpleasant incident several months earlier, when Malmberg, on Commissioner Roland Brandt's orders, more or less demanded that she resign. This was because of an obscene email that had been sent to Brandt from Westman's account, and which Sjöberg wished he had never seen. But the whole thing was now apparently forgiven and forgotten on both sides, and that was just as well, for there was no room here for any internal controversies.

'Bella's not coming, for understandable reasons,' Sjöberg began. 'But she has delivered some material anyway that we can work with.'

He held up a transparent plastic bag containing various papers, a passport and some postcards.

'She's too damned quick, that woman,' Sandén observed.

'Yes, and we're grateful for that.'

'So where's our friend Mr Eriksson today?' asked Rosén, looking around with a hint of a smile on his lips.

'He seems to be off today,' said Sjöberg. 'Has anyone seen him?'

'Do you think Einar is on holiday?' Sandén grinned. 'Skiing trip to Italy perhaps?'

Hamad let out a quiet laugh. The image of the unapproachable Einar Eriksson, who only reluctantly left his place behind his desk, on a pair of skis was undeniably laughable. Westman smiled at Sandén, but Sjöberg let the comment pass without visible reaction.

'Okay, well, that's too bad,' he said. 'We need him.'

He stood up and went over to the whiteboard, took a pen from the holder and wrote 'Catherine Larsson' at the top, after which he underlined the name.

'Catherine Larsson, formerly Calipayan, thirty-four years old, born in 1973. The children are hers, Tom and Linn Larsson, aged four and two respectively.'

He read from a handwritten slip of paper and while he spoke wrote the information on the board.

'The apartment where they were found is hers. She is Filipino, a Swedish citizen since 2005, has lived in Sweden since 2001, married to a Christer Larsson, born in 1949, who is listed as the father of both children. He is registered at a different address, so they don't seem to live together. She was registered at that address until June of 2006, when she moved to Trålgränd 5.'

'How did she support herself?' asked Rosén.

'She is listed as seeking employment and has been since the children started going to preschool in August 2006. Before she had children she had a short-term job with a cleaning company, which let her go after four months "due to lack of work". Her first child, Tom, was born a few months later, so one might think that had something to do with it.'

'Did she own the apartment?'

Sjöberg nodded.

'It seems to be rather expensive housing for an unemployed Filipino woman,' Rosén pointed out.

'Yes, we'll have to investigate that, but she is . . . was actually still married.'

'I would guess that she cleaned for cash in hand,' Sandén interjected. 'You can earn a lot of money that way. She may have had money before she came here besides, because it's not too hard to guess how she supported herself over there.'

Sjöberg rubbed one eye with his knuckle and let out a slightly dejected sigh.

'Shall we try to proceed a little more objectively,' he attempted, but the amused gleam in his visible eye did not get past Sandén.

'Someone has to say what we are all thinking,' he said, pretending hurt feelings. 'But sure, let's proceed now by all means to laboriously unearth this already known information.'

As he spoke Sjöberg noticed a shadow pass over Sandén's features, his face suddenly turning completely grey. Sjöberg checked himself and tried to make a quick assessment of his colleague's health – a reflex that had developed since a stroke almost took Sandén's life last year. It was hard to tell whether Sandén noticed his concern, but almost instantly his customary grin was back in place.

'You and I will take Christer Larsson,' said Sjöberg as if nothing had happened, pointing directly at his old comrade. 'Petra and Jamal get to knock on doors,' he continued. 'Jens will join in later. I'll go through the contents of this bag and then I guess I'll have to play Einar, until he's back. Any thoughts?'

His gaze wandered between his colleagues at the table.

'I have a feeling she lived alone with the children, without any man in her life,' said Westman.

'I have a feeling she had a man,' said Hamad.

Westman gave him a sullen glance.

'She was married, damn it,' said Sandén.

Sjöberg raised the hand he was the holding the pen with in a deprecatory gesture.

'What do you mean, Petra?'

'You have to assume that the relationship with this Christer Larsson was over, because she had moved out,' she began. 'I saw no signs that any man was usually around. No clothes, nothing in the bathroom, and then, as I said to you, Conny, it was so impersonal somehow; there was no soul in the furnishings. It's just a feeling I have.'

'Two things,' said Hamad. 'First, she actually had a double bed.'

'But she might have had that on account of the children,' Westman said sharply. 'Perhaps she liked having them with her in the bed.'

'Or perhaps *they* liked having *her* with them in the bed,'

Sjöberg interjected, in his mind's eye an image of himself, Åsa and five children of various ages in their own double bed.

'It may also have been for practical reasons,' Westman continued. 'She may have brought it with her in the move. The double bed doesn't tell us anything.'

'Secondly,' Hamad continued unperturbed, 'there was a man's green jumper hanging on the rack in the hall.'

Sjöberg raised one eyebrow.

'One swallow doesn't make a summer,' said Westman. 'Christer Larsson visits them sometimes in all likelihood.'

'The approach,' said Sjöberg. 'What does that say to us? Violent, bloody, brutal. Hatred? Revenge? Passion?'

'He was obviously after the children,' Hamad said. 'Why else would he have attacked them? They appeared to be asleep.'

'We don't know if they were,' said Sjöberg. 'Zetterström will have to confirm it, but I agree that a great deal argues for that scenario. If the woman was murdered in the bathroom, it seems strange that the children would stay nicely in bed waiting their turn.'

'They may have been murdered first,' Hamad continued. 'But it's not likely that he would do it in that order. She was actually in the bathroom. They may have known each other. Whatever, I think it was the children he was after. Just the children or both the mother and the children.'

'Is it a he?' asked Sjöberg.

Everyone around the table nodded.

'This wasn't done with some little pocket knife, not this,' said Sandén. 'It must have been heavy-duty equipment. And the slaughter in the bathroom must have been carried out by a man. Catherine Larsson probably offered some resistance, even though she was not large. A woman would have slashed, I imagine. This is a man's work. Strong. Single-minded. Ice-cold.'

'Agreed,' said Sjöberg. 'But why does someone murder two children? Why don't you air a few more prejudices, Jens, so I don't have to.'

'Because you're the father of the children and tired of the whole mess,' Sandén answered willingly. 'Or because you wish you'd been the father of the children and are tired of the whole mess.'

'Who called the police?' the prosecutor asked.

Sjöberg glanced at the slip of paper he had in his hand.

'One of the neighbours did, a Bertil Schwartz. Catherine Larsson had reserved the laundry room this morning, but she didn't show up. Schwartz rang her doorbell to ask if he could take her time, but no one answered. He wrote her a message, and when he opened the letterbox to put the note through he noticed an unpleasant smell, so he peeked in through the slot and thought he saw blood on the floor. Then he called the police. You'll have to check that the thing about the laundry room tallies.'

The latter was directed at Hamad and Westman. To Sandén he said, 'You'll take the children's preschool too. But first we'll go and see Christer Larsson. Let's start like that, and then meet again here tomorrow at the same time.'

* * *

To spare his back he lay on his side in the semi-darkness. A ray of late-winter light made its way in through the

13

window opening above the dirty heavy-laundry sink. If he looked towards the light, everything else in the room turned black. He preferred to see the objects that surrounded him, so he fixed his gaze on a few cans on a shelf. He looked, but still did not see. In his mind it was *May, a radiant spring day long ago. He stood with his arm around his wife's waist by the living-room window on the third floor and looked down at the neighbours' boys playing in the communal garden. A ventilation window was open and the breeze fanned the white curtain beside them. Was it white, though, or was it perhaps the case that all memories from that day were shrouded in a kind of milky haze?*

They could have sat out on the balcony if it hadn't been for the planting project in progress out there. Both of the chairs and the table were neatly folded up, leaning against the wall, and the concrete floor was covered with newspapers. A sack of soil was half spilled out on the layer of newspaper, and around it stood a dozen pots in piles and a couple of cartons of plants. The aroma of earth from the balcony was mixed with the odour of freshly cut grass from down in the garden.

It was Saturday and a few older children had occupied all the swings, so the two little boys had to be content with the sandpit for the time being. They each dug absent-mindedly with a little shovel in the dry sand and cast furtive glances towards the swings. But they did not dare approach the bigger children, even though their mother was sitting right next to them on a bench, browsing through a magazine.

'Would you like to have a couple of those?' he said, letting his hand wander up her spine until it reached the soft hairs on the back of her neck.

'No, I want a couple of these,' she answered, turning towards him and pinching him on the cheek. 'Although smaller,' she added with a laugh.

He put his arms around her and pressed her against him. They stood that way for a while without saying anything. His gaze stopped once again at the two little boys in the sandpit, so he noticed when both of them suddenly stood up and ran off towards something outside his field of vision. After a few seconds they came back, dragging their father by each hand. The mother stood up and said something to him. She rolled up her magazine and started walking away from them. The last he saw of her was when she called something to the boys. He saw her calling something every day, unsentimental, over her shoulder before she disappeared from them, and they from her. He thought – not now, but later – that she didn't hug them, that she didn't kiss their rosy cheeks before she left, that she didn't stroke their hair and tell them how much she loved them. Then he thought, of course, it's almost ten o'clock, she has to go to her job at the beauty salon.

'Your stomach is growling,' his wife said, releasing herself from his arms. 'Come on, let's make breakfast.'

She fried eggs and bacon while he set the kitchen table. Through the window he saw the older children finally leave the swings, and the little boys' lightning-quick rush to take them over. Another man had joined their father on the bench, and they were conversing, their body language showing that they already knew each other.

When they'd finished their breakfast they let the dishes be and crept back into bed for a while. It was twelve-thirty before they got dressed, cleaned up in the kitchen and put on the gardening gloves to resume the planting project on the balcony.

Then the doorbell rang.

* * *

Without speaking much, they walked side by side back towards Trålgränd, to question the neighbours. Hamad made a few awkward attempts at conversation, but Petra was not in the mood to play-act, to behave as if nothing had happened. He did not exist for her, not as a person. As a police officer, yes. Sjöberg persisted in constantly pairing them up, putting them on the same assignment, and Petra was professional. She would never let her emotions carry over into her job. But it could never be like before. It was not possible to just whitewash over what he had done to her. And to the other women on the video recordings from Peder Fryhk's basement.

It was as good as proven that it was Hamad who had been holding the camera. He was the one who convinced her to go along to Clarion's bar and sent her right into the arms of the rapist Fryhk. And it was Hamad who had taken her pass card, lured her to the Pelican where he poured a lot of beer into her, then made his way into the police station with her card and sent an erotic email to the police commissioner. From her email address and her computer, whose password only she and the rapist could have known. And the image that was sent to Roland Brandt she had also found on Hamad's own computer.

And if that weren't enough evidence, at any time she could get her suspicions confirmed in black and white. Håkan Carlberg at the national forensics lab in Linköping had both fingerprints and DNA from the Other Man, as she had called him before he got a name. The Other Man – the one holding the camera when Peder Fryhk raped drugged, unconscious women, the one who also raped but never let himself be filmed, never left any memories with the victims.

But she hadn't. She had not sent Hamad's fingerprints

to Linköping. Because it wasn't necessary; she already knew. And because it felt too late to bring it to court, she had decided once and for all not to report the crime. And perhaps it was also the case that there was a kind of security in the situation as it was right now. Because how would she react if the forensic evidence definitively established that it was Jamal Hamad, her close friend and confidant, who was the Other Man? Or even worse: if after all this time it turned out that he was innocent. Either way, her world – which she had worked so hard to rebuild after these events – would come crashing down . . . No, she could not handle these questions.

So Petra kept Hamad at arm's length, tried to behave neutrally and matter-of-factly towards him and gave him no opportunities to feel triumphant or injure her. Because that was what he was after; Sjöberg had confirmed that when she had revealed some of the details of the rape to him. Power and revenge – that was what was motivating the Other Man. Power because that was what rape was really about, and revenge because she had seen to it that Peder Fryhk was behind bars. Sending the porno image to Brandt was an attempt – which had been a hair's breadth from succeeding – to get her fired. Revenge. Power.

He had been ingenious, that Hamad. Before, when he had the chance, he had made sure to always be around her. A rock in her existence. He had gladly touched her, put his arm around her, looked her deep in the eyes, interested her. But never more than that. No passes, no violations. And she would not have needed any pressing. He was smart, good-looking, warm and charming – what more could you ask for? He was recently separated besides. But the whole time he had been interested in only one thing: doing whatever he wanted with her, against her will. That was all it was about; she had been only a plaything for him, a wet dream.

But exult? He would not get to do that. She had never shown herself weak to him. She had recovered quickly, got back on her feet almost immediately. Her interest in men had been rather non-existent since the rape, almost a year and a half ago, but now she was back on track there too. How on earth had that happened? She smiled at the absurdity of the situation. There would never be anything, never *could* be anything more, but it had been nice. Good for her self-confidence. A one-night stand with a mature man in his prime. A family man. It had never been her intention when they met a week or so earlier, while she was out partying with some friends. At first she had been properly unapproachable, but he had driven such a well-placed wedge in her armour, had had such interesting things to say that at last she let herself be talked into a cup of tea at her place. And one thing led to another. But she did not regret a thing, was completely sensible about the situation and had no hopes for the future – on the contrary. And the same seemed to apply to him. They had spoken in passing a couple of times, in a mature way and without denying anything. Like proper grown-ups.

Once on Trålgränd Petra and Hamad called on Bertil Schwartz, a single man in his sixties who knew nothing about the dead woman and her children. He claimed never to have even noticed them, and Hamad and Westman found nothing about him that gave them reason to suspect otherwise. The list in the laundry room confirmed for them that Catherine Larsson really had reserved a morning slot on Tuesday.

Her nearest neighbours – the ones on her floor – did not have much to add either. Neither of them had a close relationship with the Larsson family, but everyone in the building was in agreement that they were quiet, that the children were sweet and that their mother was always friendly.

It had been noticed that a man of Swedish appearance figured in her life, but no one knew whether it was Mr Larsson or somebody else. The man was taciturn, although he greeted those he met on the stairwell. Possibly he stayed the night there sometimes, though there was no one who knew for sure how things stood with that. He was much older, which perhaps argued against them being lovers, but on the other hand it was quite impossible that he was her father. Occasionally this man had been seen going out or coming home with the two children.

Catherine Larsson was also visited from time to time by a woman her own age, also of Asian appearance. None of the neighbours had ever noticed either quarrels or loud voices from the Larsson family's apartment. At the time of the murder, which had now been established by forensic investigation to have occurred at some time between Saturday evening and Sunday morning, no one in the building had noticed anything unusual, or noted either that Catherine Larsson had a visitor.

In the neighbouring building, where Bertil Schwartz also lived, the two detectives questioned a young woman aged about twenty-five, Elin Lange. She was rather small, with short blonde hair, and looked energetic and athletic in tight jeans and a T-shirt in the Brazilian colours. It turned out that Elin had run into Catherine Larsson once in the laundry room. Because she had recently been travelling in Asia, Elin had asked Catherine out of pure curiosity about her origins and found that she had grown up on an island in the Philippines that Elin herself had visited during her trip, Negros. Negros was, according to Elin Lange, a very poor part of the Philippines, so it seemed natural to her that Catherine had gone to work in the tourist industry on another island, Mindoro. There, by and by, she had met a Swedish man with whom she fell in love and followed him to Sweden, where they got married and had children. Catherine had revealed to Elin that the couple had separated, but told her that the children were rooted in Sweden and that she herself was also happy among the friendly Swedes. But deep down, Elin thought, she probably would have wanted to move home again, if it hadn't been for the children.

'The tourist industry . . . ?' said Westman.

Elin Lange looked at her from under her fringe before hesitantly giving expression to her thoughts.

'Well, that is . . . We didn't go into any details, it was just nice to talk to her. Filipinos are an amazingly gracious people and you can't help loving them. But, yeah . . . If you've visited the tourist district on Mindoro, then perhaps hotel receptionist is not the first thing you think of . . . But it's not everyone who . . . And you shouldn't be prejudiced . . . Uh, I really have no idea.'

Westman nodded thoughtfully.

'Anything else you were thinking about? You are actually the only person we've talked to so far who has exchanged so much as a word with Catherine Larsson, besides hello.'

'She was really nice,' Elin Lange replied. 'As they always are. But she was homesick and I can understand that. Cold and miserable and isolated . . . The only thing this country has to offer if love ends is our social security system.'

After a few seconds of silence she added, 'How could anyone take the lives of two small children?'

'If you think of anything you've forgotten to tell us, we'd like you to call us,' said Hamad, handing her his card.

'Sure, I'll do that,' she said, giving the card a quick glance and putting it in the back pocket of her jeans.

'Don't forget that next time you're in the laundry room.' Hamad winked at her, and she laughed in gratitude because he had lightened up the depressed atmosphere.

Westman smiled guardedly.

* * *

Christer Larsson was almost sixty, but even with his greying hair he looked considerably younger. He was tall and rangy, well built with rough hands, and had a slightly absent look in his brown, sorrowful eyes.

Showing no surprise, he invited them into his apartment, which was located on the fifth floor of a high-rise in Fredhäll. Despite the small scale of the little studio it was neat and tidy and smelled clean. On the windowsill were a couple of flowerpots with thriving plants and there were some framed photographs and posters hanging on the walls. Along one wall stood a relatively large bookcase, full of books and nothing else. As they passed the kitchen on their way in, Sjöberg noted that it was also clean with things put neatly away.

The two police officers sat down on the couch, which Sjöberg figured out also served as a bed at night. Larsson sat down in an armchair, leaning forward with his legs spread, his big hands hanging between his knees. His gaze was directed down at the rug.

'You are married to Catherine Larsson?' Sjöberg began.

'Yes,' Christer Larsson answered, without raising his eyes.

'But you no longer live together?'

'No, she moved out.'

He spoke very slowly and Sjöberg suspected that he was under the influence.

'Are you sober?' he asked.

Christer Larsson did not look surprised now either, but gave them a searching look.

'Yes,' he said simply.

'Do you take any medication?'

'No, I don't,' he replied drily. 'Was there something you wanted to know?'

'But you still see Catherine?' Sjöberg continued on his original track.

'No, not really. She's been here a few times with the kids.'

'A few times? When most recently?'

'Twice, I think. About a year since the last time.'

'You are the father of the children, aren't you?'

'Mmm.'

'So haven't you visited them?'

'No, I haven't.'

'But you know where they live?'

'I'm sure I've got the address, but I don't know where I put it.'

Sandén, who was not known for his patience, felt some frustration at the slow pace of the conversation and interrupted.

'So you weren't there, for example, on Saturday evening?'

'No, I've never visited Catherine and the kids at home.'

Larsson met Sandén's gaze with a hint of defiance in his tired eyes. Sjöberg made a calming gesture at Sandén with his hand and took a deep breath before he started speaking again.

'We're sorry to have to tell you, Christer, that Catherine and the children . . . are deceased.'

A doubtful smile swept across Larsson's face.

'Are you pulling my leg?'

'Unfortunately no,' Sjöberg answered seriously. 'They were found dead in their apartment this morning.'

'Accident?'

Sjöberg shook his head.

'No, we suspect they were murdered.'

'But by who?'

Christer Larsson's tone of voice was unchanged, but his gaze looked somewhat sharper now.

'We don't know. We thought perhaps you could help us.'

'You think of course that it was me?'

'We would like to rule that out, but we need your help. What were you doing between, let's say, six o'clock on Saturday evening and six o'clock on Sunday morning?'

'I wasn't doing anything that anyone can confirm. I was at home and ate and watched TV and slept. I did go down to buy something for dinner, but that's probably not something anyone will remember.'

'Where did you do that?'

'At ICA down on Stagneliusvägen.'

'Did you pay with a credit card?'

'Yes, I'm sure I did.'

'Good, then we can verify that at least.'

'Do you have anything against me taking a look in your bathroom?' Sandén interjected.

Larsson shook his head.

'And rooting in your laundry a little?'

'Do what you have to,' Christer Larsson answered, without looking up.

Sandén got up from the sofa bed, went over to the little hall and disappeared through the bathroom door.

'Can you tell me a little about your relationship with Catherine?' asked Sjöberg. 'How you met, why it ended, how it happens that you no longer see each other, your relationship with the children, and so on.'

After a heavy sigh and a moment of silence, Christer Larsson started his story. Sjöberg decided to let it take the time it took, without interrupting or pressing.

'Someone at work had been to the Philippines and came back really positive about it. I wasn't that interested then, I had never been on any long trips, but a few years later I got the idea that I should pull myself together and do something different, so I decided to go there. And I did: bought a guidebook and just went there. Travelled around to a few different places and on Mindoro I met

Catherine. I hadn't been with a woman for ages and I guess I wasn't particularly interested then either, but she was rather forward, you might say, and it was like she didn't give up. I didn't get what she wanted with an old bore like me, but she was persistent. And gradually I took a liking to her too. She brought life back to the old man. It's a bit like being born again.'

He looked a little shamefacedly at Sjöberg, but there was also a glimpse of something reminiscent of happiness in his eyes.

'We travelled around for several months and we were actually really in love. She put me in a good mood. Then I brought her home to Sweden, she moved in with me here and we got married. Then the children came. Fine kids. Nice, easy to deal with, no shrieking and quarrelling. Catherine was good with them, a good mother. But it was like I ran out of steam after a while. There was really no reason for it, but I'm just that way. I became more and more my old self again and I guess Catherine wasn't able to put life into me any more, so finally she got tired of it. There was no arguing or anything, but one day she and the kids moved out and it was probably only right. She has to live, even if I am the way I am.'

They sat quietly for a while, listening to the sound of Sandén's rooting around in the bathroom. Sjöberg wondered if and when the news would sink in. Something was wrong with the guy. Whether he was depressed or lacked empathy in general Sjöberg could not judge. What was that called? Autistic characteristics? Could it be connected with violently flaring aggression?

'How did they die?' Christer Larsson asked calmly.

Sjöberg tried to meet his gaze, but once again it was aimed down at the rug between his feet.

'Their throats were cut,' Sjöberg answered factually.

No reaction now either.

'The children too?'

'The children too.'

Christer Larsson still did not raise his eyes. Sandén came out of the bathroom shaking his head.

'Are you the one who bought the apartment for Catherine?' Sjöberg asked.

'I don't have any money.'

'So what do you live on yourself?'

'I'm retired.'

'On what grounds?'

'Depression.'

'Since . . . ?'

'For many years.'

'But you don't take any medication?'

Christer Larsson shook his head.

'Didn't think it helped,' he replied.

'Do you pay any child support?'

'That's never come up for discussion.'

'No, really?'

'No, I don't pay any support.'

'And Catherine, what kind of work did she do?'

'I don't know. She was unemployed since she had to leave that cleaning company.'

'I can tell you,' said Sjöberg in a rather sharper tone of voice now, 'that the apartment on Söder that she is listed as the owner of and where she and the children lived cost an awful lot of money, more than two million. How do you think she came across such a sum?'

Christer Larsson did not answer.

'Either,' Sjöberg continued, 'she earned a lot of money somehow or someone else paid for that apartment. Do you have any comments about that?'

Larsson shook his head. Sandén felt a tougher edge was needed.

'She may have won the lottery, she may have robbed a bank, she may have been a prostitute or she may have met a rich man who took care of her. She seemed to have had frequent visits from a man your age; could it have been you? Or do you think it was her pimp?'

Sjöberg glared at Sandén, but had to admit to himself that he was curious about the response. Larsson defiantly met Sandén's gaze.

'She was not a prostitute,' he said in the same drawling way as before, but with a more acid tone. 'She didn't rob banks. But sure, she may have met a man. I haven't talked to her for ages.'

'Perhaps you got jealous and took matters into your own hands?' Sandén continued, but Larsson sat quietly.

'Did she have any circle of friends that you know of?' Sjöberg tried the friendly angle again and Larsson seemed to respond to it because he answered in his normal, flat voice.

'She had a girlfriend who was also from the Philippines. Vida is her name; they were co-workers.'

'At the cleaning company?'

'Yes, and afterwards too.'

'Cash-in-hand jobs?' asked Sjöberg.

Larsson nodded lamely.

'You didn't say anything about that when I asked a while ago.'

'You're the police, damn it. I'm saying it now.'

Sandén reluctantly swallowed a snide comment and asked instead, 'Who did she clean for? How did she get customers?'

'As I understood it she cleaned for individuals that she met at the companies where she cleaned as an employee.'

'How much did she bring in for that?' Sandén continued relentlessly.

'Seventy kronor an hour, I reckon. It might be a couple of thousand a week.'

'Cash in hand!' Sandén exclaimed. 'That's what nurses earn, for Christ's sake.'

'In any event, it's not enough for an apartment in Norra Hammarbyhamnen,' Christer Larsson pointed out.

Sjöberg and Sandén exchanged glances.

'Do you own any weapons?' asked Sjöberg.

'No,' Larsson answered quickly.

'Do you have any objection to us looking around a little?'

'You've already done that,' Larsson replied, clenching his hands and hitting his knuckles against each other.

'We would like to do it a little more thoroughly,' Sjöberg answered in his friendliest voice.

Do you mean a house search?'

'No, but it can be if you don't cooperate,' said Sjöberg threateningly, hoping to frighten Christer Larsson into submission.

'Do as you wish,' said Larsson dejectedly. 'I'll sit here.'

'May I ask for the key to the cellar storage room?' said Sandén with a crooked smile, reaching out his hand.

Forty-five minutes later they left the peculiar man without having found anything that shed the slightest light on the case. Sjöberg did have his fingerprints, however, in an envelope in his inside pocket.

'That was one really shady character,' said Sandén as they got in the car.

'Well, he's obviously depressed,' said Sjöberg doubtfully. 'It seems to add up, don't you think?'

Sandén turned the key in the ignition and cast a glance over his shoulder before he backed out of the parking spot.

'He wasn't exactly in floods of tears when he found out that his wife and children had been murdered.'

'Depression can be a kind of emotional paralysis. If he'd had strong feelings for them, he probably wouldn't have let them disappear from his life,' Sjöberg thought out loud.

Sandén turned the steering wheel and drove slowly ahead, out on to the street.

'Maybe that was just what he didn't do. He did away with them instead. In a classic manner. He was lying to us. What reason would he have for that if he doesn't have anything to hide? Why didn't you call him to account for that, by the way?'

'You mean he knew where they lived? That was not exactly a direct lie,' Sjöberg replied. 'We can chew on that a little.'

'He is big and strong and could easily have carried out the murders,' Sandén observed. 'Didn't need to force his way into the apartment; he was certainly let in with no problem. And he has had plenty of time to do laundry. There was a washing machine in the bathroom, the laundry basket was almost empty and there was nothing in the bin either.'

Sjöberg glanced towards the DN skyscraper. It looked naked and gloomy in the cold grey March light.

'I can't get over how slow that guy talked! I was about to explode.' Sandén grinned, shaking his head.

'Yes, I noticed that,' Sjöberg muttered. 'It's a good thing we're not both as impatient as you. No tablets in the bathroom cabinet?'

'No tablets in the bathroom cabinet,' Sandén confirmed. 'He's probably like that without any help.'

'Speaking of medicines, how are you feeling yourself?'

Sandén hesitated a moment before he answered. He preferred to avoid the subject, Sjöberg knew that, but it could not be helped. It was only six months since his colleague had had a stroke and collapsed during a witness interview. An ambulance had been called promptly, which had saved his life. He had been rushed in for treatment, was on sick leave for a couple of months and came back to work part-time. The stroke had limited the mobility of the left side of his body, but with a single-mindedness that Sjöberg had hardly believed Sandén capable of, he had worked his way back, and was now physically almost completely recovered. He would, however, have to live with the threat of another, more serious stroke hanging over him. But every cloud has a silver lining: Sandén had changed his eating habits and must have lost twenty kilograms.

'Good,' he answered. 'It's okay. I take my warfarin, otherwise everything is as usual. No stress.'

'Any plans to go up to full-time again?'

'Damn it, I'm already working full-time,' Sandén replied with a crooked smile.

'Yes, but then see that you get paid for it too.'

It was starting to snow. Big heavy flakes floated down from the sky, but before they reached the police station on Östgötagatan the snowfall had turned into rain. Catherine Larsson would not have liked that, thought Sjöberg.

* * *

When Sjöberg got back to his office at the police station a box was sitting on his desk. Bella Hansson had, not unexpectedly, kept her word and sent over Catherine Larsson's life in words and pictures, neatly packaged in what resembled a shoebox. The little plastic bag he had got earlier was next to it. He closed the door and sat down.

He started with the photographs and soon determined that Catherine Larsson did not seem to own a camera. The pictures she had were all either taken by family in the Philippines or by Swedish professional photographers. He sat for a while with a group of portrait photos of the children at various ages in front of him, presumably from preschool.

With a sigh he set them aside and took out a photograph of the whole family and a few from the wedding day, those too taken by a professional. He devoted a few minutes to thoughtfully studying the loving couple. Christer Larsson's greying hair was well combed, he was tanned and looking into the camera with a vague smile. He was wearing a dark suit with a red rose in the buttonhole. Catherine, in a simple white dress, looked up in semi-profile at her new husband. He was more than a head taller than her and his big right hand enclosed her entire bare shoulder.

Was he a murderer? He didn't look like one here, but how much had happened since the picture was taken? People change, circumstances change. Christer Larsson had reverted to his old self again, whatever that might mean.

And what was it that had happened with Sjöberg himself? He had jeopardized his and his family's future. He had put his relationship with his life's great love, his best friend, his life companion, his beloved Åsa, at risk for the sake of an unknown woman. A woman who had come out of nowhere, who could not reasonably mean anything to him.

Margit Olofsson was the woman in his dreams, but not in any way his dream woman. It was not often he allowed himself to think this thought through, but now it was there and he could not stop it. What was he playing at? He summoned all his mental powers to convince himself that this story had to end. Now. Or the next time they met. He and Margit did not meet often, but when he felt shaken it was her embrace he sought. Why, he did not know. Åsa had always been a good comforter, but since that dream started coming to him he had changed. He had become a different person. He had become a scared, desperate, treacherous little piece of shit.

In the dream he is always standing on a lawn wet with dew, looking down at his bare feet. He does not dare look up although he knows he should. His head feels so heavy that he can hardly lift it. He gathers all his courage and all his strength to turn his face upwards, and then he sees her. The beautiful woman with the dazzling red hair like a sun around her head. She takes a few dance steps and her gaze meets his with a surprised expression. He reaches up his arms towards her but loses his balance and falls suddenly backwards. The woman is Margit, had become Margit since he met her for the first time during a serial murder investigation over a year ago. Rationally he knew he had to end it, but she had such unfathomably great significance for him. She awakened something in him; what, he did not know. Something new? Something old?

With a shiver he shook off the unpleasant thoughts and continued browsing through the photographs. He cleared his throat, cleared away the feeling of shame about his own behaviour. The throat-clearing somehow made him a grown man again and he straightened up as if to further confirm his authority.

A strip from a photo booth aroused his interest. It was Catherine and another Asian woman in four colour pictures. In the first two they just looked pleasant and happy, in the third they were pulling funny faces and in the fourth they were no longer sitting down but instead appeared to be dancing around in the booth with their arms in the air and new grimaces on their faces. So this is Vida, thought Conny Sjöberg. We have to find her.

He guessed that the rest of the photographs depicted friends and relatives from Catherine Larsson's homeland. She herself did not figure in any; presumably they had been sent to her since she moved to Sweden. There were no pictures from her life with Christer Larsson. The letters and postcards she had all came from the Philippines and were written in a language unknown to him. He would see about having them translated.

Sjöberg quickly went through the contents of the box and placed everything that had to do with Catherine Larsson's finances in a separate pile: receipts, bills, account information and tax documents. As he set to work on them he still had not found even a hint of a lead in any direction whatsoever.

Needing to stretch his legs, he got up and went out into the corridor. He glanced into Einar Eriksson's office. Still unoccupied. Sjöberg swore quietly at the thought of now having to run the type of enquiries himself that normally would be Eriksson's job: telephone calls to the authorities, searches in computer registers, and other things that Sjöberg was not skilled at.

A few hours later, despite his reluctance, he had managed to discern a structure in Catherine Larsson's financial activities. Her apartment had been paid for, by her, on the first of June 2006, when a sum of 2,115,000 kronor had been transferred from her account with SEB to the seller's. This was after a down payment of 235,000 had changed hands in the same way a few weeks earlier. The money had been deposited in her account in cash, by Catherine herself, 20,000 kronor at a time over a six-month period, at various Stockholm branches. In addition, since she had taken possession of the apartment, at the end of every month 5,000 kronor had been deposited into her account. By ringing round the various bank branches, Sjöberg managed to speak to a couple of employees who thought they remembered a few of those transactions, and they were in agreement that it really was Catherine who had made the deposits. The question was: where had this money actually came from?

In other respects too she managed her financial affairs on her own. Besides the 5,000 kronor, child benefit was also deposited into her account every month. She had not received any benefits beyond these payments. She paid her own bills on time, once a month. The money in the account covered almost exactly the fixed expenses she had. Day-to-day expenses she seemed to have paid for with her current earnings.

With the help of a colleague in the financial intelligence unit, Sjöberg also investigated Christer Larsson's finances, and found nothing to suggest that Catherine's money could have come from him. He too had an account with SEB, and he could have made transfers from his own account to hers without attracting attention, if he had wanted to. Which obviously he had not, because there was no trace of any such support to be seen.

Had there been a mysterious benefactor in Catherine Larsson's life, and if so, who could it be? Someone who loved her? Someone who exploited her somehow but still paid his way? Someone who was in debt to her? Or was it really her own money – no doubt dubiously earned, but still hers?

Sjöberg reached for the phone and, absurdly enough, called Information to be connected to Telia, the phone company. After a number of wrong turns he ended up talking to the right department, and after many ifs and buts managed to obtain a list of incoming and outgoing calls on Catherine Larsson's line during the past six months. He would have it by fax twenty minutes later.

Then he clipped off the top picture from the photo-booth strip, pasted it on to a piece of white paper and with a ballpoint pen drew a circle around the unknown woman. Then he wrote in legible handwriting under the picture: 'Does anyone know who this woman is? The Hammarby Police need to contact her in connection with a murder investigation as soon as possible. Please call the number below . . .' Then he put on his jacket and rushed along the corridor and down the stairs with the paper fluttering in his hand.

Fifteen minutes later he was on Skånegatan, at the Catholic ministry for Spanish-speakers, pinning up his homemade search enquiry on the notice board. A short, middle-aged, South American-looking man appeared beside him.

'Hi, my name is Conny Sjöberg, Hammarby Police,' Sjöberg said, extending his hand.

'Hi. Joseph,' said the man, responding to the greeting with a smile.

Sjöberg ran his hand through his hair, wet from the rain, to push a strand back into place.

'We're investigating a murder,' he explained. 'Or to be more precise, three murders. This woman and her two children were found dead in their home this morning.' He pointed at Catherine Larsson's happy face and continued. 'She did not seem to have a large circle of friends, but this may be her best girlfriend. They both came originally from the Philippines. Do you have many parishioners from there?'

'Yes,' Joseph replied with a heavy accent, while he studied Sjöberg's notice. 'Many Filipinos come here, although most of them don't know a word of Spanish. The Philippines is of course an old Spanish colony.'

'You don't recognize either of the women?' Sjöberg attempted.

'No, not immediately. A whole family murdered? That's a dreadful story. How old were the children?'

'Two and four.'

'How will the funeral be arranged?'

'To be honest, I don't know,' Sjöberg answered. 'We'll have to speak to the woman's family about that.'

'Well, if you need our services, you're very welcome. I'll ask around, see if any of our parishioners recognize these women.'

'I would be very grateful for that,' said Sjöberg. 'It's really important that we get hold of her friend here.'

He pointed at the circled smiling face on the photograph.

'Her name is Vida apparently,' he added.

'Vida? Then I'm sure we'll find her,' the little man said cryptically.

*

37

Forty-five minutes after his call to Telia Sjöberg was back at his desk and the fax had still not arrived. By phone he muddled his way back to the man he had spoken to before and ten minutes later he had the list in his hand. He wondered to himself how long it would have taken if he hadn't called and exerted pressure. This is what it's like for Einar all the time, he thought. It's Telia's fault that Einar's always so damned grumpy.

He sat down at the desk and scanned through the list of telephone calls. It was not long. He imagined what the Sjöberg family's list would look like: two adults and five children constantly gabbing into that receiver. Well, you could blame a lot on his twin sons, Christoffer and Jonathan, who were almost three, but not the high telephone bills.

From the employee at Telia he found out that Catherine Larsson did not have a mobile phone account with them. No mobile had been found in the apartment either, but Sjöberg made a note to ask the other providers too. It took him over an hour to make a list of all subscribers who had called or been called by Catherine Larsson. None of them was named Vida. He printed out the list on the laser printer, attached a yellow Post-it note with the text 'Check what relationship these people have to Catherine Larsson' to it and set it on Einar Eriksson's desk.

*   *   *

Only a small number of children were left at the preschool when Sandén made his entry. The teacher, a charming woman in her sixties, appeared to belong in a very different workplace. She was dressed in a pair of tight jeans and a patterned blouse that looked expensive, with an elegant scarf around her neck. She was heavily made up and draped with baubles – rings, necklace, bracelets and earrings – but Sandén was not the right person to determine whether the jewels were genuine or not. She had a cheerful, warm voice that reached Sandén even out in the cloakroom, and he recognized the story she was reading. It was the one about the little rabbit Spotty. He had read it many times to his own children when they were small. She was sitting on a heap of soft pillows on the floor and had a child on each knee. A third child lay with a thumb in her mouth right alongside. As he stepped into the room, the teacher broke off and looked up at him with a surprised smile.

'Jens Sandén, police detective,' he said, suddenly realizing that he had barged into the children's cosy corner in his wet winter shoes. 'I need to speak to you, but finish reading the story, while I take off my shoes.'

She had a worried look on her face and followed him with her eyes as he left the room.

'I'll clean up after myself,' Sandén called from the cloakroom before she had managed to resume the storytelling.

He put his shoes inside the front door, searched for the staff toilet and tore off a long piece of toilet paper from the roll. Then he carefully wiped up his wet footprints, flushed the paper away and tiptoed in his stockinged feet back to the children and their teacher.

'So, we'll read the rest tomorrow!' the teacher said, closing the book with a bang that suggested the continuation of the story would be unbearably exciting. 'I have to talk to the nice policeman who has come to visit us. Can you help me pick up the pens on the table? Then we can divide up the last banana.'

The children obediently did as she said, which Sandén presumed they would not have done if it had been their parents who asked them.

He did not feel like an especially nice policeman, with the business he had. Only now did it occur to him that he was not just there to snoop for information, but that he actually had been sent to break the awful news of the deaths of the two children, to one of the people who perhaps had been closest to them.

'Margareta Norlander,' she said, extending a hand in greeting, while with the other she ushered him out of the room. 'We'll go a little further away, so we can talk undisturbed. What's this about?'

He followed her through the cloakroom and into the kitchen without answering her question.

'Let's sit down,' said Sandén, gesturing towards some chairs around a table.

Obviously worried, she watched his face as she sat down across from him, her fingers laced in front of her mouth.

'I don't think I want to be part of this,' she said anxiously.

'Well, this has nothing to do with you personally.' Sandén tried to calm her. 'This is work-related.' He could hear how bureaucratic he sounded, but continued seriously, 'Tom and Linn Larsson – is it correct that they come to the preschool here?'

'Yes, but they've been absent this week and we haven't heard anything.'

She put her hands to her cheeks and her eyes filled with tears before he had even started.

'Kate is always so careful . . .'

'Is it Catherine you call Kate?'

She nodded in response.

'All three of them were found dead this morning,' said Sandén in as neutral a voice as he could muster. 'We found them at home in bed, beside each other. They died together and the children do not seem to have been aware of what happened.'

'And what was it that happened?'

Margareta Norlander could not keep from crying; the tears ran in torrential streams down her cheeks and her voice broke.

'This is terribly difficult for me too,' Sandén excused himself. He was also having a hard time holding the tears back. He took her hands in his and continued, 'They were murdered. Someone cut their throats.'

'Did you see them?' she wanted to know between sobs.

'Yes,' answered Sandén. 'But I promise you that the children did not feel anything, the whole scene looked quite peaceful. And at least they were all together.'

'And poor Kate?'

'The crime scene investigation is not yet finished, but unfortunately most signs indicate that she was conscious when it happened. But in all likelihood she didn't see her children die.'

Sandén sat quietly for a while and let Margareta Norlander take in what he had said. She pulled her hands out of his and reached across the table towards a roll of paper towel. He anticipated her and tore off a piece which he handed over.

'How in the world will I be able to explain this to the children?' she asked while she dried her cheeks.

The front door banged outside and she made a half-hearted effort to get up from her chair. Sandén stopped her with a gesture, stood up and asked, 'Is that a parent coming now?'

She nodded.

'I'll go,' he said. 'Stay here. I'll ask them to mind the children for a short while. I need to talk to you a little more.'

He left the kitchen and went out into the cloakroom, where the three remaining children had come out to meet a rain-soaked mother. He pulled out his police ID from the inside pocket of his jacket and showed it to the mother, who already had her own child in her arms.

'I'm afraid I've come with bad news, so I would like to ask you to stay here for a while and take care of the children who are left. Margareta and I are sitting out in the kitchen talking, and it would be nice if we could be undisturbed. What's your name?'

'My name is Anna,' she answered with a serious expression. 'Anna Åkesson. I'm the mother of Isa here.'

'Good, Anna,' Sandén said authoritatively, putting his ID back in his pocket. 'Then that's what we'll do for the time being. Margareta will be in touch later. Okay?'

'Okay,' she said, puzzled, but asked no questions.

Sandén went back into the kitchen where Margareta Norlander was still sitting exactly as he had left her. She was still crying and staring listlessly at the refrigerator door. He sat down again in the chair across from her.

'And Erik?' she asked quietly.

'Erik?' Sandén asked in turn. 'Who is that?'

'He helps her with pick-up and drop-off sometimes.'

'I must ask you to tell me what you know about Erik,' said Sandén. 'Do you know what his last name is?'

'No, I've never asked. He's about my age. We never really understood what kind of relationship he and Kate had. They may of course have been a couple and perhaps that's most likely, but they never showed any physical intimacy in front of us in any event. He must be at least twenty years older than her . . . He was amazingly good with the children and they were crazy about him. But he isn't their father, as far as I know.'

'Have you met the father?'

'No, he's never appeared. Kate said they were divorced.'

'Separated anyway,' Sandén interjected.

'Yes, it's possible that's how it was. Have you told him . . . ?'

'Yes, but according to him he no longer saw either Catherine or the children. He must not have known about this Erik. We are extremely interested in getting in touch with him.'

The front door closed again and then several adult voices were heard outside.

'Perhaps we have his telephone number in the office,' said Margareta Norlander. 'The parents have to provide phone numbers for someone who can step in if anything happens and they themselves can't be reached. But I don't want –'

She gestured towards the voices and Sandén calmed her. 'We'll do that later, when everyone has left. Anna

43

Åkesson is running the show out there for now. Perhaps you could call the parents and your colleagues this evening . . .'

'Yes, of course, I'll have to do that.'

Then the preschool teacher broke down and the tears were now running unchecked down her cheeks.

'Who could have done something so terrible –'

'I wanted to ask you about that,' said Sandén. 'You here at the preschool perhaps know the family better than anyone else. Who did Catherine socialize with? Did the children have any friends outside preschool? I want to find out everything you know about Catherine Larsson. Could she have had any enemies?'

'She was friendliness itself. Always happy and positive. And Erik likewise. He wasn't here that often, once or twice a week perhaps.'

'Since when?'

'Ever since the children started here. It must have been in August 2006. They were so small then: little Linn had just learned to walk when they started. I'm not aware that Kate socialized with any of the other parents. And the children are so little in this group, it's seldom they go home with each other and play. Tom and Linn didn't do that anyway, as far as I know. It was always Kate or Erik who picked up and dropped off.'

'What was Catherine like as a person?'

Margareta Norlander thought for a moment before she answered.

'Sweet and friendly, as I said. A little shy, I think you could say. Rather quiet. Her Swedish was not all that great.'

'What kind of work did she do, do you have any idea about that?'

'She cleaned, she said; more than that I don't know.'

She tore off another piece of paper towel from the roll and tried with little success to wipe off some mascara that had run.

'How were the children doing?' asked Sandén.

'They were very happy and harmonious; there were never any worries with them. They were clean and well looked after. Kate was organised and careful about being on time and all that kind of thing.'

'Did the children ever talk about their father?'

'I've probably heard Tom brag a few times about how strong his dad is and such like, but children do that. I don't think I've ever heard them *tell* anything about their father.'

'And this Erik, what does he look like, what kind of work does he do?'

'Average height, ash-blond hair, glasses. Swedish appearance. He looks rather ordinary with ordinary clothes. Trousers and jumper.'

'So not a suit and not labourer's clothing,' Sandén filled in. 'White-collar worker?'

'Yes, something along those lines. I don't know what kind of work he does.'

'Green jumper?' Sandén suggested.

'Yes, now that you mention it . . . He often had a dark-green jumper on. He's very fond of children, Erik,' she continued. 'Not just Tom and Linn, he always had a word to say to the other children too. He would play ball with them, throw them up in the air, you know, the kind of things kids like.'

The voices outside got louder and then stopped completely. The front door closed again with a slam. Margareta Norlander cast a glance at her watch. It was just past five.

'The last ones probably just left,' she observed with a sigh.

'Can you help me check on those telephone numbers?' Sandén asked.

'Of course,' she answered tiredly.

She got up from the chair laboriously, looking suddenly much older. He had not noticed the feebleness in her gait as she walked ahead of him through the corridor earlier. She had been transformed from a preschool teacher to a woman who had lost two children.

A young man in washed-out jeans and a discoloured tank top that nicely set off a pair of sturdy upper arms stood leaning on a mop behind the glass door to the adjacent section of the preschool. Sandén nodded a greeting, but Margareta Norlander took no notice of the indolent cleaner and instead searched out a key she had on a ring in her jeans pocket and unlocked the office door. From a row of binders on the desk she pulled out one with a grey spine and flicked to the Larsson children's paperwork. There were two telephone numbers listed, one of which was a mobile number. The landline was Catherine Larsson's home number, but whose mobile number was it? Erik's?

Tuesday Evening

'But you could do this, da— You could do it last week and last year and . . . You can't simply have lost all your knowledge of subtraction!'

'You were going to swear.'

'No, I was going to – Yes, I was going to, but I didn't.'

'You were going to lie.'

'You can think what you want, it's a free country, Simon. Stop being silly, and let's try again.'

'There's freedom of speech too, you can say what you want.'

'Shall we drop the law and devote ourselves to mathematics instead? If I draw this on an axis . . . Oh, what the he– Åsa!'

'You were going to swear.'

Conny Sjöberg looked in distress at his ten-year-old son and got up with such haste that the kitchen chair almost fell over behind him.

'Åsa!' he shouted again.

He heard a door being carefully closed in another part of the apartment and then Åsa's feet on the parquet floor, first tiptoeing and then almost stomping, carrying her into the kitchen.

'I was just putting the boys to bed!' she hissed. 'They just fell asleep!'

'So are they awake now?'

'No, but they could have been.'

'But what kind of pseudo-discussion is this!'

Then Simon started giggling and it rubbed off on Åsa and finally all three of them were laughing.

'Is it maths?' asked Åsa.

Simon looked with feigned embarrassment at his mother.

'Yes, the law, which is my field, he has no problem with,' said Sjöberg. 'But maths . . . And since we already have a trained maths teacher in the family, I don't see why I should have to sit here –'

'Because the two of you are on the same level, darling. It's easier for you to understand what's difficult.'

Åsa winked teasingly at him and gestured with her hand as if to wave him away from the kitchen table. Sjöberg was rescued by his mobile ringing somewhere in the apartment. He rushed out of the kitchen and finally found the phone in the inside pocket of his jacket in the hall.

'This is Vida,' said the woman on the phone, with an obvious accent. 'You were looking for me.'

It took Sjöberg a few seconds to switch into the role of detective chief inspector, but once he'd gathered his wits he said in a firm and definite voice, 'Yes, it's good that you called. We would really like to speak to you.'

'I was at work and my phone battery was dead. A friend saw at the church that I should call this number. The police have also left me a message.'

The police? Shit. So the mobile number Sandén got hold of at the preschool was not Erik's.

'What is this about?' Vida asked.

'Are you aware of what has happened?'

'Happened? No, I'm not.'

'Then it's best that we meet.'

'Can it wait until tomorrow? I'm tired.'

'No,' said Sjöberg. 'Unfortunately it can't wait. Are you at home?'

'Yes . . .' the woman said hesitantly.

'I'll bring another officer with me and come over in about half an hour. Is that okay? It's very important.'

'Okay. I live at Rusthållarvägen 31 in Bagarmossen. The entry code is 5110.'

After some hesitation he called Sandén, who immediately got in the car to drive from Bromma in the direction of Skånegatan to pick him up. Then Sjöberg went into the room that their two daughters, Sara and Maja, shared to kiss them good night. They were sitting on the floor, diligently making up questions for the nature-trail board game to which they would soon subject their mother and big brother. In the kitchen, to his mother's delight, Simon was spitting out solutions to one subtraction problem after another at a furious pace. Sjöberg kissed his son on the head and gave him a commending pat on the shoulder.

'Well done, Simon,' he said. 'I said you could do this.'

'Mum explains it much better than you,' said Simon.

'I know,' said Sjöberg. 'It's her job.'

Åsa got a kiss on the mouth.

'Are you leaving?' she asked.

'The girlfriend called. She doesn't know what happened, so we'll have to see her now. Jens is on his way here.'

'I see. Jens, who works part-time and is avoiding stress?' Åsa said sarcastically.

'Hmm.'

'Poor thing,' said Åsa, tilting her head.

'Jens or me?'

'The Filipino woman. Will you be late?'

'I don't believe so,' said Sjöberg, leaving them with a hint of a wave.

* * *

Vida Johansson was a very beautiful woman in her thirties and lived in a two-room apartment with her husband, who was watching TV when the two police officers showed up. He seemed to have just showered; his hair was still damp and he smelled of perfumed soap when he got up to greet them. He appeared to be around the same age as his wife and was dressed in jeans and a checked shirt, which was unbuttoned all the way down to his navel, revealing a well-toned torso. Vida had long, shiny black hair, gathered in a thick braid. She too was dressed in jeans, with a chunky knitted jumper. She held her arms crossed over her chest and looked guarded.

'Can we sit down somewhere?' Sjöberg asked.

Vida nodded and looked around a little confused.

'Should Göran stay or do you want to talk to just me?' she asked.

'It's probably good if Göran is here too,' Sjöberg replied. 'Perhaps we can sit here?' he suggested, sitting on the beige leather couch without waiting for an answer.

Göran reached for the remote control and turned off the TV, and sank back down on the chair. Sandén sat down beside Sjöberg on the couch and Vida perched on her husband's footrest. She looked uncomfortable with the situation.

'Something very unfortunate has happened,' Sjöberg began.

Vida put her hands in front of her mouth and her eyes darted, terrified, back and forth between the two policemen. Göran raised his eyebrows in curiosity.

'I've been told that you are a close friend of Catherine Larsson,' said Sjöberg, and Vida nodded in agreement. 'Do you know her too?' he asked the man.

'Sure, very well,' answered Göran Johansson.

'She was found dead in her apartment this morning,' said Sjöberg.

'Dead? No!' Vida exclaimed. 'She was my best friend!'

Göran looked at the policemen with alarm and pulled his wife to him. Sjöberg cleared his throat as if to brace himself and then recounted the circumstances as carefully as he was able. Göran Johansson looked at his wife, who was crying loudly, still with her hands in front of her mouth. He caressed her hair and held her tight to get her to stop shaking. When Sjöberg was finished, Vida sat motionless with her face buried into her husband's chest. Göran Johansson had nothing to say either, and only looked imploringly from one policeman to the other. Sjöberg did not say anything for a while, letting the news sink in. He cast a resigned glance at Sandén, and finally took a deep breath.

'We have to ask you a few questions,' he said.

'But we don't know anything about this,' said Göran Johansson.

'And we know nothing about Catherine,' Sjöberg

retorted. 'We need you to help us form a picture of her family life. How long have you known one another, Vida?'

Vida wriggled out of her husband's grasp and looked at Sjöberg with clouded eyes.

'Since 2002. We worked at the same cleaning company. We were pretty new in the country, both of us, but she had been here a few months longer than me, so she took care of me a little.'

'Do you still work there?'

'No, now I work in the office at Göran's company.'

Sjöberg looked questioningly at Göran Johansson.

'A couple of guys and I have a decorating company,' he explained.

'You're not cleaning for cash in hand any longer, Vida?' Sjöberg asked.

She stared at him in dismay without answering.

'We'll turn a blind eye to that sort of thing today, but you must understand we have to know the truth.'

'I've stopped cleaning,' she said quietly. 'But Kate cleans. Cleaned. Cash in hand.'

'Kate – is that Catherine?'

Vida nodded and ran the back of her hand under her nose.

'Do you know who her customers were?'

'I know a few of them. We helped each other some-times when there was a lot to do, window-cleaning, moving furniture and so on.'

'You'll have to help us make a list of the customers you know about.'

'Now?'

'Now would be good.'

Sjöberg thought it might help to divert her thoughts for the moment. He flipped to the first clean page in his note-pad and handed it to her along with his pen. She started writing.

'Do you have any idea who might have done this? Anyone who had it in for Catherine?'

'Had it in for her?'

'Someone she didn't get along with.'

'Everyone liked Kate,' said Vida.

Her husband nodded in agreement.

'Tell us about her relationship with Christer Larsson,' Sandén asked.

Vida Johansson and her husband exchanged glances.

'He was a real wet blanket,' said Göran at last.

'Presumably Catherine didn't think so, because she married him?'

'Well, maybe that's not always how it works.'

'Kate liked him, she did,' Vida interjected.

'What do you mean, that isn't the way it works?' Sandén asked.

'The Philippines is a poor country and many will do anything at all to get away from there,' Göran explained. 'Such as marrying a Westerner, for example.'

Both of the police officers involuntarily cast a glance at Vida, but chose not to probe deeper into the Johansson couple's motives for having entered into marriage.

'But Catherine and Christer Larsson liked each other?' Sandén asked Vida instead.

'In the beginning. Kate was never in love with him, I think, but in the beginning they liked each other. She really tried. But after a while he got strange.'

'What do you mean, strange?' asked Sjöberg.

'In the beginning all four of us socialized,' said Göran Johansson. 'Not that Christer talked that much then either, but he was there and would laugh when you made a joke and so on. But he got more and more withdrawn and the last few times we met he sat completely silent and just stared out of the window.'

'He reportedly suffers from depression,' Sjöberg clarified.

'Sure,' said Göran Johansson. 'Kate told us that. We tried to include him in the conversation, but, you know, finally you give up.'

Vida nodded in agreement.

'Then he sat at home alone, didn't want to see us any more,' she continued. 'Finally Kate and the children moved out.'

'I don't think we've seen Christer since Linn was a new-born,' said Göran.

'He's probably not suited to being married,' said Vida. 'He wants to be alone. He was married before, but he got a divorce then too. Kate told us that she was the first woman he'd been with in twenty years.'

Sjöberg raised an eyebrow.

'Was he ever threatening, aggressive?' he asked.

'We didn't notice anything like that,' Vida replied. 'And Kate didn't say anything. He didn't seem to be that way.'

'Not to the children either?'

'He didn't care that much about them. Kate had to take care of them herself.'

'Did she seem unhappy?'

'I think she was very homesick. But she probably felt that she couldn't leave Sweden – for the children's sake.'

'Did she ever go back to the Philippines to visit?' Sandén asked.

'No, it was too much money. Alone with two kids,' Vida commented.

'So she didn't have much money?'

'No, but she saved almost everything she earned. Only bought what was necessary.'

'Where did she get the money for the apartment in Hammarbyhamnen?' Sjöberg asked hopefully.

'We've also wondered about that,' said Göran Johansson, scratching his scalp with his index finger. 'We couldn't really figure that out. The apartments there are outrageously expensive.'

Vida seemed to have thought of another customer and wrote on the pad in front of her with rapid movements.

'Did she prostitute herself?' Sandén asked, straight to the point.

'No, she didn't,' Vida said firmly, looking Sandén right in the eyes.

'And you're completely sure of that?'

'Quite sure.'

She lowered her eyes back to the pad and jotted down another piece of information.

'Did Kate meet a man who took care of her and the children financially?' Sjöberg asked on a sudden impulse, turning towards Vida.

'No, she –' Göran began, but Sjöberg made a dismissive gesture at him and said in a commanding voice, 'Vida?'

A tear dropped from her cheek on to Sjöberg's pad and she hurried to wipe it away with the tip of her middle finger. Göran Johansson looked questioningly at his wife.

'I promised Kate . . .' she began, looking sorrowfully at her husband. 'I promised never to tell anyone.'

'Kate is dead,' Sjöberg said urgently. 'We have to find out the truth.'

Vida took a deep breath before she started her story.

'There was a man. A man she happened to meet somewhere. He helped her one time when she was attacked by skinheads. I found this out long after,' Vida pointed out. 'They started meeting. Kate said they didn't have sex, but I don't know . . . What else could it have been? They used to meet outdoors, never at his home. He must have been married, but she never said anything about that. They didn't meet at her home either – she was living with Christer at the time. Kate thought this man was really good to talk to; they talked about everything, she said. He comforted her when she had problems with Christer, and he wanted to help her when she finally decided to leave him. At first she didn't want to accept so much money – it was more than two million kronor – but he convinced her. It would be good for the kids there, he said. Playground in the area, and a lot of friends. She was worried at first that she would be forced to do things she didn't want to, but it didn't turn out that way. He seemed to be an amazing person. And the kids loved him, Kate said. And he loved them. He used to take care of them sometimes when she worked long days.'

'You've never met him?' asked Sjöberg.

'No, I wanted to, but he was a little mysterious. She felt that she was betraying him, when she told me. And I feel that way too, now I'm telling you.'

Vida started crying again and her husband stroked her hair.

'Was this man's name possibly Erik?' asked Sandén.

'Yes, his name was Erik. Do you think he's the one who –'

'We don't think anything so far, but naturally it is very important that we make contact with him,' Sjöberg replied.

He reached for the pad and pen and noted that Vida Johansson had contributed six names. After routinely taking the Johansson couple's fingerprints, Sjöberg stood up, and Sandén did the same. Sjöberg pulled his wallet from his back pocket, took out a business card and set it on the coffee table.

'We're truly sorry,' Sjöberg concluded. 'You've been a great help. Please give us a call if you think of anything else.'

The rain was pattering against the windscreen and thousands of diffused light sources swept past in the darkness outside. Sandén's controlled driving made the car seem a safe place in the late-winter evening.

'What was it that happened before?' asked Sjöberg. 'At the meeting.'

Sandén did not reply at first, which convinced Sjöberg that the question was relevant. It would be heavy-handed to clarify what he meant any further; he didn't want to risk the brief change in his colleague that afternoon being brushed off, as if it had never taken place.

'I don't know if I want to talk about it.'

'That's okay. We'll forget it.'

In the few minutes of silence that followed Sjöberg convinced himself that there was no cause for concern. Sandén took care of himself. He was eating better, drinking less and exercising in moderate doses. Worrying yourself unnecessarily was the quickest route to the morgue. Sandén was not that type and Sjöberg too did his best to be rational.

'I suddenly wished I hadn't made that comment.'

Unexpectedly Sandén picked up the thread again.

'You know me, I spit out droll remarks without thinking. It's just words. Prostitution. But suddenly I could visualize it. And I didn't like it.'

'Catherine Larsson?'

'No.' Sandén sighed. 'Jenny.'

Sjöberg did not understand, did not know what to think. Sandén drove on to Nynäsvägen. There was a fair amount of traffic, despite the weather and the late hour, but he took his time. He stayed in the inside lane all the way into the city, let himself be passed and splashed by motorists who were in more of a hurry. And then he told Sjöberg about those few days in September when his life had fallen apart. How his beloved daughter Jenny, vulnerable because of her learning disability, had been lured into a form of prostitution. How that utter bastard Pontus, her live-in (at the time) so-called boyfriend, had sold her for money that she herself never saw a trace of. And how this horrifying discovery almost killed Sandén, while Pontus had left his life with Jenny behind him without a backward glance or any consequences other than a considerably fatter wallet. Sandén had managed to buy him out of his life – and Jenny's – for the hair-raising sum of

50,000 kronor, tax free, and since then fortunately he had not been seen. Sandén felt unable to initiate any legal proceedings against Pontus, mainly because certain less flattering facts about his daughter were best buried.

Sjöberg could do nothing but agree. And cross his fingers that now it all really was over, and that Jenny's life had taken a new and better turn with the job with Lotten on reception, which he had arranged for her.

'And you? Are you doing okay, you and Åsa?'

Sandén had had enough of his own troubles, leaving it open for Sjöberg to share what worried him. That was the closest he would come to an invitation to familiarity. Curious questions or insinuations were not something Sandén resorted to. Straight shots or complete discretion, that was Jens in a nutshell. Sjöberg had always had the feeling that his entanglement with Margit Olofsson had not passed unnoticed by his colleague as he had hoped. Sandén had been there when the relationship began; if he had the least bit of intuition, he must have noticed the spark between them there in the piano bar.

And he had, of course. Despite his boorishness Sandén was a person with a lot of warmth and a well-developed sense of nuance. He must have noticed what was happening that unfortunate evening when Åsa and the children were with her parents in Linköping. He had never said anything, but hadn't he been unusually attentive, unusually . . . considerate, in his brusque way, in the months after that first transgression? Yes, that's how it was, thought Sjöberg. Jens Sandén had been his best friend for a long time – ever since they were at the police academy – and he felt warm inside at the thought that maybe Sandén understood a little of what was going on in his lost soul. Although he had been sensitive enough all this time not to bring the subject up.

And perhaps it was the rain, the cold and the glistening lights outside, in contrast to the darkness and warmth in the car, that did it. Perhaps it was the emotional situation, or just the obvious security in a solid friendship of many years. But an overpowering need for complete frankness came over Sjöberg, and he told him.

When the car turned into Skånegatan, passed Nytorget and then stopped, everything had not yet been said. They remained sitting in the car for a long time, across from Sjöberg's building. It was an evening for painful topics of conversation, and perhaps they would never be touched on again. But now the two of them could go on, a little stronger, a little richer. A little less alone.

'No,' Sjöberg concluded the conversation. 'What good would it do to tell Åsa? It would only stir up emotions unnecessarily. And do damage.'

* * *

It was cold, really cold, in the shed at night. There was a little heating element in the room, but it was placed by the inside wall, where there was no window. The wintry air streamed in through the crack under the door and through the small window opening alongside it. The room was pitch black and around him it was completely silent, but in the distance he could hear the noise of the city.

He tensed all the muscles in his hands and arms and tried to prise loose the rope around his wrists. He repeated the exercise ten times, but it made no difference. There was nothing to do other than continue trying until his time was up. That was his only chance and it was as good as non-existent, he realized that.

Afterwards he lay exhausted, staring up into the darkness. The back of his head and his back both hurt, but that could not be helped. It had to hurt somewhere. It always hurt somewhere. *Then the doorbell rang. He was startled by the new, modern ding-dong sound that the landlord had spoiled them with since the old doorbell fell apart. An agreeable, welcoming sound, instead of the previous angry buzzing. She rolled her eyes and looked at him with an expression that was supposed to convey resignation, but he saw only the glistening blue eyes under the blonde fringe. He did not see what she expressed, only how beautiful she was.*

'I'll get it,' he said with a smile, taking the few steps from the balcony door out to the hall.

Still with his gardening gloves on, he turned the lock and pushed down the handle to open up for the visitor.

'Hi! Listen, I've got a little problem . . .'

It was the neighbour. His door was wide open behind him in the corridor and from inside the lively voices of the boys could be heard. He broke off when his eyes fell on the gardening gloves.

'Am I disturbing you in your work?' he said jokingly.

'Yes, we're making the balcony nice, planting a few flowers. What can I help you with?'

'How nice, how nice. Well, the wife is working a half-day and a friend is wondering if I can help him bring in his boat. If we're going to get it done today, it would be good if we could get going right away. You couldn't look after the boys for a while?'

'Sure, no problem.'

It was not the first time they had taken care of the neighbours' boys; they used to help out when it was needed. The boys were two whirlwinds aged three and five, but they were fun little rascals, affectionate and charming.

'She'll be finished at the salon in an hour and a half so you can drop them off there, if that's convenient. She was thinking about shopping for shoes with them.'

'No problem. Shall we have them here or stay at your place?'

'Whichever you like. I'll leave the door open, so you can do what you want. Oh, wait a minute . . .' He rushed into his apartment and came right back with a bottle of Rioja in his hand. As he handed it over, he bowed solemnly. 'To brighten up Saturday evening with your beautiful wife!'

She materialized in the background and waved cheerfully.

'Thanks in advance for the help!' the neighbour said, already on his way out.

'No problem; it's fun!' she called after him as he disappeared down the stairs. 'Go in to the boys now and see what they're up to, then I can carry on with the planting,' she said to her husband.

He handed her the gloves and went in through the neighbours' open door.

The boys were sitting on the floor in the children's room, setting up Brio train tracks.

'Hey there, boys! Can I play too?'

They threw themselves at him happily and then all three of them tumbled around on the floor for a while, before returning to the building. It was part of it; you always had to wrestle a little first. He thought that if he had a son of his own he would wrestle and build with him but his wife could do the playing. He loathed the train driving itself, but the track building he had developed into an art. It had to take its time; he let the boys think and guided them with a careful hand, so that they got the feeling that they had built the track without his help. At last it was done and then there was no going back; then you had to play long-drawn-out train games. But he was rescued this time by little Tobias, who asked, 'Where is the lady?'

'Listen now, my young man,' he answered with an offended look. 'That lady is no lady, that lady is a girl.'

'So where is the lady girl?'

Big brother Andreas and he laughed so hard they fell backwards on the floor, and then it was time for a little wrestling again.

Wednesday Morning

Sjöberg, with his thoughts elsewhere, studied Petra Westman as she closed the door and sat down at the table. She stirred the spoon a few times in her cup before she brought it to her mouth. The tea was still too hot, so she set the cup down again, stirred a little more and then let it stand. Sjöberg woke up from his musings and started the meeting.

'Everyone here? Hadar is in court today and isn't coming. But Bella has taken the time to join us and also has Kaj's preliminary report with her, is that right?'

Gabriella Hansson held up a black folder and nodded affirmatively.

'Then perhaps you can begin, Bella. After that you can leave, if you want.'

'Okay. Catherine Larsson was murdered some time between nine o'clock on Saturday evening and three o'clock in the morning on Sunday. The murder took place in the bathroom where she was standing turned towards the sink when she was cut across the throat with a single cut, deep enough that she would die pretty much immediately. The bruises on her upper arms and across her ribcage confirm that she was held from behind. The murderer is considerably taller than the victim and right-handed. He – though it could have been a tall woman – had a good view in the mirror when he did the deed, and Catherine

Larsson probably could have seen it all too. Then he carried – not dragged – her to the bed, where he placed her alongside the children. After that, bending over the woman, he did the same to the girl, who was in the middle. Then he went around to the other side of the bed and killed the boy. Both children were certainly asleep; there were no marks on their bodies to indicate that they might have put up any resistance. The weapon had a long, sharp blade – at least twenty centimetres long, probably longer – like a sturdy hunting knife, machete or sword.'

'How did he get into the apartment?' asked Sjöberg.

'There were no signs of violence. Either he was let in or else he got in on his own. He may have had his own key, he may have picked the lock or the door may have been unlocked. He left the apartment without locking up. The door can be locked from inside, with or without a key, but from outside only with a key, so the fact that the door was unlocked possibly indicates that he did not have one.'

'Wouldn't he have been covered in blood himself?' Hamad wondered.

'That's hard to say,' Hansson replied. 'He must have got quite a bit of blood on him, but how much I don't know. He certainly had blood on his arms and hands, but he seems to have washed himself off in the sink before he left, although without using any of the towels. He may have had protective clothing on, which he took off before he left the apartment.'

'There was a jumper hanging in the hall –' Hamad began.

'We have found hair strands on it which we have sent to

Forensics,' Hansson responded quickly. 'It was too big to be hers.'

'Brand?' Sjöberg wanted to know.

'Åhléns' own brand.'

'I saw a shoeprint too,' Hamad tried again, but the efficient crime technician was a step ahead.

'We have secured a number of impressions. All come from the same pair, gym shoes of some type. We have not been able to establish the brand yet, but the size is about 43 or 44, so that also indicates that the murderer is a man. We found the same impressions in the stairwell, but they obviously ended as soon as we were out in the courtyard.'

'Fingerprints?'

'Sure, there are fingerprints from several different people in the apartment. The majority are the family's own, naturally, but we have found a few other sets too. However, not on the bathroom taps or the door handle, as one might have hoped. I'll compare them with the ones I got from you, Conny.'

Sjöberg nodded.

'Do you have anything to tell us from the autopsy?' he asked.

'Yes, three autopsies, and they're not finished yet. But Zetterström says that none of the victims was subjected to sexual assault. Catherine Larsson had not engaged in sexual activities in the final days of her life. Forensics has not found any trace of assault, either on the children or on the mother. Anything else?'

Hansson started gathering up her things.

'I would actually probably like to take samples of these

children and of Christer Larsson to establish paternity,' said Sjöberg musingly.

'Oh,' said Sandén with a self-righteous smile. 'Exciting.'

'Shall I pass on your request to Zetterström or were you thinking of taking the blood samples yourself?' said Hansson with a smile.

'Yes, thanks,' said Sjöberg. 'Thanks for the report, Bella.'

Hansson pushed the black folder with the preliminary autopsy report over to Sjöberg, packed up the rest of her papers in her briefcase and left the room.

After the four police officers around the table had recounted the facts that had emerged from their respective interviews, Sjöberg sat with his hands behind his neck and leaned back, balancing his chair.

'What kind of murder is this really?' he wondered. 'What type of murderer are we dealing with? This is extremely clinically performed. Could it be a contract job?'

'The shoeprints argue against that,' Westman suggested. 'It's unprofessional to leave tracks behind.'

'Who said that hired killers are professional?' Hamad interjected jokingly. 'Have you seen that on TV or . . . ?'

Westman gave him an irritated look.

'Joking aside, it may have been a pair of shoes he incinerated afterwards,' Hamad continued. 'A pair of ordinary shoes that are in every store. Or else he didn't care if he left evidence, just wanted to get the job done.'

'Then he wouldn't have been so careful about the fingerprints,' Westman pointed out.

'Maybe,' said Sjöberg. 'Admittedly, the murders themselves are brutal, but despite that they were carried out without any sign of personal involvement, don't you agree? No unnecessary violence, no humiliation, no mutilation. It can't be a question of an ordinary break-in that got out of hand, because then he hardly would have attacked the children. Not a sex crime. Quick and efficient, no fumbling, no unnecessary suffering.'

'But a contract job?' Sandén hesitated. 'Money laundering comes to mind, thinking about the apartment transaction. Could she have had connections to the underworld?'

'Whoever took out the contract would have the connections, in that case,' said Sjöberg. 'We'll have to check on her customers.'

He scratched himself under his chin with his thumb and index finger.

'So Einar isn't here again today,' he noted despondently. 'Has anyone seen him?'

Only head-shaking.

'I guess I'll have to check if he's taken leave,' Sjöberg muttered.

'It's good for you to try your hand at pen-pushing sometimes too,' Sandén sneered. 'You'll get to see what it's like to be Einar. Doesn't he already look a little sullen . . . ?'

He looked around at his colleagues and gestured towards Sjöberg, whose self-conscious drumming of his fingers on the tabletop released a salvo of laughter from his subordinates. Sjöberg let them have their fun for a moment, before he took command again.

'As punishment, Jens, you get to track down someone who can translate Catherine Larsson's correspondence.

Get to work on the list of customers too. Check them out, contact them and see whether they in turn know any more of her customers. Petra and Jamal, you'll sit down with the list of phone calls that I put on Einar's desk yesterday evening. Get an overview of her telephone habits, especially the last few days. Who did she talk to and about what? Is Erik there anywhere? In addition I want you to find out whether she had signed up for a mobile phone contract. She did not have one with Telia, that much we know. I'll investigate the Johansson family's finances, and the decorating company and so on.'

An hour and a half later Sjöberg had managed to chart both the Johanssons' personal and the decorating company's finances, without discovering any irregularities. No large withdrawals, no deviations from the normal receipts and revenues. Absent-mindedly he swung his pen back and forth between his index and middle fingers, staring vacantly ahead. Finally he picked up the phone and dialled Einar Eriksson's mobile number. He immediately got voicemail and listened to the concise message. At Eriksson's recorded request he left a message after the tone:

'Hi, Einar, Conny here. You haven't been seen for a couple of days and I haven't heard anything about you taking time off. Please give me a call as soon as possible. We need you here,' he added before he finished.

Then he searched for Eriksson's home number in the contacts on his mobile and called it. Eriksson's landline had no answering machine. After ten rings he gave up. He also tapped a brief text message to Eriksson's mobile, with the same request he had just left on voicemail. Finally he entered the speed-dial number for the police switch-board and asked to be connected to the payroll office.

'Conny Sjöberg, Violent Crimes Unit. I need a little information concerning one of my subordinates, Einar Eriksson.'

'Yes?' said the woman on the other end.

'Is he on holiday now or on sick leave or anything like that?'

'Let's see here,' she said obligingly, and Sjöberg heard her tapping on the keyboard in the background. 'What is his civil registration number?'

'No idea,' said Sjöberg. 'You can tell me that. There can't be that many Einar Erikssons in the police.'

'Let's see . . . Yes, here he is. He's not sick and hasn't requested any leave.'

'Could you give me his address?' Sjöberg asked.

'We don't give out that kind of information,' she answered amiably but firmly. 'You'll have to get author-ization.'

'Get authorization? I'm his boss, for crying out loud,' said Sjöberg sullenly, but at the same moment realized that she was only doing her job.

'I can call you back,' she said just as amiably.

'Okay, my number –' Sjöberg started.

'I have it,' she said, hanging up on him.

Authorization, thought Sjöberg. What kind of awful word is that? He had no time to ponder this further because the phone rang.

'Sjöberg.'

'Yes, that's good. You wanted information about Einar Eriksson?'

'Correct,' said Sjöberg.

She gave him Eriksson's civil registration number and his address, and he thanked her for her help and ended the call.

It struck him that he actually had no idea even what part of the city Eriksson lived in. Now it turned out that they lived very close to each other. Einar's home was on Eriksdalsgatan, only a short walk from the police station on Östgötagatan and just as close to Sjöberg's apartment on Skånegatan. They knew so little about each other, thought Sjöberg. They had worked together for – what was it? – twelve years, and he knew nothing about Einar. Yes, he knew he was married and that he didn't have any kids, but what else? Nothing, now he came to think about it. Einar Eriksson was an inaccessible character, contrary and difficult to deal with, so the conversations they did have dealt exclusively with work. Eriksson never went out for lunch with his colleagues, usually an excellent opportunity to talk about things other than work. No, he stayed in his office and ate the packed lunch that his wife had prepared. Presumably, thought Sjöberg, smiling at the absurdity of Einar Eriksson at the stove, busy throwing together a piping-hot sausage stroganoff for the next day's lunchbox.

These thoughts led him to his own life. There were certainly things his colleagues did not know about him. He imagined that the possibility of a Margit Olofsson in his life must seem extremely foreign to the others. Except for Jens, who was now in the know and who had sensed something was going on from the start. But Sjöberg's mother – what would she say if she found out? He couldn't bring himself to think about it. She was so anxious about the facade she presented to the neighbours and so worried about what they would think.

His mother was a case in point, with all her secrets. 'Secrets' was perhaps the wrong word, rather it was her taciturn way of refusing to talk about anything that had any significance. He remembered how he had tried to press her to tell him about his father, the father that he had never got to know. All he had were vague impressions of a man who had died when Sjöberg was only three years old, of some mysterious, unmentionable disease.

He happened to think about the title deeds he had found among his mother's papers when he was helping her pay some bills after she had fallen off a stool and broken a couple of ribs. A title to a plot of land somewhere: Björskogsnäs 4:14. His mother claimed not to know where this property was located. It must be something from his father. But was it really possible that she – if she hadn't known about the property at his father's death – had not been curious enough to find out what kind of place it was? It seemed improbable, but he would not get anything out of his mother, detective inspector or not; he had already tried.

Suddenly he was struck by an intense desire to get to the bottom of that old property mystery. If he had to sit here anyway, playing Einar and pen-pushing, as Sandén had put it, he could certainly find out where that land was too.

He dialled the number for Information and asked to be connected to the Registration Authority at Stockholm District Court. After a few minutes' wait it was his turn. Sjöberg introduced himself and explained his business.

'I have a title deed with a property designation, but I have no idea where in Sweden the land is located, so I'm sure I've called the wrong registration authority. Can you help me anyway?'

'Sure,' said the woman on the other end. 'It may take a while, but just give me the property designation, then we'll see.'

'Björskogsnäs 4:14,' said Sjöberg.

She spelled it out to make sure she had the right information, and after a few minutes she was back.

'Björskogsnäs 4:14 is in Västmanland,' she said. 'In the vicinity of Arboga.'

'Arboga?' mumbled Sjöberg.

'Arboga,' the voice confirmed. 'Do you want me to fax you a map of the area?'

'Please,' said Sjöberg, without having a clue what he would do with the information.

* * *

He woke with a start. Even though he slept for the better part of the night, he still managed to doze a little in the morning too. He slept only intermittently because he was forced to change position every ten minutes or so. Otherwise the pain was almost unbearable for hours afterwards. But now he woke himself when it was time. It had become his body's instinct to wake up after a short period of rest to change position. Life on the chilly, splintery wooden floor in the tool shed had fallen into a routine.

He slid up into a sitting position against the cold outside wall, moving slowly, almost listlessly, and spent a few minutes trying to stretch the rigid rope. He knew that he had to do something, and this was what he was capable of. He no longer hoped, he did not look ahead. There was nothing in his future worth seeing; he looked backwards instead. He saw himself with *the two little boys draped over him like small warm pillows, downy chicks that you could pinch and snap at, roll around with. It was like they had no edges and if you got an elbow in the eye, for some reason it didn't hurt. Your body was prepared for it not to hurt, and so it didn't.*

'*Lady Girl is planting flowers on the balcony,*' *he replied, holding Tobias at arm's length above him.*

'*Oh,*' *said Andreas,* '*can we help her? I love planting!*'

'*Of course, I'm sure she'll be happy to have help. She can put you each in a flowerpot so that you grow and get big, so I don't dare wrestle with you any more.*'

'*Come on, Tobias!*' *Andreas called, already on his way out of the room.*

Tobias freed himself and rushed after his brother. He himself got to his feet, adjusted the rag rug on the floor of the children's room with his foot and brushed off his trousers and jumper. He closed the outside door of the neighbours' apartment and went into his own.

On the balcony Andreas was standing, his little hands in the much-too-big gloves, with a stranglehold on his younger brother's throat.

'*No, no, no,*' *said his wife.* '*Not like that. Do you want to plant or shall we do something else instead?*'

'*I want to have my own flower,*' *said Tobias.*

'*Yes, let's do that! Decide which flower you want, Tobias, and then Andreas can choose one too. Then you get to plant them very carefully. But you have to remember to water them often too.*'

'*I want that red one,*' *said Tobias.*

'A geranium. Yes, it's going to get really big and nice when it grows. And you, Andreas?'

'The blue one,' he answered, pointing down into the carton.

'Perfect! A petunia for Andreas. Then we do it like this . . .'

She gave each boy a terracotta pot with a shard in the bottom and set one in front of herself.

'Take a little soil, like this, and place it in the bottom of the pot . . .'

There was not room for all of them on the small balcony, so he stood in the doorway admiring his wife's easy dexterity and enjoying her and the boys' gentle voices. The aroma of freshly cut grass from the garden below and damp earth from the balcony filled his nostrils. Life had just begun.

* * *

Sjöberg left the police station without telling anyone where he was going. A gnawing unease followed him the whole way to Eriksdalsgatan. If Einar answered when he rang the doorbell, what should he say? He did not want to have to confront a dishevelled Eriksson reeking of alcohol and with his hair on end . . . He interrupted himself in mid-thought. Why should it be like that? Eriksson had never smelled of booze at work, which he himself, on the other hand, conceivably might have on a few occasions. But what else could it be? He wouldn't just not come to work one day, after having done his job irreproachably, as far as Sjöberg could tell, for twelve years. Could he have hurt himself or got really sick? Then he should have been in touch; Mrs Eriksson would have called and reported him sick. If she hadn't been injured herself, of course. They could have been in a traffic accident . . .

An old man with a toy poodle came out of Eriksson's entrance and Sjöberg ran the last few steps before the door closed.

'Excuse me,' said Sjöberg, and the old man looked up at him with a watery gaze. 'Do you live here in this building?'

'Who's asking?' the old man wanted to know.

'Yes, excuse me . . .'

Sjöberg pulled his wallet out of his back pocket and took out his police identification.

'Conny Sjöberg. I'm a colleague of Einar Eriksson, who lives here too.'

'I see. Is he a cop? I had no idea.'

The old man peered at him with a knowing smile, which Sjöberg reciprocated.

'Have you seen him recently?' Sjöberg asked.

The old man thought for a moment and then answered, 'Recently? No, not since Saturday when he drove away in his car.'

Sjöberg felt a stab of worry; was it as he feared, that Eriksson had been in a car accident?

'He always drives off in his car on Saturday mornings when I'm out with Topsy,' the man continued. 'And he comes home late in the evening, but then usually I'm asleep.'

'And last Saturday?'

'I didn't see him come back,' the old man filled in. 'That's correct.'

'Was he alone in the car or did he have his wife with him?' asked Sjöberg.

'Wife? Eriksson is a bachelor, as far as I know. I've never seen a wife, or any other woman either for that matter,' the old man chuckled.

The old man must be senile, thought Sjöberg. He had heard Eriksson mention his wife on a number of occasions. True, they had never talked specifically about her, but on the other hand they never talked about anything else either, if it didn't have to do with work. Besides, he was as good as certain that Eriksson wore a ring on his finger. As if to refute Sjöberg's assumption that he must be confused, the man continued.

'But he must have come back, if that's what you're wondering about, inspector. The car is parked over there, and it was there on Sunday morning.'

He nodded towards an old Toyota Corolla, which at this time of day was almost alone in the car park.

'Thank you very much for the information,' said Sjöberg, relieved in any event not to have to ring around the various hospitals in search of his missing colleague.

The old man tugged lightly on the leash, and the little dog took off single-mindedly with him. Sjöberg wondered whether the animal would have been approved of by Lotten, their receptionist, and Micke, one of the caretakers at the police station. Both were crazy about dogs, in the proper sense of the word; the pooches sent Christmas cards to each other and likewise celebrated each other's birthdays. And now Sandén's daughter, the easily led Jenny, had joined in this hysteria.

He went into the stairwell and made his way a half-flight up. Outside the door with 'Eriksson' on the letterbox he stopped and rang the bell. He heard it ring from inside the apartment, but that was all that he heard. After another two attempts he looked guiltily around before he took his lock-picking tools out of his jacket pocket. Eriksson had a very common lock, thank God, and it took Sjöberg only a few minutes to get inside.

He called Einar's name, but was met by silence. The first thing he saw was a golf bag. Sjöberg knew nothing about golf, but his instinctive judgement was that it looked old. He had never imagined Eriksson as a golfer. On the wall in the hall a framed black-and-white photograph was hanging, depicting a considerably younger version of Einar and a beautiful young woman, in all likelihood Mrs Eriksson, because it was a wedding photo. He had never imagined Eriksson as young either. Or happy. But he looked undeniably happy in the picture. There was no trace of worry on the smiling face, which testified to an openness that Sjöberg had never even seen a glimpse of.

Einar Eriksson's apartment proved to be a studio with a small hall, a rather large room with bed, couch and armchair, a little bathroom and a kitchen with a dining area for one person. He noted that the bed was a single. Sjöberg sighed in relief, having quickly gone over the apartment without finding his co-worker alone and drunk, injured or even dead. In a policeman-like way, he browsed through the post on the hall floor and determined that Eriksson had not made the effort to read – or even pick up – the newspaper since Saturday. Where in the world could the man be hiding himself? He tried to recall what outdoor clothing Eriksson wore this time of year. Neither the heavy shoes nor the black winter jacket were to be found anywhere in the apartment. So Eriksson must have come home in his car late on Saturday evening, as he usually did according to the neighbour, and then disappeared before breakfast on Sunday morning. The whole thing was incomprehensible.

But what worried Sjöberg most was the awful fact that no one seemed to miss Einar Eriksson. Neither his neighbours nor his colleagues – besides himself, but that was primarily because he had been forced to perform the tasks that were normally Einar's and had started getting annoyed about the whole situation. And Mrs Eriksson – where was she?

For a moment he considered calling Sandén, but he stopped himself. Perhaps he had been over-hasty, after all, to break into Einar Eriksson's apartment; he had only been absent from work for two or three days unannounced, it was no more than that. It was nothing to do with Sjöberg; he was just a co-worker. And to intrude on his colleague's personal life in this way was unforgivable. This was what he said to himself as he strode up to the bookshelf and without hesitating pulled out a binder with a wine-red aluminium spine marked 'Important Papers'.

Behind the first tab in the binder was a plastic sleeve and on it a handwritten label read 'Solveig'. Carefully he pulled out a bundle of papers and skimmed over the one on the top. It was a bill, dated quite recently. The bottommost paper in his hand was a similar bill, dated ten years earlier. The bills had been sent from a nursing home called Solberga, which according to the address on the letterhead was located in Fellingsbro. At the back of the plastic sleeve he found a brochure that described the nursing home as a gem in Bergslagen, in picturesque surroundings close to the water. In addition, twenty-four-hour care by nursing staff was promised and daily contact with doctors as needed.

Sjöberg could not remember Eriksson ever having mentioned his wife by name, but he thought that Solveig could possibly fit a woman of his own generation and consequently Eriksson's too. It was quite clear that no Mrs Eriksson was living in this small apartment. Did she maybe live at the Solberga nursing home, and if so, why? Sjöberg cursed himself for having been content over the years with Eriksson's muttering in response to his curious questions about how his leave or Christmas holidays had been, but his colleague's grim expression and brusque manner effectively kept everyone at a distance. It was obvious that he was not prepared to share his life, and perhaps the reason was simply that he thought he had no life to share. Einar's reticence and sulkiness were perhaps only an expression of general disappointment with a life that had not turned out as he had hoped, as he had perhaps imagined it when the photograph in the hall was taken.

Sjöberg closed the binder without investigating its contents further. He already felt sufficiently ill at ease after the little insight he had got into his colleague's personal life. Before he left Einar Eriksson's apartment, however, he made a detour into the kitchen. He stopped in front of the cooker, which like the worktop and the little kitchen table was clean and tidy, and it suddenly struck him that actually it must be Einar himself who made his sausage stroganoff at this stove. Earlier that morning he had laughed to himself at the thought of Eriksson in an apron among the saucepans, but now he had no problem not laughing. The fact that Einar kept things clean and tidy around him and managed his personal hygiene – which he did, although he was always dressed in the same boring, cheap clothes – indicated that he had not given up. Although at 'given up', Sjöberg then thought: who was he to have any opinion about whether Einar Eriksson's life was worth living? But there was something about Eriksson – there had always been something about Eriksson – whose sullen manner gave an impression of being sorrow-stricken and resigned. It was not something Sjöberg had immediately noticed, instead the feeling had grown stronger as the years passed, and he had never really been able to put his finger on what it was. That was why he always refrained from joining in his other colleagues' rather harsh talk about Einar and the pointed remarks that were constantly made behind his back.

On the little work surface to the right of the stove were a few cookbooks. One of them he recognized from his own mother's kitchen. It must be at least fifty years old, he thought as he pulled it out, careful not to let the other books fall over. He turned to the title page to find out when the book was printed. He didn't find that information, but there was an inscription inside the cover: 'Sincere congratulations on your graduation to our clever dear Solveig from Grandma and Grandpa, May 1968.'

So now we know where to find Mrs Solveig Eriksson, Sjöberg noted, but where the hell is Einar?

* * *

Hamad and Westman had divided up the work on the phone list between them, and when Hamad was finished with his half of the job he went over to Westman's office and invited her to come and eat. But she obviously had something else going on – when had they had lunch together lately? – so he decided to go out on his own, got his jacket and went down to street level. Sandén's daughter Jenny was sitting alone on reception and her face lit up when she caught sight of him.

'Hey, good-looking!' she called loudly, so that it echoed in the marble hall.

'The same to you. How are you doing? Are you by yourself?'

'Yes, Lotten is at lunch.'

'So when do you get to eat?'

'I already ate. I brought my lunch.'

'Too bad. Otherwise you could have come with me.'

She gave him a sunny smile, happy to get some attention.

'I have to stay here anyway, until Lotten comes back.'

Good, she knew what was expected of her. Lotten was the perfect mentor for Jenny: definite about how she wanted things, appreciative and instructive. And Jenny was like a marionette in her hands, doing everything she was told.

'Are they nice to you? No one is treating you badly?'

'No one is mean to me.'

'Of course, everyone likes you, Jenny. You're a great girl.'

Hamad saw how a little frown appeared on her forehead as she shifted her gaze towards the entrance.

'But I don't like everyone,' Jenny said sullenly.

He cast an eye over towards the doors to find out which police officer it might be who was apparently not highly regarded by the new receptionist. With a smile, he leaned towards her and whispered confidentially, 'It doesn't matter. A lot of girls don't like Holgersson.'

While they were still on speaking terms Petra had said on several occasions that she could not stand the guy.

'But I'm sure he's just joking,' Hamad continued. 'What sort of thing does he do?'

'I think he's making fun of me,' Jenny whispered back.

'Don't worry about it. There are idiots at all workplaces.' Hamad straightened up and continued in a normal conversational tone. 'And otherwise? Are things going okay? Do you need help with anything?'

'No, I know exactly what to do. Although I have a problem at home that you can help me with.' She lit up again as this thought occurred to her.

'I see. What's that then?'

Holgersson had now made his way up to reception and Hamad nodded to him as he passed.

'My computer,' Jenny replied. 'There's something wrong with it. It's so slow.'

'Can't your dad help you with that?'

'Dad? He doesn't know anything about computers either!'

Hamad could only agree with her.

'Okay, I can look at it sometime.'

'Tonight, please!'

Hamad capitulated before her childish eagerness and answered with a sigh, 'Okay, Jenny. I'll come over after work. Now I'm going to lunch.'

As he left, he cast a glance over his shoulder towards the stairs, where to his surprise he saw Westman standing talking to the odious Holgersson. Hamad noted dejectedly that he himself had sunk lower than he thought was possible on her list, and continued on towards the doors.

Petra Westman was hungry too, but she had been working on the same things as Hamad all morning; that was more than enough. Hearing his steps die away down the corridor, she decided to take a break too, pulled on her jacket and left her office. She was just at the stairs when Jenny's voice echoed in the reception hall down below: 'Hey, good-looking!'

Well, Jenny was the way she was, but Hamad answered in the same spirit. And then there was some jolly small talk. Almost at the bottom of the stairs, she stopped at the sight of Hamad leaning over the reception counter whispering something in Jenny's ear. Credulously Jenny whispered back, radiant with happiness. Nothing surprised Petra any more, but that Hamad needed so much self-affirmation that he couldn't even keep his paws off Jenny Sandén, that took the biscuit. Yet another creep showed up in reception when Holgersson stepped in through the door. Which made Hamad immediately conceal his intentions; he straightened up and abandoned the pathetic whispering game. After which it was loudly and clearly decided that he would go round to Jenny's in the evening. Unbe-fucking-lievable.

Holgersson was almost at the stairs now, eyeing her lasciviously up and down. She shuddered, but at the same time started moving so that her reaction would not be noticed.

'He'd chase anything in a skirt, Hamad,' Holgersson noted with a meaningful smile when they met on the stairs.

'Oh, yes,' Westman replied tiredly, without really being clear what she meant by that.

'She is good-looking, so it's not that.'

Westman stopped reluctantly.

'So what is it then?' she hissed, even though she was actually not at all interested in hearing the answer.

'Well, I guess the lift doesn't go all the way up. You know?'

She considered making some scathing comment, but could not decide in what direction she wanted to direct her disgust, so with a look of contempt she just shook her head and left the asylum.

Wednesday Afternoon

Sjöberg had just hung his jacket over the back of his chair when Sandén walked into the office.

'How's it going?' Sjöberg asked, sitting down.

Sandén sighed and sat down in the visitor's chair opposite.

'I've managed to get hold of a translator. An old American officer, Sverker Ivarsson.'

Sjöberg raised his eyebrows. 'Sverker Ivarsson?'

'Yes, he was born in Sweden, but emigrated to the US in the thirties. He was stationed at an American base in the Philippines during the Second World War and evidently learned the language then. After the war he moved back here again. He's sitting in my office reading those letters, but they contain nothing of interest. The brothers and sisters are doing fine, and this or that cousin got married, and the roof has blown off and so on. It's leading nowhere.'

Hamad and Westman appeared in the doorway. Sjöberg waved them in.

'Catherine Larsson did not have a mobile phone account,' said Hamad.

'And the calls she made,' Westman continued, 'were almost exclusively to the preschool and Vida Johansson. Vida's home number and Vida's mobile. Incoming calls we have from the Child Welfare Centre, the National

Dental Service, preschool, Vida, naturally, and a few of the customers on the list we got from her. None of them is named Erik.'

'You'll have to keep researching those calls,' said Sjöberg. 'Especially the later ones. Considering Catherine's narrow circle of acquaintants it's probable that this Erik is there somewhere after all. Maybe he works at the Child Welfare Centre or the Dental Service.'

Sjöberg turned to Sandén.

'Have you been able to contact the customers on the list?'

Sandén shook his head.

'It wasn't the easiest thing to find a translator. But I'll get going on that. And as you said: somewhere there perhaps we have our man. I would rather look them in the eyes when I talk to them.'

'That's a good idea,' said Sjöberg. 'Take Petra with you. Jamal, you can keep working on the phone calls on your own. Find out who called and what was discussed.'

'And the chief inspector himself is fully occupied, do I understand?' Sandén said with a roguish smile.

Much too quickly Sjöberg answered that nothing out of the ordinary had emerged from either Göran and Vida Johansson's private finances or the decorating company's. Sandén's face resumed a neutral expression as if on command, but a slight frown revealed his surprise.

'I'll make enquiries about Christer Larsson's first wife. Was there anything else?' Sjöberg asked, standing up decisively.

Hamad and Westman left the office, but Sandén lingered.

'You have something going on . . . ?' he said hesitantly, making no effort to get out of the visitor's chair.

With a sigh Sjöberg let himself fall back into his chair. It rolled backwards a little, but he pulled it up to the desk and rested his chin on his palms. The drumming of his fingers over his temples possibly revealed to Sandén that something was not really as it should be. But he did not want to talk about his visit to Einar Eriksson's apartment. Not yet anyway. Hopefully Einar would show up soon and then he could forget the whole thing. If on the other hand he did not reappear in the next few days, Sjöberg would involve his colleagues in the search. He decided to give it until Friday morning.

'You've been gone the better part of the morning,' Sandén pointed out, now with more concern than curiosity in his voice.

Sjöberg did not like his tone – it suddenly struck him that Sandén perhaps suspected it was something personal that was preoccupying him, and that it had to do with Margit. That thought caused him to abandon his police instincts in order to clear himself of all possible suspicion in that direction.

'This stays between us,' said Sjöberg, raising a finger to underscore his seriousness.

'Obviously,' said Sandén with surprise. 'But you don't have to say anything if you don't –'

'You will not breathe a word of this,' Sjöberg continued sternly.

Sandén nodded soberly in response.

'I was at Einar's place,' said Sjöberg in a low voice,

casting a glance in the direction of the open door to the corridor.

To be on the safe side he went over and closed it. Sandén followed him with his eyes, now with a slightly amused expression.

'This is nothing to laugh at,' said Sjöberg seriously. 'The man's been absent for three days now without getting in touch. He hasn't called me or anyone else here either. He hasn't phoned in sick or requested leave.'

'So what explanation did he have for that?' asked Sandén.

'He wasn't at home! I still don't know where he's hiding himself. I talked to one of the neighbours, who told me that he drives off in the car every Saturday morning and comes home late in the evening. As he did last Saturday, although the neighbour did not see him return that particular evening. But the car was there anyway, so he must have. So we can rule out a traffic accident.'

'But he must be inside,' Sandén interjected. 'He just doesn't feel like talking to you.'

'Wait and you'll hear,' Sjöberg continued. 'I asked the neighbour if Einar usually takes his wife along on those outings, but he just laughed and answered that Einar Eriksson doesn't have a wife. Didn't you have the impression that Einar is married?'

Sandén thought for a moment before he answered.

'Well, yes, he has mentioned a wife a few times, but he has never talked about her directly. Or about anything private, for that matter. Although I definitely recall that he wears a wedding ring.'

'I broke in, Jens.'

Sandén formed an inaudible 'oh' with his lips.

'I picked the lock on the front door and went in.'

'Yes, well, you're not allowed to do that, of course. The police will come.'

'Well, what the hell was I supposed to do? He has no friends that I know of, no family.'

'So he doesn't have a wife?'

'Yes, he has a wife. But she's in some bloody home in Fellingsbro, wherever that is. And she's been there a long time. I found ten-year-old invoices from there. Ten years! No wonder he's peevish.'

'So you rummaged through his apartment. Naughty, naughty, Conny.'

'I felt I had to. For Einar's sake. We can't just let him disappear; we're the police, damn it. Who's going to help him with whatever has happened to him if not us?'

'But don't you think it's a bit early to –' Sandén ventured.

'I don't think so. There were newspapers on the hall floor from Sunday morning. He's been gone for four days and if he had anyone who cared, he would have been reported missing several days ago.'

'If he weren't so damned contrary, perhaps he would have someone who cared,' Sandén pointed out.

Sjöberg looked dejectedly out of the window, where snow was falling heavily from a grey sky. Neither of them said anything for a while.

'Did you know that he plays golf?' Sjöberg asked at last.

Sandén shook his head.

'Or has played, at least. The golf bag looked old.'

'Where does he live?' Sandén asked.

'Over there,' Sjöberg answered with a nod in that vague direction. 'Eriksdalsgatan. In a small studio. Neat and tidy. All alone, without a wife. Single bed and *one* chair at the dining table. And the wedding photo was hanging on the wall. A very beautiful and happy couple, I would say.'

'Unbelievable,' said Sandén seriously.

'And now you keep quiet about this. Go back to what you're supposed to be doing, and I'll devote myself a little to this on the side, so to speak.'

Sandén nodded and stood up.

'And listen,' Sjöberg added. 'No insinuations, please.'

Sandén nodded compliantly and left the room.

Christer Larsson's first wife had not remarried. After the divorce she took back her maiden name and was now known as Ingegärd Rydin. She turned out to be registered at an address in Arboga, of all places. When Sjöberg heard this the first thing that occurred to him was that perhaps he should take the trouble to go there to question her. Then he rejected that thought. He realized that it would only be a pretext for investigating that property mystery, which was gnawing at him. He had enough on his plate as it was, with a butchered family and a colleague who had vanished off the face of the earth.

He picked up the phone and dialled the number for Ingegärd Rydin, but got no answer. So he stood up and left the room. When he reached Eriksson's office he peeked in, as he had so many times before during the past few days, but his colleague was not sitting at his desk now either. He looked quickly up and down the corridor. No one saw him hesitantly take a step into the darkened room, but he moved with greater decisiveness after he had closed the door behind him. He turned on the ceiling light, which blinked a few times before drenching the office in inhospitable white glare. Sjöberg did as he usually did in his own office; he went over and turned on the desk lamp, then went back to the door and turned off the fluorescent ceiling light. Then he went over to the bookshelves that flanked the desk, and stood for a while letting his gaze run across the binders and book spines. He saw nothing there that did not appear completely ordinary. Eriksson's desk chair stood properly pushed in under the desk and when Sjöberg pulled it out he discovered that although it had wheels like his own it lacked armrests. He asked himself whether that had to do with his colleague's lower rank or if Eriksson simply preferred a chair without armrests. He sat down in the chair rather cautiously, partly so as not to change the setting in any way but mainly because he felt deeply uncomfortable. Once again he was trespassing on Einar Eriksson's territory and this time too he felt a knot of unease in the pit of his stomach.

The desk was just as tidy as his own. There were a few piles of paper in a neat row in the upper-right-hand corner; picking up the top few papers from each of the piles he could quickly tell that they had to do with the cases Eriksson was working on or had recently worked on. He pulled out the top drawer in the pedestal under the desk and found only office supplies: pens, rubbers, stapler, tape, scissors, hole punch, a can of colourful plastic paper clips and a few notepads in various sizes. The two bottom pads were blank, the one on top contained notes from a number of meetings that Sjöberg himself had led. The next drawer contained a variety of other things, such as a mobile charger, a few packs of CDs, a tin of metal paper clips and a torch. The bottom drawer was locked, but it took Sjöberg less than a minute to pick the simple lock with the help of a paper clip.

What first drew his attention was the little card with one-time codes from Nordea that stuck out from under a plastic folder in the drawer. He picked it up and studied it while his thoughts churned in his head. So did Eriksson pay his bills at the office? But Sjöberg quickly realized that it would be completely natural for him to do that. Einar Eriksson was a computer person and as such he would use the Internet and nothing else to pay his bills. Sjöberg had not seen a computer in Eriksson's apartment, so consequently he must manage his affairs from here. He cast a furtive glance over at the computer, then another at the credit-card-sized rectangle he held in his hand. Eriksson had used only two of the four-digit codes, so there were lots left to scratch off.

Then he decided. With his free hand firmly gripping the desktop he moved the wheeled chair over to Einar Eriksson's computer. The green light on the screen indicated that it was on and the dull hum from somewhere under the desk convinced him that the computer was on too. He moved the mouse a little to activate the dark screen and a log-in icon with the text 'Einar' against a sky-blue background appeared for him. With low expectations he clicked on the icon, only to be met by the request to enter a password. Sjöberg let out a deep sigh and slumped down in the chair. Naturally Eriksson was not logged into the computer; you were automatically logged out if you did not show it proper attention for half an hour or so.

He clasped his hands behind his neck and looked around the room. It was impersonal, like everything else that had to do with Einar. The office was considerably smaller than his own, and because two walls were taken up by bookshelves and the door and a third by windows, only one wall remained to hang anything on. But nothing was hanging there, except a jumper on a traditional institutional hook.

He rolled back to the pedestal and dug deeper among the objects in the bottom drawer. Under a bundle of papers from an old course he found a small metal trophy with the inscription 'PISS, 1st Div. VI 1976'. The sport concerned was obviously football, for on the side of the engraved plaque at the foot of the trophy stood a little man with arms robustly crossed over his chest and a ball under his right foot. Sjöberg thought that the team couldn't have been that piss-poor if they had won the division. He drew the conclusion that PISS must have stood for 'Police Interdepartmental Sports Society' back then. He didn't actually know where Eriksson had had what would have been his first job, back in the mid-seventies. In any event Eriksson had evidently once been an athletic type who played both golf and football, and Sjöberg had a hard time imagining that. Eriksson was not actually overweight, like many men his age, but he definitely made a rather unhealthy impression with his pale skin, poor posture and sunken eyes that testified to too little sleep.

He put the trophy back in the drawer and pulled out a

plastic folder that seemed to contain bills, the bills Eriksson had not yet paid or had paid recently, Sjöberg assumed. He set the folder in front of him on the desk and pulled out the contents: a rent notice from HSB for the apartment on Eriksdalsgatan, a deposit card from the ICA bank, a minimal phone bill and the familiar and considerably larger bill from the Solberga nursing home. He had a sudden inspiration and rolled back to the computer, whose screen was still illuminated and still ordered him to enter a password. He typed in 'Solveig', and bingo! He was in.

With rising pulse he double-clicked on the icon for Internet Explorer, made his way to the Nordea website and on to the page for private customers, where he was asked to provide civil registration number and yet another password. He tapped in the civil registration number he had got from the woman at the payroll office, tried 'Solveig' again, and finally scratched off a four-digit one-time code from Eriksson's little card. This time too luck was with him and he suddenly found himself in the middle of Einar Eriksson's personal finances. A shiver passed through his body as he started systematically going through his colleague's financial transactions over the past year, which was as far back in time as he could access.

Every month a sum of over 5,500 kronor – which Sjöberg decided must be Eriksson's wife's disability pension – was deposited in Eriksson's account by the National Agency for Social Insurance. In addition he took home about 20,000 kronor in salary. Of this money about 11,500 kronor went on his wife's stay at the nursing home, 4,500 on rent and 2,500 on other fixed expenses.

The remaining 7,000 kronor he took out via ATMs and used for day-to-day expenses, Sjöberg assumed. Eriksson did not have a credit card connected to the current account at Nordea, nor did he seem to have taken out any loans. Einar Eriksson's finances were easy to understand to say the least, and as far as Sjöberg could see he lived exactly according to his means and had nothing saved for the future.

He made sure that Eriksson's computer was set up to use the same printer that he himself always used and checked that the queue was empty. Then he printed out all the information from Eriksson's Nordea account and logged out of the bank's website and the computer. He put the card and folder of invoices back in the bottom desk drawer, locked the drawer with the paper clip and pushed the chair back in under the desk. After turning off the desk lamp he groped his way over to the door in semi-darkness, opened it and slipped unseen back into the corridor.

Quickly he made his way to the printer, which was located in an alcove off the little kitchenette where the coffee machine was. Instead of waiting until all the pages had printed out he picked them up one at a time so that no passer-by could happen to see what they were. When all the pages had printed out he folded them twice and quickly slipped them into his back pocket.

* * *

It was really windy now and the clouds were hanging heavily over the city, apparently prepared to release their contents at any moment over the already freezing inhabitants of Stockholm. The blanket of clouds also effectively prevented the promising rays of the March sun from peeking through, and even though it was only just after three o'clock in the afternoon it already felt like twilight.

Jamal Hamad walked with his shoulders hunched up and his hands in his pockets. Not so much due to the weather as to how he felt. He was making a fuss about nothing. He hoped. This little excursion was a real long shot; it was an odds-on bet that he would have to trot back to the station without having accomplished anything. But that didn't matter, because in this particular case he wanted nothing more. Besides, it was nice to get out. Westman's march past in reception, not even condescending to look at him, gave him cold shivers. There was certainly an ice age at the office. Why, he did not really understand, but it was annoyingly unsettling.

The whole thing had started about six months earlier when he sat and lied to Westman for an entire evening at the Pelican. As usual they had lots to talk about and the mood was crude but hearty. It was late, almost midnight, by the time they'd left. She'd suggested they could carry on drinking, but he had steeled himself and declined, because he was going to get up and play golf early the next morning. That it was Bella Hansson he was playing with, and that she was waiting for him in her car a block or two away besides, had nothing to do with anyone. Not even Westman. There was a slight possibility that she had put two and two together and suspected that there was something between him and Bella. Rightly so, there had been too. It had started as a semi-serious pentathlon, comprising bowling, golf, tennis and whatever, and, yes, it had developed into something a little more. Which was now over, no more to it than that, for those involved in any case. But perhaps Westman felt there was more to it? Because she had not said a friendly word to him after that evening, and he could not interpret that as anything other than jealousy.

Not that he had ever noticed her showing any interest in him – although that could have something to do with the fact that he had been married until rather recently. But wasn't she smart enough to notice that she was special to him? And when she did not show any interest herself, she could hardly expect him to live in celibacy. Or was that maybe exactly the way it was? She just wanted to own him, would not share him with anyone else?

And the punishment for defying her unspoken rules was cruel. Shunning him, not speaking, and making little digs whenever the occasion arose. Subtle and deliberate. Old-womanish. Not at all like the Petra he knew, but his transgression had obviously been serious and maybe he should be grateful that she did not punch him in the jaw. Or perhaps not. It might actually be better to clear the air and put their cards on the table.

But the annoying thing was that the more she persecuted him, the more he wanted her back. To have her. Sick world, thought Hamad as he finally managed to outwit the complicated lock mechanisms and the gate he was trying to open gave way at last.

He pulled a few times on the door without getting it to open before he noticed the knob right above his head – an additional security arrangement to prevent the children from slipping out in some unguarded moment. He stepped into the cloakroom, locked the door behind him and obediently placed his own boots next to the children's.

The first thing he saw when he looked up was a large poster on the wall with portrait photos of Catherine Larsson's two children, framed by flowers made from small pieces of crêpe paper in various colours. Below the pictures, in gold paint, was clearly printed: 'Tom and Linn, we miss you.' Below the text the staff and children, to the best of their ability, had written their names. Hamad swallowed the lump in his throat. On a little table below the poster they had placed a vase with a lovely bouquet of flowers in happy colours, surrounded by stuffed animals.

He tiptoed into the room, trying not to interrupt the activity going on inside. A woman about his own age was doing a puppet show for the children. She stood with her back to him, hidden from her audience behind a large sheet of plywood with a window cut out at face height. Her hands were stuffed into two glove puppets: a crocodile and a king, eagerly conversing with each other in funny voices. The children sitting on the floor in front of the handmade theatre looked up, wide-eyed, towards the puppets and not a sound escaped them until the crocodile suddenly made a comment that made everyone laugh. Then the preschool teacher took the opportunity to turn towards Hamad, quickly looking him over, and asked in a low voice, 'Are you from the police?'

He wondered to himself if it really was that obvious, but confirmed her assumption. She fixed her eyes on some indeterminate point behind him and nodded quickly in the direction from which he had come.

'Maud is doing dishes out in the kitchen, talk to her,' she whispered, whereupon she turned her back to him again and continued with her performance.

He slipped out of the room and went past the cloak-room and the little shrine again. He heard the clatter of dishes and followed the sound along the corridor to the kitchen. At the sink stood a woman in her sixties, short-haired and dressed in jeans and a navy-blue T-shirt with rolled-up sleeves. She stood deeply immersed in her own thoughts and did not notice Hamad as he entered the kitchen. He cleared his throat as he pulled out his wallet with the police badge from his back pocket.

'Oh, I didn't notice anyone was here,' she excused her-self, letting go of the washing-up brush and plastic mug she had been cleaning, and drying her hands on her jeans.

'I apologize for disturbing you,' said Hamad, holding up his identification in front of her with his left hand and extending his right hand in greeting. 'Jamal Hamad, from the Hammarby Police.'

She took his hand, introduced herself as Maud Fah-lander and gestured towards the chairs around the kitchen table.

'Yes, nothing's the same here,' she sighed, sitting down on the edge of one of the chairs.

Hamad sat down on another one.

'I understand that,' he said sympathetically, 'and I'm truly sorry about what happened.'

'You just want to stay at home and cry,' she said, shaking her head dejectedly, 'but all three of us are here. For the sake of the children. Almost all the children are here too. We conferred with each other and with the parents and decided that it would be best. To be able to talk about it together and explain it to the children.'

'I saw the poster out there,' said Hamad. 'And . . . the shrine. It was nice.'

He felt his eyes getting damp and tried to blink it away.

'We did that this morning, with the children. As a way of processing the grief,' Maud Fahlander explained.

'How are they taking it?'

'They're so little, for most of them it's really not so easy to take in the information. We haven't gone into any details . . . about how they died and such. But you have to tell them something . . . They are going to hear about it anyway. We say that it was a nasty man with a knife who cut them. That has created worry, naturally, that something similar could happen to them.'

She took a deep breath before she continued.

'They ask a lot of questions. Some of the children cried. We hug a lot and talk quite a bit about Tom and Linn, in positive terms. The children are taking it well, I think, anyway. It was worse for the parents. And for us on the staff, of course.'

She fell silent. Hamad struggled to think of anything sensible to say, so they sat for a while in silence. The door into the neighbouring section opened and shut again with a bang. The preschool teacher was startled by the sudden sound.

'Are you getting anywhere?' she asked.

'Unfortunately I can't answer that,' said Hamad. 'But we haven't arrested anyone. You should know that we are prioritizing this case. And naturally you will be informed in due course.'

Maud Fahlander sighed and shook her head despondently.

'It doesn't make any sense,' she said. 'Completely incomprehensible.'

Hamad agreed.

'Occasionally I've been involved with children who have got sick and died,' she continued. 'Or been in an accident. But slaughtered like this . . .' She shook her head again. 'What did you want to talk to me about?'

A shiver passed through Hamad.

'I actually have just one question,' he said.

* * *

With the release of tension after his risky prying in Eriksson's office, Sjöberg felt a headache coming on. He decided to try to cure it with a large glass of water and a couple of dry biscuits, which he got from the kitchenette. He brought them with him into his own office and sat down in front of the computer. When the glass was empty and the biscuits consumed his headache had got worse. He stared listlessly at the black screen in front of him. After some hesitation he finally decided to do something else that he did not have the right to do.

He logged into the crime register and searched for Einar Eriksson, whose civil registration number he had by now learned by heart. He was aware that his search could be traced, and if it turned out to be unfounded – which it would be if Eriksson were to suddenly reappear – he would lose his access to the register. His suitability as a detective inspector and as a policeman would naturally be questioned. Sjöberg tried to console himself with the thought that this offence seemed relatively insignificant after the break-in and computer intrusion he was already guilty of that day. But it worried him that the offence he was now in the process of committing, in contrast to the previous ones, would probably be discovered. Fortunately Einar Eriksson had no criminal record, and Sjöberg hoped that Eriksson himself, when he showed up, would not be interested in pursuing a lawsuit against him.

Then, without knowing what he was really looking for, he called the population registration office. He introduced himself as a chief inspector, whereupon he was asked to hang up to be called back by the official in question. After a few minutes the call came and Sjöberg discovered everything there was to know about Einar Eriksson and his wife, which was not much. He took notes while he listened and when the call was over he went through the information on his pad.

Eriksson had no siblings and his parents were no longer alive. He was, as Sjöberg had correctly guessed, married to one Solveig Eriksson, née Jönsson, and they were born in the same year. She had no living siblings or parents either. They had been married since 1976, had no children, and she was registered at the same address as her husband. Eriksson had changed address in April of 2006, when he moved to Eriksdalsgatan from an address in a townhouse area in Huddinge, where he had lived since 1980. Prior to this Einar Eriksson had been registered for census purposes in Arboga.

This admittedly new but not particularly interesting information reminded him that he should once again try to get hold of Christer Larsson's first wife, Ingegärd Rydin. He picked up the phone and entered the number, but got no answer this time either. After letting the phone ring ten times he gave up.

Sjöberg sighed quietly, clasped his hands behind his neck and spun the office chair a quarter-turn towards the window. He stretched his legs out in front of him and tilted the backrest as far back as it would go. Spring seemed to be holding off and large snowflakes whirled around outside the window. The wind was starting to pick up. Although the days were getting longer all other signs of spring were conspicuous in their absence. He had not seen a single snowdrop so far, but perhaps he was just inattentive. The thermometer had been at minus five degrees this morning when he left his apartment on Skånegatan, and there was still ice on the Hammarby canal, even though the boats drove up the channel in the middle all the time.

He was thinking along these lines when the phrase 'frozen solid' flashed into his mind. He no longer recognized himself. How could he so cold-heartedly betray his beloved Åsa? True, it had only happened a few times, but still, it had been with the same woman and that meant that it was a question of a relationship and not some isolated tryst. He tried to convince himself that he was ashamed of himself and his actions, but emotionally he was neutral. Shameless. Ice-cold. What happened was in some way inevitable and he sealed it away from himself in a way that he did not recognize. Perhaps he ought to see a psychologist, someone who could explain the constantly recurring dream to him, put labels on his emotions and give him a shove in the right direction. Or even better, a direct order, an exhortation to immediately end the relationship with that woman. 'That woman,' he repeated to himself. Now he had gone so far as to reduce Margit to 'that woman' in his thoughts. He had shifted the burden of guilt over to her.

He sighed again. A whole family had been put to death and Einar was missing as well, and in neither case had they really got anywhere. Sjöberg was struck by a feeling of impotence. And here he sat, dwelling on his own worries. An image suddenly came to him: Einar waking up alone in his little apartment every morning, even though he had been married for more than thirty years. Einar, who every day struggled off to a job that he was obviously not happy in. But it was a job he was trained for, and work he needed so that he could pay for his wife to stay in the nursing home. It struck him that Einar Eriksson must really love his wife, in spite of the miserable circumstances, if he was prepared to spend so much money on her care. He had not put her just anywhere, instead he had chosen that 'gem in Bergslagen, in picturesque surroundings'. Nor had he abandoned her, but instead conscientiously got in the car every Saturday morning and drove all the way to Fellingsbro. Because wasn't that most likely how he spent his Saturdays?

Sjöberg turned his chair back towards the computer. With his right index finger he went to the Eniro website. He clicked on the 'Maps' tab and after a few attempts managed to find a map of Västmanland with the little community of Fellingsbro marked on it. It turned out to be just outside Arboga, on the way to Lindesberg. Suddenly it occurred to him why Eriksson had chosen that particular area for his sick wife: that was where she came from. He wanted her to be nursed, for whatever condition she might conceivably have, in her home district. Einar Eriksson grew in Sjöberg's estimation. But why had he moved away from there?

A tactful knock on the doorframe woke him from his musings. Sjöberg waved in Jamal Hamad, dressed today in a pair of chinos with a wide belt and a light-blue shirt. His dark eyes flashed in the subdued lighting from the desk lamp, and Sjöberg recognized that look. It usually meant eagerness and excitement: Hamad had come across something. But despite this his steps were hesitant and Sjöberg did not see the little hint of a smile that was usually there when Hamad had made a discovery. Gesturing towards the visitor's chair, he asked Hamad to sit down. Hamad sat, cleared his throat, but said nothing.

'How's it going?' Sjöberg began.

'Not a nibble on either the Dental Service or the Child Welfare Centre. Their calls concerned quite everyday matters and they have no Erik among their employees.'

'But . . . ?' Sjöberg said encouragingly.

'But what?'

'I can see that you have something.'

Hamad sighed, but even though Sjöberg smiled his younger colleague did not respond to it. Instead his gaze wandered dejectedly around the room.

'You're going to be angry with me.'

'Angry?' Sjöberg laughed. 'Good Lord, I don't think I've ever been angry with you. Let's hear it.'

'It was a hunch,' said Hamad. 'Far-fetched, but it was just a feeling I had –'

'I'm usually the one who believes in following my intuition,' said Sjöberg, still smiling. 'You're supposed to represent the objective type.'

'This is unfortunately probably not totally non-objective either –'

'Unfortunately? Out with it now.'

Hamad straightened up and Sjöberg could see how tense he was. He had never seen him that way before.

'Conny, do you remember that jumper that was hanging in the hall at Catherine Larsson's?' he began.

Sjöberg felt as if an ice-cold gust of wind rushed past him and he got goosebumps all over his body. Suddenly he knew what Hamad was going to say, and he realized that he had subconsciously had the same thought himself. Even so, before Hamad had time to continue he had already decided to oppose it. He nodded, a guarded look on his face.

'I think it's Eriksson's jumper,' Hamad continued, lowering his eyes.

'Which damned Eriksson?' Sjöberg spat out.

The harsh tone riled Hamad. His eyes met Sjöberg's defiantly.

'Einar, damn it. I did say you would get angry.'

'Of course I'm angry,' Sjöberg answered condescendingly. 'It was a completely ordinary jumper from Åhléns. How many like that do you think there are in Stockholm?'

'Hundreds, perhaps thousands, I know. But I think it's his anyway.'

'And what makes this "not totally non-objective"?' Sjöberg asked sarcastically.

'I sniffed the jumper,' Hamad replied, his eyes flashing again. 'It smelled of Old Spice. And I can tell you that there are not many men who use that these days.'

'But Eriksson does?'

Hamad nodded.

'I'm imagining that it's roughly the same clientele using Old Spice who buy their jumpers at Åhléns,' Sjöberg said dismissively.

'That's a bit snobbish,' Hamad appealed, but Sjöberg was not in the mood for banter, and simply looked at him coolly without saying anything.

'Erik Eriksson on Eriksdalsgatan,' said Hamad knowingly.

'Is that the objective part of your argument? A silly name game?'

'Einar is Erik.'

'Einar is missing.'

'Which makes my discovery seem even more reasonable then.'

'But Jamal, damn it! What is it you've discovered?'

'That Einar is Erik.'

'Based on the Åhléns' jumper?'

'Based on witness statements from the preschool staff.'

Sjöberg turned completely cold inside and he felt a lump growing in his throat. He got up quickly from his chair and went over to the window. The sun was shining now from a clear blue sky, which did not match his mood.

With his back to Hamad he asked in as controlled a way as he was able, 'What have you done, Jamal?'

'I've shown a photo of Einar to the preschool staff. And they confirmed that Einar is Erik. That Einar definitely is Erik. There's no question, Conny.'

'You've defied my orders, Jamal.'

'Or you could say that I've followed your orders and done a little extra. And I think it was a damned good thing, because now we know for sure.'

Sjöberg put his hands in his trouser pockets and sighed dejectedly. A large crane in the industrial area on the other side of the canal swung around a half-turn with a construction shed hanging from it on a wire some fifty metres above the ground.

'You felt it too, right?' Hamad asked carefully.

'I wouldn't say that,' Sjöberg replied. 'But I understood what was coming when you started talking about the sweater. I guess it must have been gnawing away somewhere at the back of my mind.'

He turned back to his colleague.

'Why didn't you come to me first?'

'I wanted something more solid. Which was just as well, considering you reacted as expected.'

Sjöberg sat down again. Neither of them said anything for a while. Sjöberg drummed his fingertips on the desk. His eyes were fixed on something far beyond his assistant.

'What do we do now?' Hamad finally dared to ask.

'We have to put a search out for him.'

'On what grounds?'

'That he's been missing for four days.'

'Four – where did you get that from?'

'The night between Saturday and Sunday.'

'You mean when the murders were committed?'

'I mean that certain investigations lead me to conclude that he came home in his car late Saturday evening, but he did not pick up Sunday morning's *Dagens Nyheter* from the hall floor.'

'Oh damn it,' said Hamad with admiration.

'Another of Einar's sweaters is hanging in his office. Send it to Forensics and ask them to compare any hair strands and so on.'

'So you've been thinking along these lines too?'

Sjöberg did not answer the question. Suddenly he started thinking clearly.

'I'll contact Einar's bank to get confirmation that he was the one who financed Catherine Larsson's housing.'

'Do you think he was?'

'I'm convinced he was. Einar lives on nothing. Each month, anything left over after he's paid for his own and his wife's housing goes to Catherine Larsson. He sold his townhouse in Huddinge in the spring of 2006, right before Catherine bought her apartment.'

Hamad looked at him with alarm.

'But what about his wife? She must have noticed that two million kronor was missing from the bank account?'

'She doesn't live at home. For at least ten years she has been living in a nursing home, which is also paid for out of Einar's police salary.'

'So Einar is living a double life! Who would have thought . . . But that explains his secrecy in any event. And his gloominess.'

Sjöberg happened to think just then of Sandén's account of how the preschool staff viewed 'Erik'.

'He plays ball with the children . . .' he blurted out.

Hamad looked at him questioningly.

'Einar was happy with Catherine Larsson,' said Sjöberg. 'The children loved him. What went wrong?'

They had avoided the core issue for long enough now. Hamad did not mince his words.

'Do you think it was Einar who murdered them?'

Sjöberg thought for a while before he answered.

'What do you know about people actually? Most murders happen at home, behind closed doors. I find it extremely hard to see Einar as a merciless child-killer. But I have to admit that I have almost as much difficulty seeing him as a conscientious father.'

Hamad nodded thoughtfully.

'With two wives as well,' he added.

'Are you criticizing him for that?'

'Well . . . No, not if the wife has been sick as long as you say. What is it that's wrong with her?'

'I'll have to find that out. I'm going to Arboga tomorrow morning.'

Sjöberg made the decision as he said it.

'Arboga?'

'The home where she is being treated is outside Arboga,' Sjöberg clarified. 'And Christer Larsson's first wife lives there and I can't get hold of her by phone.'

'Shouldn't we focus on finding Einar?' Hamad said.

'Absolutely. That's the point of the trip. I can imagine a number of different reasons why Einar is missing.'

He tempted his young assistant and Hamad obligingly took the bait.

'He may have murdered Catherine Larsson and her children and fled. The wife may be able to tell us something that will help us find him. Or understand him.'

Sjöberg nodded approvingly, and Hamad continued his speculations.

'Christer Larsson may be the murderer. Then it's probable that this is a classic crime of passion. Einar may be . . . hard to find. You've met Christer Larsson, do you think he's capable . . . ?'

'He's depressive. Lives alone, and lacks an alibi for the night of the murders. He's a real strapping fellow; Einar would not have much of a chance against him. I have to get hold of Larsson's ex-wife.'

'He has no criminal record,' Hamad interjected.

'Neither does Einar.'

Hamad raised an eyebrow but refrained from commenting. 'If it's Einar who did this, as you said, he's had four days to get out of the country,' he pointed out.

'I don't think he has the financial resources,' said Sjöberg. 'He's already skimping on food. But I'll look into his finances immediately.'

'You already seem to know a lot,' Hamad said.

'As I said, I've made certain investigations.'

'Nice anyway that he doesn't abandon his lawful wife. Especially since he's met another woman.'

'Or cowardly. Jamal, you call in the others for a meeting at five o'clock. Rosén too, say it's important. Don't mention this yet; we'll let them carry on unbiased with what they're doing for the time being. And then you'll arrange a search for Einar.'

'As a suspect?'

Sjöberg looked at Hamad with ice in his gaze.

'As a missing person.'

* * *

Just before five they came back to the police station for the meeting that Hamad had called. Sandén stopped inside the doors to brush off the snow he had brought in with him on this unpredictable March day. Westman strode purposefully over to the reception counter as soon as she saw that Jenny was there.

'I heard you're going to have a visitor this evening,' she said, getting straight to the point.

'Yes,' Jenny answered naively. 'Jamal is coming to see me.'

Sandén tried to get rid of the damp snow in his hair by shaking his head, to Lotten's amusement, in an almost dog-like way.

'I would advise you against that,' said Westman.

Jenny looked at her with surprise.

'I don't understand . . .'

Lotten was laughing loudly at Sandén, which made him ham up his performance even more.

'It's a bad idea,' Westman continued. 'He's not a good guy.'

'He's not?'

'No, it's best that you look out for yourself.'

Sandén was done with his one-man show and barged over to reception.

'But why? What has he done?' Jenny wanted to know.

Petra Westman leaned a little closer and said, 'He eats girls like you for breakfast.'

Whether it was down to this information or her father's boisterous arrival was hard to say, but a little smile spread across Jenny's face.

'That's harsh,' Sandén said with a laugh. 'Don't listen to what she says, honey. She's our tattletale here at the station.'

He cast a glance at the big clock on the wall.

'Forty seconds until show time, Westman. We'll have to make it snappy.'

* * *

'The investigation has taken an unexpected turn.' Sjöberg opened the meeting.

It was a quarter past five and in the middle of the table in the blue oval room was a tray of sandwiches that Jenny had set there a few minutes earlier.

'Help yourselves, by the way,' said Sjöberg, gesturing towards the baguettes.

He himself felt on the verge of nausea and contented himself with the bottle of mineral water he already had in his hand, but his colleagues fell on the food with pleasure.

'First I just want to hear if anyone has anything. Petra and Jens?'

'Catherine Larsson was involved in cleaning in this country, nothing else,' said Petra Westman.

'And she did it masterfully, according to one of the customers we talked to,' Sandén added. 'She got ninety kronor an hour and it seems she could have been working up to thirty hours per week. That's 2,700 kronor cash in hand a week. Good money, but not enough for an apartment in Hammarbyhamnen.'

'Nothing strange about the customers,' continued Westman. 'They are rather spread out in Stockholm and the suburbs, seemed quite normal, were dismayed by what had happened. We should check the families against the crime register, but there's nothing suspicious so far. None of them knew anything significant about her on a personal level.'

'That's good,' said Sjöberg. 'Continue with the customers and run them through the register. Despite what I'm going to tell you now.'

A sudden tension became perceptible in the room. They all stopped chewing and Sandén straightened up in his chair. Westman stroked a strand of hair back behind her ear. Hamad set his sandwich to one side on the table and crossed his arms over his chest. Rosén looked up from his notepad. Everyone's eyes were directed towards Sjöberg.

'Jamal has made another visit to the Larsson children's preschool,' Sjöberg began. 'The mysterious "Erik" has now been identified and it seems probable that he was the one who bought Catherine Larsson's apartment.'

Sjöberg paused briefly before continuing. All that could be heard in the room was the faint hum from the ventilation system.

'What I am now going to say is very sensitive information and I want you to treat it as such. It is confidential and I want all of you to keep it between these walls until we know more. The case should also be handled without prejudice and professionally, as always. This is completely independent of any conception you might have personally.'

You could have heard a pin drop. Sjöberg clasped his hands in front of him on the table and let his gaze wander over his listeners, as if to take in their unspoken promises of respect and professionalism.

'Catherine Larsson's benefactor is not actually named Erik,' said Sjöberg. 'His name is Einar Eriksson.'

No one moved or said anything for several seconds. Then Rosén dropped his pen on the table and leaned his long body back in his chair. Hamad reached for his ham and cheese sandwich and brought it to his mouth. Westman shook her head and gave Sjöberg a look that seemed to ask him to take back what he had said. Sandén spoke for all of them.

'I'll be damned,' he said simply.

Sjöberg let the news sink in for a while before he spoke again.

'We have the following facts: the murders of Catherine Larsson and her children were committed some time between Saturday evening and Sunday morning. Some time around then Einar also disappeared. He has been married to Solveig Eriksson since 1976 and she is in Solberga, a nursing home in Fellingsbro, just outside Arboga. She has been cared for there since 1977, for what reason we don't know. According to one of Einar's neighbours, he drives off in his car every Saturday morning and does not come home until late in the evening. I have verified with the nursing home that Solberga is where he goes. Every Saturday he sits by his wife's sickbed. In addition he always spends Christmas Eve, New Year's Eve and her birthday there. Like clockwork. The neighbour did not see him return last Saturday, but early the next morning his car was in its spot again, so he must have. He has not picked up Sunday's paper from the hall floor. That's what we have to go on.'

Rosén, Westman and Sandén were diligently taking notes. Hamad devoted himself to his sandwich.

'Concerning the financial aspect, the monthly deposits of 5,000 kronor to Catherine Larsson's account tally with withdrawals made by Einar. The apartment purchase itself was financed by money that Einar got when he sold the townhouse in Huddinge where he lived until April 2006, that is, right before Catherine Larsson's apartment transaction took place. Almost all of Einar's salary has gone to cover the Larsson family's needs and to pay for his wife's nursing home. The little that was left over has gone on food and lodging for himself. That's what we know. Comments?'

Three voices tried to make themselves heard at the same time, but Sandén's was strongest.

'How did you arrive at this?'

'Jamal recognized the jumper in the apartment and connected it to Einar. The preschool staff identified Einar from a photo. Forensics will now investigate the hair strands and so on to produce more objective evidence that the green jumper is Einar's.'

'Is it possible that the Larsson children are actually Einar's?' asked Rosén.

That thought had not occurred to Sjöberg.

'Naturally there is that possibility,' he replied. 'I'll consult with Bella when we get the results of Christer Larsson's paternity test. If he isn't the father of the children, we'll test Einar. Hadar, I want you to issue a warrant to search Einar's apartment. Jens, you will conduct the search, together with Petra. Don't forget the car, it's in the car park outside the building. You'll have to take the opportunity to question the neighbours too, when you're there. The ones who live in the same building will be enough. We are especially curious to know whether anyone saw him come home with the car on Saturday evening or if anyone saw him take off again. All shoes in the apartment should be sent immediately to Bella for comparison with the prints at the crime scene. Also material for comparison of fingerprints. Take whatever seems appropriate: the book on his bedside table, if there is one.'

Sjöberg tried to recollect whether he had seen any such thing, and decided that he would have remembered it if there had been. 'Or a well-thumbed cookbook,' he added to be on the safe side. 'Jamal, you get to go through Einar's computer. I'll go to Arboga tomorrow morning to question Einar's wife, Solveig, and Ingegärd Rydin, Christer Larsson's ex. We won't completely let go of the other threads, but the focus of the investigation will now be to locate Einar. His disappearance probably has major significance in this case.'

'He's either a murderer or murdered,' Sandén clarified. 'If he's a murderer, he's lying on the beach in Uruguay right now. If he's murdered, he's at the bottom of the

Hammarby canal. Just as bloody impossible to find him, whichever it is. Is there a search warrant out for him?'

'Since about an hour ago. As far as we know, he doesn't have the means to spend a long time abroad, but you never know. Jamal, you also have the task of finding out whether he has left the country by air, train, boat or any other means that can be traced. And then I want you to monitor his bank account.'

'Why would he call himself Erik in his relationship with Catherine Larsson?' Westman asked.

'Well, we can only speculate about that,' Sjöberg replied. 'For some reason he wanted to keep his identity secret. From her or from the outside world or both. For his wife's sake, presumably.'

'Everything around this relationship is secret,' Sandén observed. 'No phone call has ever been made between Einar and Catherine Larsson. And just look at the way the money was transferred from his account to hers. Completely impossible to trace. Yet he happily shows up regularly at the preschool.'

'Shouldn't we notify the press about this?' the prosecutor asked.

'I want to delay that for as long as possible. Out of concern for Einar.'

'And if he's the murderer?' said Westman.

'I prefer to see him as a victim until the opposite is proven. He's a policeman. He has no record. How would you want to be treated yourself, in a situation like this?'

Westman nodded thoughtfully and none of the others had any objections either.

'Doesn't he have any friends?' Sandén ventured to ask. Sjöberg shrugged.

'I don't know Einar personally. If any of you know anything personal about Einar that might be of interest to this investigation, then you are more than welcome to tell me. Privately,' he added, in order to further underscore the importance of loyalty to their colleague. 'We'll have to see what emerges from the search. Addresses, phone numbers, correspondence . . .'

'Shouldn't we question Catherine Larsson's neighbours and Vida Johansson again?' Hamad pointed out. 'With respect to Einar, I mean.'

'Absolutely. Above all we should question Christer Larsson again, but I want us to wait until I've talked with Ingegärd Rydin. Will you take on those interviews too?'

'Sure. How long will you be away, Conny?'

'I'm coming home as soon as possible. When I've done what I have to. No later than Friday afternoon. We'll keep in regular contact.'

Sjöberg stood up and the others followed his example. Petra Westman squirmed self-consciously as she closed her notebook.

'You don't think Einar is dead, do you?' she said in a low voice, meeting Sjöberg's gaze, her forehead in a worried crease.

Despite the scraping of chairs against the parquet everyone stopped in mid-motion and all eyes were again directed towards Sjöberg. He straightened his back and pushed his chair in with such decisiveness that it slammed into the edge of the table.

'He's alive,' he answered in a steady voice. 'And he's counting on us to help him.'

* * *

The sun had been out for a while, he was sure of that, because a little more light than usual had managed to make its way in through the narrow opening. Now that it was starting to get dark outside he could barely make anything out. He had managed to keep himself awake ever since this morning. Not because existence had become more tolerable in any way, but rather because he longed so much for the night, when he hoped to be able to sleep for hours. True, it would be in ten-minute shifts, but still.

Now he was leaning against the ice-cold outer wall, listening for sounds from outside. He heard the muffled bellowing of a fire engine, followed by sirens. To the sound of the emergency vehicles he rhythmically stretched the rope he had been tied up with as much as he was able. That is, almost not at all. The rope felt completely rigid and he was convinced that he was not making any progress. But what else was there to do? The slim hope that the stretching would give results by and by was what still kept him mentally strong. He could not bear to do any more; pain throbbed in every joint in his body and he was wet and cold right down to his marrow.

He braced his toes against a crack between a couple of floorboards and managed to push himself up a little bit against the wall. It was enough to allow him to tip his frozen-stiff body down on to his knees. Then he let his body, his right shoulder first, fall against the floor. It hurt, but he tried not to attach much importance to the pain. He pushed with his bound feet against the wall, and in that way managed to move his cocoon-like body the short distance to the water bowl. With an effort he raised his neck enough to put his face to the water and lap up a few of the life-giving drops. Afterwards he was so exhausted by the exercise that he lay on his side and panted for several minutes. He could have fallen asleep any time now, but he staved it off for as long as possible. He wanted to keep himself awake for another few hours before he let himself sink into the sweet embrace of sleep.

There was crunching under his head and when he had recovered he kicked himself away from the hard bread, just far enough away to be able to reach a piece with his mouth if he rolled over on to his stomach. The rapid movement that turning involved meant his right shoulder burned and he moaned in pain. Like a reptile he extended his tongue a few times towards the piece of bread, until it finally stuck enough to be pulled into his mouth. Carefully he lowered his head and chewed slowly with his forehead against the floor, before he bent his neck back and swallowed.

He tried to scream, but only a faint hiss came from his throat. He had screamed his voice away already during the first night. It didn't matter anyway, because no one seemed to ever pass outside there at this time of year. But soon, in just a few weeks, the shed would be opened for the season and the tools inside would be out in the spring earth. *Earth, the knees of your trousers were always black with earth, but what did that matter? Earth was clean dirt and the smell of potting compost* filled the car as he reversed out of the parking space at the end of their apartment building. The boys squabbled in the back seat and suddenly a little foot shot out between his own seat and his wife's.

'Stop that!' he said as sternly as he was able. 'That's dangerous. You have to sit still in the car, so that you don't touch any of my controls. That might make us crash and we don't want that, do we?'

'What is that control for?' little Tobias asked curiously.

'That's the handbrake.'

'Can I pull on it?'

'No, you mustn't touch anything in the car. It's really dangerous.'

'What would happen?'

'If you tug on the handbrake, the car will stop suddenly and then someone might run into us from behind.'

Tobias turned around to look out through the rear window.

'But there's no one behind us!' he exclaimed eagerly. 'So I guess I can —'

'Andreas, keep your little brother under control,' his wife interrupted.

Then she turned towards her husband and said with a wry smile, 'Two hours are more than enough . . .'

'Listen, this sort of thing takes eighteen years,' he sighed with pretended resignation.

The boys were lively the whole way into town, and several times they were given friendly but firm admonitions to quieten down a little. The road they were driving on now ran parallel to the river and the rays of the sun glistened animatedly on the black water. Right where the city centre's somewhat denser development began he slowed down to finally stop completely and park the car alongside the playfully rippling river.

'I'm just going to run into the cobbler's and pick up my shoes,' he explained. 'I'll be right back, boys, and then we'll drive you to Mummy.'

'Can I drive the car? Please, I get to sit in front!' Tobias asked.

The sorely tried babysitter closed the door to the driver's side behind him with a slam and stuck his head in through the window he had left half rolled down.

'No, little man, you may not. Be nice to Lady Girl now!'

Before he pulled his head out he blew her a kiss and had time to see it answered before he turned around and began to cross the street. Only then came the reaction from the older of the brothers.

'Okay!' he heard Andreas call out after him from the back seat, no doubt with the best intentions.

Wednesday Evening

Modesty Blaise – or Blaisy, as she was called – came to meet him eagerly but calmly at the door. She was a two-year-old female Silken Windhound and Jenny's current live-in partner, and she had given extra energy to the hysteria in the support staff dog lovers' club. The dog nosed Hamad curiously with her tail wagging but refrained from jumping up or barking. Jenny on the other hand threw herself around his neck, which Hamad felt somewhat dubious about, before dragging him into the apartment.

There were lighted candles on the kitchen table and it was attractively set with tea and sandwiches. Hamad had thought that he would fix the computer in fifteen minutes and then leave, but when he saw the effort Jenny had made he realized he would have to think again.

'You've arranged things very nicely,' he said as he stood in the kitchen doorway, convincing himself that his body could manage without hot food that evening and that his fatigue was just an illusion caused by the weather and the solstice. 'That looks good. I'm really hungry!'

She took him by the hand and led him the few steps to one of the chairs at the table, and it happened so quickly that he did not have time to wriggle out of her grasp before she released him of her own accord. He sat down and Jenny sat down on the chair beside him.

'Sit across from me instead. It's easier to talk then,' Hamad suggested.

'It doesn't matter where we sit, does it?' said Jenny, placing her hand on his arm. 'We can talk anyway.'

He noticed that she had put on make-up. Maybe she wore it every day, but now it was definitely more clearly visible. For some reason he did not like that. He got up and went around to the other side of the table.

'You talk better when you can see each other properly,' he repeated, sitting across from her.

She looked at him with a worried expression.

'Not when you're dating. Then you sit next to each other.'

'No, not then either,' Hamad persisted. 'And this is not a date.'

'It isn't?' she asked, with a surprise that seemed genuine.

It struck him that everything about Jenny was probably genuine for that matter. This was not some crappy role play. The most honourable thing he could do, of course, was to be honest in return.

'No, it's not. I'm only here to help you with the computer. You've made tea and that's sweet of you. We'll sit and talk for a bit while we have our tea, then I'll try to fix your computer and then I'm going home. Okay?'

'But don't you like me? Don't you think I'm pretty?'

Jenny looked a little sad, but Hamad suddenly felt completely relaxed. He felt that he could do something about this, something that her father was apparently not able to do. Simply because he was her father.

'I think you're super, Jenny. You know that. And you're very pretty.'

She lit up again. Hamad poured tea for them both and continued.

'But that's not why I like you. Because you're pretty. That's not important. And there are different ways to like someone. I like you as a friend. Because you're nice. And capable. And a good friend. I'm not in love with you and you're not in love with me.'

'Yes, I am,' said Jenny, looking completely sincere.

'You only think you are. Maybe because you think I'm nice?'

'Mmm.'

She tucked a golden wisp of hair behind her ear and brought half a rye roll with liver sausage and cucumber up to her mouth.

'Maybe not everyone is nice to you, but you shouldn't worry about that. Not everyone is nice to me either. But you don't fall in love with every person who is friendly to you. Then you would be in love with lots of people, and carry on and kiss and hug all those people all the time,' Hamad said with a laugh.

Jenny laughed too, but he doubted whether she really understood what he meant.

'And I would really like to be your friend,' he continued. 'You can come to me and tell me if someone is being mean or if you're in love or just want to talk, so I can help you. Does that sound good?'

Jenny nodded, seemingly satisfied. Hamad could not think of anything else to say about it, so they drank their tea, ate a few sandwiches and talked about other things.

'So, what's wrong with the computer?' Hamad asked when they had finished eating.

'It's so slow.'

'You probably have a slow connection. Because I guess you mean that the Internet is slow?'

'Yes,' Jenny confirmed.

'When you send email?'

'No, that works fine. It's when I watch movies that it stops all the time. I can't stand waiting.'

'Okay. We can try installing the latest version of Adobe Flash Player. Otherwise I don't know what to do.'

They got up from the kitchen table and went into the combined bedroom and living room. Hamad sat in the armchair and turned on the laptop that was on the table. Jenny sat on the arm of the chair and watched as he brought up the Adobe website and downloaded the most recent software. It went reasonably fast – there did not seem to be any problem with the broadband connection itself.

'What is it you want to watch?' Hamad asked. 'Shall we go on to YouTube?'

Without waiting for an answer he searched for the site and clicked on one of the day's most popular clips: something from a Champions League match. They were able to watch the whole clip without being left hanging.

'It wasn't any harder than that!' said Hamad, who in no way felt he was a computer specialist, and turned towards Jenny.

'I should check if it works with another film too,' she said and got up.

Hamad did the same and made room for her on the chair. A little breath of a nice-smelling perfume or soap swept past him when she moved. She looked under her favourites and chose one of them. While waiting for the page to come up she turned on the sound, and Hamad decided to make a visit to the bathroom before he left. But he stopped in mid-step when the screen suddenly changed. It was now occupied by an image that was anything but expected. In the middle of the image was a 'play' symbol and before he had time to react she had clicked on it and the film had started. To human sounds and something monotonous that was reminiscent of music a partially blurred man was pleasuring himself with a young girl. Whom the heading designated 'Lucy in the sky'. And in this age of public exposure of almost everything it probably would not have been particularly sensational. If it weren't that the girl was Jenny.

Hamad suddenly broke out in a cold sweat. Why had she recorded such a video at all? Why had she put it out on the Internet? And why was she showing it to him? The last question was the easiest to answer. She had obviously not understood a word of the conversation they had just had. Holy shit.

He leaned over her and turned off the screen, after which he turned the volume down to zero. Then he went over to the bed and sat down with a sigh. Jenny looked at him with big expectant eyes, but he only shook his head, not knowing what he should say.

'Didn't you like it?' she asked uncertainly, perhaps noticing that something was wrong.

He hesitated to answer, forcing himself to order his thoughts before he took a deep breath and replied, 'No, Jenny, I really didn't. I thought it was awful.'

'But why? You say you think I'm pretty.'

'You're pretty like this, Jenny! With clothes on and . . . I don't want to see you that way! What do you think your dad would say if he knew? He would go completely crazy!'

'But you don't have to tell him, do you?'

'That's not the point. Everyone else who knows you would also . . . Why did you do that, Jenny? Why did you put this on the Internet? Do you want a lot of dirty old men to sit and . . . well . . . when they look at this, do you want that?'

Jenny almost looked scared.

'I'm not the one who put it up, it was Pontus,' she answered, looking as if she might start crying at any moment.

'Which Pontus?'

'Pontus Örstedt. My boyfriend. Who I lived with before.'

'He's not your boyfriend any more?'

'No, he moved out.'

'Yes, that was just as well. He exploited you, Jenny. You don't do this to someone you like.'

Hamad had calmed down somewhat, and tried to think rationally.

'But it doesn't matter –' Jenny began, but was interrupted at once.

'Of course it matters. You were lucky that it was just me who discovered it. Your mother would cry blood if she knew about this. And your dad would maybe get sick again; you don't want that, do you?'

He was piling it on now, trying to get her to change her attitude.

'And your friends at work,' he continued. 'What would

they say? They would laugh behind your back, Jenny, and you would –'

'But everyone does it!'

Jenny was looking wounded, as if she felt she had been treated unjustly.

'Not everyone does it. No one I know exposes themselves like this on the net. It's only –'

'Yes, they do,' said Jenny.

'No,' said Hamad.

'I'll show you,' said Jenny.

'Don't do that, I don't want to know.'

'But you don't believe me! I have to show you . . .'

She reached towards the computer and turned the screen back on, went in under her favourites and brought up a new film. Hamad let her have her way; he would spend the whole evening making this lost child see reason if he had to. Nag about the same things over and over until they stuck.

The film had started: yet another unprofessional amateur porno sequence of the genre 'considerably older man whose face is not seen screws young woman'.

'I don't want to see any more of this sort of thing, Jenny. I'm not interested. Turn it off.'

'But don't you see who it is?'

An expectant smile spread across Jenny's face.

'No, I don't. And I don't want to know. Turn it off.'

'But look carefully. You see who it is, don't you?'

The intimate scene came closer as the camera zoomed in on the girl who, with eyes closed and mouth half open, was being screwed from behind with great intensity. She did not seem to react, she was just a piece of meat that swayed back and forth with the tempo of the man's movements. She was not really with it: she seemed drugged, unconscious or simply indifferent. It took several seconds before the penny dropped and Hamad suddenly realized who the film's protagonist was, who the title 'Bad cop, good cop' alluded to. And it hurt. He almost felt like crying.

'Turn it off,' he said, clearly with considerably greater authority now, for he was immediately obeyed.

Jenny looked at him reproachfully.

'There, you see,' she said. 'It's not just me.'

He shook his head dejectedly, uncomprehendingly. What was happening? What should he do?

'Where did you find this film?' he asked.

'At the same place. It's on Pontus's website.'

'Amator6.nu? Is that Pontus's website?'

Jenny nodded.

'And how the hell did Petra end up there?'

She shrugged her shoulders, had no idea.

'I have to speak to him, make sure he removes these films. Where does he live?' Hamad asked, now beginning to think clearly again.

'I don't know. We're not in contact any more.'

'What did you say his last name was? Örstedt? You'll have to write it down for me.'

Jenny did as she was told while Hamad took a flash drive out of the coin compartment in his wallet and copied over both of the films, though he wasn't really sure what he would do with them.

'We won't talk to anyone about this, Jenny. Soon these

films are going to disappear, and I don't want you to tell anyone about them. Is that okay?'

Jenny nodded without understanding.

'Petra would be really sad if she found out about this. And your parents would fall apart, I promise you.'

'Why do you care about Petra?' asked Jenny. 'She doesn't like you.'

'Doesn't she? Maybe she's a little angry at me right now, but that will pass.'

'She says you eat girls like me for breakfast.'

Hamad could not conceal a little smile. Even if he did not understand what was going on in Westman's head these days.

'I see, she says that? I like her a lot anyway. And I'm sure that she does not want to be found on a website like that. And you don't want to either. Now let's go back to the kitchen. Then I'll explain what I mean.'

A couple of hours later he left Jenny and Blaisy with great hope that this time he had actually reached her. A good deed that unfortunately must be followed by one more.

Thursday Morning

By six o'clock Sjöberg had already taken off in the car from the five-room apartment on Skånegatan. When he reached Arboga it was eight o'clock and he imagined that the conscientious Hansson was already at work. He took the phone out of the front pocket of his shirt, already wrinkled after the drive, and entered the lab number. Her unmistakable voice in his ear confirmed his suspicions.

'Hansson.'

'Good morning, Bella, it's Conny. Am I disturbing you?'

'No problem. What's on your mind?'

She was one of the most competent and reliable people he had ever dealt with in his occupation. She was a very pleasant and interesting person privately too, he knew from talking to her at a few work parties and evenings at the pub. Chatting casually over the phone however was not one of her strong suits. She preferred to express herself concisely and that whoever she was speaking with did the same, leaving out polite chit-chat and other insignificant things.

'I'm calling regarding that paternity test on one of our suspects, Christer Larsson. Have you done it?'

'Yes, Linköping has received it.'

'Can you put it on twenty-four-hour response? We need the result as soon as possible.'

'I've already done that, with reference to the murders. We should have the result later this morning.'

'Good, call me as soon as you get it, please. Anything else new?'

'No, not right now.'

'You're going to be getting a number of shoes this morning. I want you to compare them with the prints at the crime scene. Look for blood. Comparison material will be coming as well for the fingerprints in the apartment. These matters have the highest priority as far as my investigation is concerned.'

Sjöberg ended the call and got out of the car in a neighbourhood of apartment buildings that he imagined must be one of the dreariest in the otherwise rather picturesque Arboga. The outside door was unlocked; Ingegärd Rydin lived on the third floor. It took so long before her door was opened that Sjöberg was about to give up, but at last she was standing there, looking at him suspiciously.

'I'm looking for Ingegärd Rydin,' said Sjöberg, extending his police ID towards her.

She took it from his hand and studied it at close quarters before she gave it back and answered, 'That's me.'

Her voice was so hoarse that Sjöberg immediately assumed that she had had a long career as a heavy smoker. He introduced himself and asked to speak to her. She shrugged and opened the door wide to let him in. He closed it behind himself before following her into the apartment.

The woman was somewhat older than him, in her early fifties, and very thin. Her bony spine and almost shuffling steps made her seem brittle. Her hair was cut short and its grey tone revealed that once it had been dark. She was dressed in a checked short-sleeved shirt and a pair of trousers that he thought might fit his seven-year-old daughter if you shortened them a bit.

The apartment seemed to consist of two rooms and after passing the kitchen on one side and a closed door on the other they ended up in the living room. Laboriously she lowered herself into the armchair he presumed she had struggled out of to answer the door. On the table alongside was a remote control, a pile of magazines and a local newspaper that was open. On the other side of the chair stood something that appeared to belong in a hospital rather than a home: a kind of wheeled stand holding what Sjöberg assumed was an oxygen cylinder. A tube led from the cylinder, with a mouthpiece at the end, which Ingegärd Rydin brought up to her face as soon as she sat down.

'COPD,' she got out between inhalations, in reply to Sjöberg's unspoken question. She explained, with a shortness of breath he had not noticed during their brief conversation at the front door, 'I suffer from COPD. Emphysema. This helps me breathe.'

Wasn't it the case that oxygen treatment was not prescribed for smokers? Sjöberg looked around curiously for evidence that she smoked, but he saw no ashtrays or cigarettes anywhere in the room. Despite that he sensed that someone had smoked in the apartment not all that long ago. He wondered if it was herself or someone else she was trying to fool, but thought he got the answer to the question in her next sentence.

'They come from social services to look after me a

couple of times a day, help me shop and do errands. I'm no longer able to go out.'

'I'm truly sorry,' said Sjöberg. 'Can you manage to exchange a few words with me?'

She nodded at him while she took a few deep breaths through the tube. Sjöberg was grateful that there was no rattling when she breathed, because he felt that would have been hard to endure. He felt sorry for this little person and suddenly in his mind's eye saw an image of her by the side of the comparatively enormous Christer Larsson. They seemed a mismatched couple, but on the other hand it was almost impossible to imagine what she had looked like in her youth, seeing now her prematurely aged face and the pale-yellow skin of her exposed arms.

'I don't have long now,' she said, unprompted. 'They've removed as much as they could of the damaged parts of the lungs. And they say I'm too weak to survive a lung transplant.'

'I'm awfully sorry,' said Sjöberg, and then could not think of anything else to say.

If it's that bad, surely she can be allowed to indulge in a sneaky puff under the kitchen extractor fan once in a while, he thought. Hopefully she wouldn't set fire either to herself or to the building. He listened to her breathing for a while with a dismay that he hoped was not outwardly visible.

Then he suddenly remembered his business, straightened up and went over to the other armchair by the table. Without being asked, he sat down on the edge, as if to show that he did not intend to stay long but that he had legitimate reasons after all for being in her living room.

'Do you have any idea why I'm here?' he asked hesitantly.

She shook her head without dislodging her breathing apparatus.

'You were married to a Christer Larsson, is that correct?' he continued.

She nodded, her expression revealing nothing about what she was thinking.

'Do you have any contact with him?'

Now she removed the mouthpiece to answer his question.

'We have not seen each other in more than thirty years.'

'Have you ever spoken over the phone during that time?'

'Not that either.'

'You didn't divorce as friends?' Sjöberg attempted.

'Not as enemies either,' she answered expressionlessly. 'There has never been any reason for us to maintain contact. It's no stranger than that.'

She put the mouthpiece back between her lips and he could see how her breathing at once became a little easier.

'Did you ever experience Christer Larsson being violent?'

'Why do you ask?' she wanted to know.

'Please answer my question. I'll explain later,' he said authoritatively.

'No,' she answered simply, through one corner of her mouth.

It bothered Sjöberg that he could not really judge her reactions when she had that contraption in her mouth.

'Never threatening or aggressive?'

She shook her head with her eyes steadily fixed on his.

'Did he have problems with alcohol or other drugs?'

'No. He drank like most people do. Nothing that could be considered a problem.'

'Did you know that he remarried?'

'No, I didn't know that.'

'Does it surprise you?' he asked.

She freed herself from the apparatus and answered without visible surprise, 'As I said, I no longer know him. Why should I be surprised?'

Sjöberg did not answer her rhetorical question, but instead continued doggedly.

'He got married in 2001 to a woman he met in the Philippines. They had two children together.'

A wrinkle that could hint at surprise appeared above one eye, but Sjöberg could not decide what he had said to cause this first visible reaction. Presumably the choice of the word 'had', he told himself. Suddenly she looked neutral again, but the breathing seemed more laborious without the oxygen.

'Then they separated a few years ago. They didn't get a divorce, but they lived separate lives.'

'Is Christer dead?' she asked, again bringing the mouthpiece to her face.

Sjöberg looked at her for several seconds before he replied.

'No, Christer is alive. But his wife and both children were found murdered in their home a few days ago. Perhaps you read about that in the newspaper or heard about it on the news?'

She nodded in confirmation with a look, behind the oxygen tube, that Sjöberg interpreted as a little thoughtful but not frightened in any way. It seemed to him that Christer Larsson truly no longer had any place in her life. And why should he have? Thirty years is a very long time, more than half a life in Ingegärd Rydin's case. Her facial expression suddenly changed.

'You asked whether Christer was violent. So you think he murdered his family?'

'We don't know. What do you think?'

'Not the Christer I knew,' she answered without taking the tube from her mouth.

'But perhaps Christer Larsson in 2008?' Sjöberg coaxed.

She simply shrugged, unwilling to speculate. Sjöberg felt a certain disappointment come over him. He had hoped to get more out of this conversation. Ingegärd Rydin herself he could easily strike from the list of suspects, for in her condition she would not even be capable of beheading a chicken. On the other hand he had to admit to himself that it would have been welcome if she had had something compromising to offer concerning Christer Larsson. But however much he wanted to be able to lead the investigation away from Einar, he could not lose his objectivity; he was quite clear about that.

'He is big and strong,' Sjöberg attempted anyway. 'On sick leave for many years for depression.'

A shadow drew over her face.

'Perhaps he hasn't got over the divorce?'

Suddenly she laughed and the tube flew out of her mouth.

'I'm quite sure he has,' she said, and Sjöberg detected neither irony nor bitterness behind the laugh.

A little later, getting out of the car and hearing the chirping of the birds, Sjöberg felt that spring was approaching after all. It was overcast, but the sun had found a gap in the cloud cover and shone hopefully both on him and the lifeless ground around him. On winding gravel roads eroded by the long winter he had found his way to the piece of property, Björskogsnäs 4:14, that had turned out to be owned by his mother. He had to walk the last stretch up to the boundary line. There was a narrow road, but it had long been overgrown by bushes and brushwood and there was no way through by car.

It was a rather large plot, approximately 8,000 square metres according to the title deed, up on a little rise. He had imagined that the undergrowth would change in character when he reached the boundary of the land, and admittedly it did, but not in the way he had imagined. Instead of meadowland he encountered dense thickets, and the only difference between the plot itself and the surrounding forest was in the age of the trees. The road, which nowadays could be considered a game trail, brought him to the part of the land that had once been developed. The ruins of some partly razed outbuildings were still standing, but based on what he could see through what had been small windows the sheds contained nothing besides the timber they had been built of. Among the indigenous trees he managed to make out several ancient apple trees. He couldn't imagine that they still bore fruit, but immediately found himself standing with his shoe on a rotten old apple that had not yet decayed into the soil.

Suddenly he was struck by a longing to use this earth. Plant new apple trees, prune the untended thicket and lay out a garden again here. It was his land, or would be his land, and he would not let it deteriorate even more. On the map he had in his hand he saw that there was a lake with a beach only a few hundred metres from the property. On the road he had passed a group of summer houses that appeared to have been constructed some time in the sixties, and there would be playmates for the children in the summer. Why had his mother held this back from him? It could hardly be the case that she did not know about this land of which she herself was listed as owner. He rejected the possibility immediately. Even if it had been his father's land to start with and she had not lived there herself, she must have had knowledge of its existence.

He left the outbuildings and the apple trees and walked on. Suddenly he came across the house itself. Or rather, what was left of it, which was not much. Brick foundations with the remnants of a chimney in the middle were all that was left of what had once been the main building. Within the outer walls, as everywhere else, a few young trees and bushes were growing. It was depressing to think that this was the remainder of what had once been someone's home, perhaps his father's or grandparents'.

On a sudden impulse he took the phone out of his pocket and entered his mother's number.

'It's Conny. How are you doing?'

'All right. How are all of you doing?'

Positive as always. He decided to get right to the point.

'I'm standing here on the land. Our land. The land you say you don't know about. Björskogsnäs 4:14.'

There was silence at the other end.

'Mother?'

'I hear you,' she said guardedly.

'It's nice here, Mother. A nice, big property. It's up on a hill. You could clear it a little, then there would be a fine view of the area.'

No response.

'Build a new house where the old one stood. It would be super for the kids, close to the beach down by the lake. Now that we have this land, why shouldn't we do something with it?'

He waited for a few seconds, but there was no reaction.

'Why don't you answer?'

'Because I don't know what you're talking about,' she said simply.

'I wasn't born yesterday, Mother. I'm just trying to understand; why can't you help me?'

'You don't understand a thing.'

'Exactly, that's just the point. Why are you being so contrary?'

Sjöberg did not often criticize his mother; he found it pointless. She was basically a negative person, afraid and cowering, but deep down she had a good heart. She was loving to the children, even if she did not often show it with physical contact. They liked her, even though she was slow to smile.

143

'The way you talk.'

As usual she dismissed everything that was not strictly mundane as nonsense.

'Did Father live here, Mother? Did Grandma and Grandpa live here? Now you have to answer me.'

He did not intend to give in so easily this time.

'What do I know, what do I know . . .'

Now she was starting the familiar grumbling which got on his nerves. She dismissed his simply formulated, direct question in a silly old person's way, hid behind the facade of some kind of dementia that she did not suffer from. At that moment he decided he would get to the bottom of this story. He would find out how and why the land had ended up in his mother's possession and why she did not want to acknowledge it. Genealogy had never interested him particularly, but now he really wanted to know how things stood. It would not be that difficult to discover who had lived on this property and when they had moved away. He was a police officer after all, even if he didn't know when his grandmother and grandfather had died. That sort of thing had not been talked about during his childhood with his reticent mother. Of his father he had hardly any memories at all.

'Oh, screw that!' he blurted out. 'I'll find out what I want to know anyway.'

Then he hung up, without the customary polite phrases or promises to visit that could have cheered his old mother up. And sure enough, his conscience overcame him only a few seconds later, while he was still recovering from his little outburst of anger. He would call her later in the day and act like nothing happened, as etiquette demanded in his family, then this episode would be forgotten. But he had no intention this time of abandoning the core issue.

He made his way back between the trees, in the direction of the car. Before he left the abandoned land and stepped out on what had once been a road he turned around and inspected his property one last time. With newfound enthusiasm Sjöberg resolved not to abandon his clearing and construction plans either.

As he got back behind the steering wheel, his sights set on Fellingsbro, his mobile rang. It was only eleven, but it was Gabriella Hansson already.

'I presume that the Catherine Larsson case is going well for all of you?' she opened.

'I wouldn't say that.'

Sjöberg sensed what was coming and felt ambivalent about it.

'It completely depends on how you look at it,' he continued, not elaborating on the emotional conflict he found himself in, his hopes of quickly arresting the murderer possibly on a collision course with a colleague's well-being. 'Do you have any results to report?'

'Sure. The paternity test is completed. Christer Larsson is the father of the children.'

It was not without relief that Sjöberg received this news.

'Good, that was expected. What else?'

'The national forensics lab has found strands of hair in both jumpers. They weren't able to do a regular DNA analysis because no living roots have been found. On the other hand mitochondrial DNA analysis has been done, but without comparison material there are no conclusions to be drawn. Besides the fact that both jumpers have been worn by the same person, of course.'

Sjöberg registered this information in silence. It hardly came as a surprise that both jumpers were Einar's.

'The fingerprints on the object Sandén sent over to me an hour or so ago match fingerprints found in Catherine Larsson's residence. They have been found both on loose and fixed objects, the refrigerator door, for example, so you can safely assume that the person in question has been there.'

This did not surprise Sjöberg either. That Einar Eriksson visited Catherine Larsson and the children was completely natural, considering how close they were. There was no proof however that he was the one who had taken their lives. On the contrary, it would have been ominous if they had *not* found Einar's fingerprints in the apartment, for that might have suggested that he had reason to conceal traces of himself from crime scene technicians, not just from his wife and any other curious people, which apparently had been the case as far as his financial transactions were concerned.

'That's good,' Sjöberg said simply. 'Anything else?'

'Then there's the shoes,' said Hansson.

Sjöberg stiffened, hoping with all his heart that the ambitious technician would not deliver unwelcome news.

'A pair of shoes, trainers to be more precise, matched the tracks we found in the apartment and the stairwell. We also found one of the victim's blood on them.'

'Catherine Larsson's?'

'Yes. Good or bad?'

'Both. It depends which way you're leaning.'

'That's all I have.'

'Thanks, Bella.'

Despondent, he ended the call and began to brood. He charted the entire course of events and went through it in his head while he drove. Einar had, as on any other Saturday, got up in the morning and taken off in the car to Fellingsbro, on the same road he himself was driving on now. Then he spent the whole day with his sick wife at the nursing home, got in the car again in the evening and drove home. He arrived some time after eleven o'clock, parked the car and went to Catherine Larsson's. Or to Kate, as he surely called her. Apparently she let him in. A little later he cut her throat in the bathroom, and immediately afterwards did the same to both of her sleeping children. After that he left the apartment at Trålgränd 5, walked back home to Eriksdalsgatan, changed his shoes and fled.

Einar Eriksson. A police officer with a spotless past. His colleague for many years. A man who never drew attention to himself, admittedly a sullen character, but who never made a fuss. Why in the world would he take the trouble to change his shoes? And then leave the bloody shoes behind in his home, as if to prove to his colleagues that it really was him who had committed the terrible murders? Perhaps he had counted on them not connecting him to Catherine Larsson – and perhaps they never would have either if Hamad had not sniffed that jumper. But even though Einar's fingerprints were basically everywhere in the apartment, they were missing from the door handle as well as from the tap on the bathroom sink, the only objects it was known with certainty that the murderer had touched with his hands.

There was something about this that did not really add up. Einar's disappearance and his involvement in this case were crucial to the investigation, but was he really the murderer? Sjöberg told himself that this was not so. But what had gone wrong? Had Einar simply been in the way, just happening to be the target of someone's violent caprices? Someone who for one reason or another had a grudge against Catherine Larsson and who took the opportunity when it arose to direct the suspicions of the police at one of their own.

But above all he wondered how those poor children came into the picture. Violence against the sleeping infants, two and four years old, was unfathomable – for a drug addict who had gone berserk, even more so for a seasoned police officer like Einar. Then only a former Congolese child soldier or someone like that remains, thought Sjöberg dejectedly. No one fitting that bill had shown up in the investigation, and in the Philippines the population's problems were of a different nature. The children's role in this story must be as witnesses: not witnesses to the murder of their mother, because they had been asleep, but witnesses to the murderer's presence at the crime scene during the evening, or witnesses to something quite different, still unknown to the police.

Unless the motive was revenge, a possibility they had touched on earlier in the investigation. Revenge would be directed either at the children's mother, in which case it was somewhat self-defeating to kill her before the children, or at the father – not particularly well thought out either, because his interest in the children had been cool for a long time. Or, it struck Sjöberg, the target could be Einar, who now suddenly appeared to be the one hit hardest by the brutal murders. To direct the suspicions of the police against him as well would be to rub salt into his wounds.

All at once it was clear to Sjöberg that this was the strategy they should work by. Revenge must be the obvious motive in a case where two small children were found slaughtered with such clinical coldness. No frenzy, no passion; the murderer apparently hadn't known his victims and had not acted in anger either. The perpetrator's emotions boiled over, but not his feelings for Catherine Larsson and her two children – with them he did only what he had to. It was in his relationship to the real object of his hatred that he abandoned himself in earnest. Sjöberg broke into a cold sweat when he thought about how Einar might be faring right now, if he was still alive. Presumably treated badly, and aware too of what had happened to Catherine Larsson and the children. He suddenly felt stressed, and an intense eagerness to move the investigation further made him step a little harder on the accelerator.

He entered Sandén's number on his mobile, and was answered almost at once.

'Conny here. Are you finding anything?'

'Not exactly. No passport, for example. Even though he reportedly has one.'

Sjöberg sighed.

'We've sent over a few shoes and other stuff to the crime lab,' Sandén continued.

'I heard. Bella called.'

'And?'

'They found strands of hair on the jumpers and there was a match. The fingerprints in the apartment likewise.'

'And the shoes – was there blood on them?' asked Sandén.

'There was. And it was Catherine Larsson's blood. Have you time to talk?'

'Sure. Have you spoken to the former Mrs Larsson?'

'That produced nothing. She's dying, so we can definitely remove her from the list. She hasn't spoken to Christer Larsson in thirty years and she had nothing bad to say about him. By the way, the paternity test showed that he was the father of the children, so we can stop speculating about that. But that wasn't what I wanted to talk about.'

'Instead?'

'I'm not satisfied with how this investigation is progressing. I think that Einar is the odject of some kind of conspiracy. The whole thing is an act of revenge against him, I sense it. I refuse to believe that he is guilty.'

'What happened to objectivity?'

'I'm being serious. There are some things that don't add up here and I would like to bounce those off you a little.'

'Shoot.'

'Why would Einar murder the family he devoted so much effort and money to help?'

'I can imagine a number of different reasons,' said Sandén. 'Disappointment, revenge, jealousy. Perhaps she met someone else. Or simply broke up with him. In some way used up his confidence. And capital. He has ploughed two million into that woman, damn it. Clearly he would get angry if she betrayed him somehow.'

'But it was all so clinical,' Sjöberg objected. 'If the motive had been one of those you listed, I think it would have been obvious at the scene. There should have been signs of frenzied violence.'

'I guess he had no feelings left.'

'Well, then why murder her?'

'Maybe he did it for financial reasons.'

'He won't get his money back. Stop playing devil's advocate now, Jens.'

'I'm keeping myself objective,' Sandén replied, without audible sarcasm this time.

'But why kill the children?'

'Because otherwise they could point him out.'

'Can you picture Einar Eriksson cutting the throats of two sleeping children?'

'I have a hard time picturing Einar Eriksson at all,' Sandén said crassly. 'Besides, I have a hard time imagining anybody on this entire planet cutting the throats of little children. But unquestionably that sort of thing happens all the time.'

'It may not have been Einar who put the bloody shoes back in his cupboard,' Sjöberg continued stubbornly. 'He's not stupid; do you think he is asking to be a suspect?'

'It can happen, we've seen that sort of thing before,' Sandén observed, and Sjöberg reluctantly had to agree with him on that point. 'But since he had murdered his witnesses there was probably nothing to suggest that we would ever make the connection between Eriksson and Catherine Larsson, right?'

'We would have,' said Sjöberg with conviction. 'Even if Jamal had not had his suspicions when he saw that jumper, sooner or later we would have linked them to each other. The preschool staff recognized him.'

'If he stays abroad, no one will ever be able to point him out.'

Sjöberg sighed despondently, changing gear and turning off the highway for the last four kilometres up to Solberga.

'Are you acting as a sounding board, Jens, or do you truly not share my thinking?'

'I think the evidence speaks for itself. If Einar's bloody shoes are at Einar's place, then it is Einar who has got blood on them.'

'Do we know that they really are Einar's shoes?' Sjöberg asked hopefully.

'We found the receipt.'

'It would be so easy to find Einar's shoes, use them during the murder and then replace them at his home.'

'In a mystery by Agatha Christie perhaps,' said Sandén sharply. 'It doesn't work that way in real life. Murderers are rash, stressed, disorganized, and often intoxicated or on drugs.'

'Not this one, Jens! That's what I'm trying to say. This murderer is ice-cold and systematic. The murders were clinically performed, without carelessness.'

'Well, now you know what I think anyway.'

Sjöberg had an uneasy feeling that Sandén was not the only one who would be against him. Maybe he alone still had hopes of Einar's innocence. Fortunately he was the one who made the decisions, and he intended to exploit that.

* * *

Pontus Örstedt was not in the phone book, but it took only a few minutes for the census registry to cough up the address for Hamad. Before ten o'clock on Thursday morning he was ringing the doorbell on Surbrunnsgatan in Vasastan. The man was obviously on his guard, because he would not let Hamad in until he held his police identification up to the peephole.

The occupant of the apartment was a few years younger than him, and answered the door clad only in underwear (he obviously kept himself quite fit) and with his hair sticking up.

'Night owl?' Hamad suggested.

'Pig,' Örstedt countered. 'What the hell is this about?'

'Your website. Amator6.nu. I would like you to take some shit off there that doesn't make anyone happy.'

Pontus Örstedt drew a hand through his hair and laughed. Loud and sincere.

'Ah, that,' he said. 'That site makes a lot of people happy, I can promise you that.'

'It's possible. But not the ones who are exposed.'

'You know what the site is called. The name shows that it's about amateurs. *Happy* amateurs who have sent those pictures to me willingly and want nothing other than to expose themselves.'

'I know of at least two films where that's not the case. And I want you to remove those.'

'Otherwise what?'

'Otherwise I'll see to it that you have problems,' Hamad replied. 'Major problems.'

'Oh, I'm really scared,' Örstedt sneered. 'Are you threatening me or what?'

'No, I'm just stating facts.'

'So what were thinking about putting me away for?'

'Procuring,' Hamad said off the top of his head.

Örstedt's face darkened, which Hamad assumed meant he'd hit home. Or close anyway.

'Open the website,' he ordered, and Örstedt closed the door behind them and with the policeman at his heels went into the kitchen, where a computer sat on the table.

Hamad looked around and noted that the furnishings jarred with the impression he had of the young man who lived there.

'Sub-letting?' he guessed. 'Nice lace curtains.'

Örstedt did not reply but brought the site up on the computer.

'What is it you're after?' he asked sullenly.

'"Lucy in the sky" and "Bad cop, good cop".'

'Oh, shit. Is it little Jens who sent you?'

Örstedt had an amused expression on his face. Hamad let out a disdainful snort.

'That's no concern of yours. Where did you get that cop film from?'

'Someone sent it to me, no idea who. Lucy I posted myself. And don't tell me she doesn't like it,' he added with a smile.

'She doesn't understand what it's about, as you well know. Do you have more?'

'No, not really.'

'Take it off then. If I catch sight of any more pictures of Jenny like that, I'm coming back. And I won't be coming alone.'

Örstedt did as he was told.

'Remove the other film too,' Hamad continued. 'And find out where you got it from. Are you the one who titled it?'

'I wouldn't think so. How the hell could I know it was a cop on the film? She's not wearing much of a uniform.'

His smile was scornful, and Hamad had to restrain himself from giving Örstedt a karate chop on the neck. After some scrolling, Örstedt clicked on an old email with a file attached.

'Here it is,' he said.

The film was, as he had claimed, already christened 'Bad cop, good cop' by the sender and was accompanied by a short text saying that he and his girlfriend would be pleased to offer curious viewers a few goodies from the bedroom at home. Hamad memorized the date and time when the message was sent. But no particular exertion was required to remember the sender's email address.

'Remove the email and empty the trash,' Hamad ordered. 'In Outlook and on the desktop.'

'Now I think it's starting to become clear.' Örstedt grinned while he dutifully did as he had been told. 'Or not . . .'

Hamad defied his impulses and left Örstedt without a word and without harming a hair on his head.

Thursday Afternoon

After a couple of rather bland sausages with completely tasteless potatoes in white sauce at a roadside tavern, and a few moments of escape from reality into a gossip magazine, Sjöberg was back in the car. Now he was almost at Solberga and found himself on a long lane that led up to a majestic building with yellow plastered walls and white corners, flanked by two free-standing wings. The buildings were surrounded on three sides by meadowland. He guessed that the lake mentioned in the brochure was located on the far side of the estate.

He drove on to the verge and turned off the engine. Before he continued up to the nursing home he wanted to exchange a few words with Hamad and get a progress report, so he took out his mobile and entered the speed-dial number.

'Hamad.'

'You answered before there was any ringtone.'

'The phone buzzed. How's it going?'

Sjöberg gave a brief and perfunctory account of his unproductive meeting with Ingegärd Rydin.

'So we can forget her. Now I'm standing outside Solberga, about to go in and talk to Einar's wife. How's it going with you?'

'No Einar Eriksson has left the country by air anyway.

He hasn't booked boat or train tickets in his own name either, so he must have bought a ticket on site, driven a car or made use of false identity documents.'

'We're working on the assumption that he is still in the country and still alive,' Sjöberg pointed out.

Hamad mumbled something inaudible in response.

'You're doubtful?'

'I think he's fled the country, because the passport is gone. Or possibly he's hiding himself somewhere in the country, but that seems a little stupid. Then we would get him sooner or later. We're finding traces of him in particular everywhere, not of anyone else. And with the blood on the shoes too –'

'Have you spoken to Sandén?'

'Yes.'

Sjöberg felt a certain irritation, but didn't show it as he presented his line of reasoning as factually as he was able for Hamad too.

'I hear what you're saying, but my experience tells me that things are usually what they seem to be.'

At this comment, Sjöberg decided to give up trying to bring his colleagues round to his point of view and to accept their scepticism. He was the one leading the investigation anyway, and they had to follow his orders. He changed the subject.

'And the computer?' he asked.

'So far I haven't found anything of interest,' Hamad replied. 'But there's a fair amount left to go through.'

'I want you to go through the papers on Einar's desk too. And the ones on the bookshelf. Investigate both the

jobs he is working on now and old cases and look in particular for someone who could have a motive to get
revenge on Einar.'

Hamad let out a long sigh but Sjöberg pretended not to
notice it.

'Okay?'

'Okay. And the interviews? What do I do about them?'

'Put those off until you're finished with the paperwork.
There isn't as much as it seems. Good luck.'

'The same to you.'

Sjöberg drove the last stretch up to the impressive manor
house. He left the car in the car park outside one of the
wings and walked across the meticulously raked gravel to
the main entrance. The snow had melted here and there
in the well-tended flowerbeds next to the wall of the
house, and for the first time this year he noticed the snow-
drops that stood in white clumps, announcing better
times to come. It was still too early for the crocuses they
would share the flowerbeds with. A few tender leaves had
worked their way up out of the hard ground, but they
appeared to be waiting until spring showed its intentions
more clearly.

Sjöberg went up the steps and rang the bell by the side
of the door, but hearing no sound from inside he opened
the door and went in.

Now he suddenly found himself in a very ordinary
reception area, which didn't fit at all with the property's
classic exterior. Behind a semi-glazed wall sat an older
woman in a white coat with a pair of glasses hanging on a
cord around her neck. She looked up at him as he

approached and opened the counter window with a friendly smile.

'Hi,' said Sjöberg. 'I'm here to see Solveig Eriksson.'

'Oh,' said the nurse, with a rather surprised expression. 'She's in room 230. You take the lift over there up to the third floor. She has the room furthest to the left in the corridor to the right as you leave the lift.'

Sjöberg thanked her and made his way over to the lift, past a group of sofas whose design went better with the institution itself than with the manorial architecture. On the way up it struck him that perhaps he ought to have brought something with him, flowers or a box of chocolates. He rejected the idea, however, remembering that he was there on business and had little knowledge of Solveig Eriksson's possible allergies or her tastes in general.

The corridor was painted white and the only window was located at the far end. Between the patients' doors hung framed posters of classic artworks, and here and there some large potted rubber plants had been placed on the floor. Sjöberg drew a leaf between his thumb and index finger and noted that the plants were artificial. Nothing living could survive with so little sunlight. He went over to the last in the row of doors on the left and knocked. Softly at first, but when he got no answer he knocked again, with a little more authority. He got no response this time either, so he pressed down the handle and the door opened.

Like a scene from a film he saw a woman with her back to him in a chair by the window, with a blanket over her legs and her forearms on the armrests. She sat without moving as he stepped into the light room, which to his surprise was personally furnished. It was a corner room and in both windows were living plants in attractive pots. The bed standing against the wall next to the corridor was carefully made and covered with a traditional patchwork quilt, and on the bedside table stood a wedding photo similar to the one he had seen at Einar's, in a lovely old silver frame. By the other windowless wall was an old-fashioned dresser, and on it stood framed photographs depicting younger versions of the Eriksson couple in various situations. In the middle of the room was a neat little group of rococo-style sofas, and a table adorned with a round lace cloth and a begonia. Books and a TV, it struck Sjöberg, were all that was missing here. This woman must read books, since she was here year in and year out, mustn't she?

He walked over to the window with deliberately loud steps, so that she would hear him or at least sense that someone was approaching. But she still sat completely motionless.

'Hi, Solveig,' said Sjöberg, who could now see her face.

She stared expressionlessly down at the grounds without responding to his greeting. He placed his hand on her shoulder to make his presence felt.

'My name is Conny Sjöberg and I work with your husband.'

No reaction.

'Einar,' said Sjöberg. 'Einar and I work together in the police.'

Her expression showed no sign that she heard him or understood what he was saying. The beautiful young woman in the bridal photo was unrecognizable in the bent, skinny creature he now saw before him. Her hair was chalk white and cut short and not a hint of life was visible in her eyes. Sjöberg asked himself what could have happened to her. Had she been sitting like this since the mid-seventies? A shiver passed through his body when he thought about Einar, who had taken the trouble to drive here and sit with her every Saturday for so many years. What did he do? Did he talk to her? Did he sit with her on the sofa and put his arm around her and tell her about his week?

Suddenly it occurred to Sjöberg what a great human being Einar must be. So loyal. 'For better or for worse' was something Einar Eriksson obviously took with the utmost seriousness. He had not bought the town-house with the intention of living there himself, but in the hope that Solveig would recover her health so that they could live there together. No one could criticize him for getting involved with another woman in the past two years. Personally Sjöberg would have given up much sooner. But Einar had still not abandoned the woman he had once married, not even since he'd met Catherine Larsson. Sjöberg took Solveig Eriksson's hand.

'Solveig,' he said, 'can you show me that you hear what I'm saying? Just move your fingers a little. I know Einar, Solveig. Einar.'

The limp fingers in his hand did not move and her gaze was still directed towards something indeterminate out-side the window.

'Do you think Einar is capable of murder, Solveig? Could Einar murder two small children?'

Still no reaction. If she had heard him, registered what

he said, wouldn't she at least have become a little curious? He asked himself how she would react if he struck her, gave her a slap. But that was not a method he intended to try. Instead he tried to seem threatening. Threats and bribes were well-proven methods where children were concerned, but in this case he felt doubtful of success. He let go of her hand and noticed how it landed limply on the blanket on her lap.

'Einar is gone, Solveig. He has disappeared. If you don't help me, perhaps he will never come to visit you again.'

But Solveig Eriksson simply stared vacantly ahead of her, so Sjöberg gave up at last and left her.

When he came back down to reception the woman behind the counter window was no longer there. He knocked on the window and a man in his thirties came out from a back room.

'I would like to speak to someone who knows Solveig Eriksson,' said Sjöberg.

'We all do,' the man said with a smile.

'Preferably someone who already worked here when she first came. Let's say the one who has worked at Solberga the longest.'

'Then, let's see, that must be Ann-Britt. I'll call her. Who shall I say is looking for her?'

'Conny Sjöberg. I'm a chief inspector at the Violent Crimes Unit in Stockholm,' he added, and the nurse raised his eyebrows in curiosity before he picked up the phone.

After a couple of tries he got a bite. He showed Sjöberg to the seating area and suggested that he should wait there until Ann-Britt showed up.

'It may take a while. She's busy with one of the residents right now, but she will come as soon as she's finished.'

Sjöberg sat down on a rather annoyingly hard waiting-room chair and, incongruously enough, browsed through an interior-decorating magazine while he waited. After ten minutes the man in reception showed up again with a glass of orange juice, which he set in front of Sjöberg.

'It's dragged on, I'm afraid,' he apologized. 'Ann-Britt is coming as soon as she can.'

Sjöberg smiled gratefully at the nurse, who left an aroma of soap behind him in the waiting room. He happened to think of Margit. Uncalled-for solicitude. Pleasant. Pleasure. Soft sound of feet in sensible shoes. But then: long corridors, stretchers, disinfectant and shiny silver bedpans. From nowhere suddenly he was imagining himself on an operating table. With Margit's face looming over him, her eyes inspecting him, her mouth covered. He was helpless and dependent; she had stainless-steel instruments and her hands were in gloves. Sterile. Threatening.

The image was so unexpected, so overwhelming that he was trembling as he reached for the glass. Terrified as he was, he noted that his subconscious was doing its part to take the life out of that . . . affair. That woman.

After another twenty minutes and another two home-decor magazines, Ann-Britt Berg finally appeared. She turned out to be the woman he had spoken to on reception when he arrived. She looked to be in her sixties, so she could conceivably have been an employee when Solveig Eriksson first came here.

'Ann-Britt Berg,' she said, extending her hand. 'I'm

sorry I took so long. I was helping a colleague shower a resident who's a little troublesome, so you can't do the job alone.'

Sjöberg responded to her greeting and introduced himself as well.

'I've never seen you here before. Are you a relative of Solveig?' asked the nurse.

'No, I'm here on duty. I need to speak to someone who has known Solveig a long time and I understand that you've been here for a while. Were you by any chance already here when she was admitted?'

'We don't usually put it that way,' Ann-Britt Berg said with a smile. 'We see it as a residence rather than a hospital. Solveig is not even bedridden, for that matter. But yes, I've worked here since 1972, for almost thirty-six years.'

'What is wrong with her?'

'That I'm afraid I cannot answer. It's confidential.'

'How about if I put it like this,' Sjöberg attempted. 'I have visited her and I could see more or less what is wrong with her. She seems catatonic, so I would guess at post-traumatic stress or something similar. Was she like that already when she came here or has that happened since?'

'You must understand,' she said imploringly, 'we really are not allowed to talk about our residents with anyone other than family. I can be reprimanded if I say too much. Even reported to the police.'

Sjöberg put on his most authoritative police face and continued in a very friendly but firm manner.

'Now it happens to be the case that her only relative,

her husband, Einar, has been missing for the past five days. I am investigating his disappearance and I imagine that it is in Solveig's interest that we find him. For that reason I need answers to certain questions.'

'But Solveig has no information to give. She doesn't talk to anyone, not even to Einar, although he sits with her every Saturday.'

'That's why I'm asking you. You can just nod or shake your head, can't you, so no one can blame you for having said too much?'

She did not reply but looked at him with a worried expression.

'Was she like this when she first came here?' Sjöberg repeated.

Ann-Britt Berg looked nervously around, but she nodded cautiously. Sjöberg felt relieved that, having had the bad luck to encounter three interviewees who were tongue-tied (including his mother), he might now get something useful out of the fourth. He cast a glance towards the counter window, but saw that it was closed and that no one could hear them right now.

'Was that the reason she was admitted to Solberga?' he continued.

The nurse nodded again.

'There is no other medical reason for her being here?'

She shook her head, starting to look more relaxed now.

'Does she have any other medical problems?'

No.

'Has her condition changed during the years she has been here?'

No, it hadn't.

'Does she function physically? Can she walk?'

Nod.

'Does she manage her hygiene herself?'

After some reflection, which Sjöberg put down to general human consideration rather than issues of medical confidentiality, he got a shake of the head in reply.

'Does she eat on her own?'

No.

'Is this a question of post-traumatic stress?'

She answered with a light shrug and looked carefully around before she dared to answer verbally.

'Possibly. It's hard to make any diagnosis in a case like this. Some doctors call it generalized mutism.'

'And how does one get it? Is it contagious?' Sjöberg asked jokingly to lighten the heavy atmosphere a little.

Ann-Britt Berg smiled gratefully at him.

'Of course it's not, but presumably it is due to stress. Because you've been involved in something traumatic or because you are unhappy and close yourself off from your surroundings.'

'So you can choose to be like this?' said Sjöberg, deliberately provocative.

'Well, you could say that, in a way, but primarily I guess it's about not being able to cope with life.'

'A kind of alternative to suicide?'

'I feel that we're out on pretty thin ice now,' she said frankly. 'I haven't studied psychology. I'm just a nurse; you should probably speak to a doctor or psychologist about it.'

'And in Solveig's case?'

'What do you mean?'

'What is the reason that Solveig Eriksson suffers from post-traumatic stress?'

'I really don't know,' the nurse replied. 'I seem to recall that I asked Einar about it a long time ago, but I never got an answer. There were probably some staff who knew, but I was only a young whippersnapper back then and they didn't tell me everything. But I remember that there was something hush-hush.'

'What is Einar like? Do you know him?'

'Of course I know Einar. He's quiet, you could say. Very friendly. And he is quite fanatical about Solveig, never lets her down. Takes her out on long walks. He usually lets her walk the first stretch, for the exercise, then he pushes her in a wheelchair. I've heard him sit and talk to her in her room, and he never gets an answer. He does not get so much as a look and yet he still visits her after all these years.'

'Do you know anything else about Einar?' Sjöberg asked. 'There at least you have no confidentiality rules to break,' he added with a teasing wink.

'Well, confidentiality applies equally to the relatives,' Ann-Britt Berg replied. 'But I don't know much. I know he's a policeman. He continued to live in Arboga for the first two or three years, but then he moved to Stockholm. Perhaps he came to realize that Solveig's condition would not change, so I guess he made a fresh start. Job-wise, I mean.'

'He didn't have a new woman?'

'I don't know that, of course. As I said he's not particularly talkative. But I do think he has seemed a little happier in the past few years.'

'Really?'

This was not something Sjöberg had noticed at work, but on the other hand Einar's reputation as a sourpuss had long been solidly established, and he was presumably routinely treated as such. Which contributed to his remaining a sourpuss.

'I have to admit that I happened to overhear something he said to Solveig on one occasion,' Ann-Britt said, a little self-consciously. 'He spoke with warmth about a woman and some small children. He took care of them when the woman was working, he said. Picked them up from pre-school and played with them. He said that it was quite wonderful and I interpreted that as more than a normal friendship. But it would be a little strange of course if he were to describe his new family in lyrical terms to his wife. Even if she doesn't care what he says. I probably misunderstood the whole thing.'

Sjöberg reflected on this for a moment. Perhaps it was still his wife Einar turned to when he needed to talk, as he had once been in the habit of doing. The reserved Einar Eriksson aired everyday concerns and the joys of life to the woman who had once, long ago, chosen to share them with him. Was it because he believed she could hear him? Because she was a person who never could abuse his trust? To fill the silent room with the sound of his voice and formulate thoughts and feelings that otherwise would never be expressed? Or could it be because he believed she might react to this particular information? In that case had he expected a positive or negative reaction? Perhaps he wanted to hurt her. Presumably he just wanted to wake her from this eternal mental lethargy.

'Does she have any other visitors?' asked Sjöberg.

'No, never. Her parents used to come, but they're both dead, have been for many years. Now it's only Einar who visits. What do you think could have happened to him?'

'No idea,' Sjöberg lied.

He saw no reason to cast Einar in a bad light with the staff at Solberga. The fact that he was missing was enough.

'So he left Solberga at about nine on Saturday evening?' he asked instead.

'Yes, he did,' Ann-Britt Berg replied. 'He comes at nine and leaves at nine. Same thing every Saturday.'

'Does he usually bring her things?'

'Sometimes. The kind of thing she may have use for: new clothes when they're needed.'

'And last Saturday?'

'Nothing last Saturday. I was the one who received him then.'

'No farewell gift then. Nothing that suggested that he intended to go away,' Sjöberg thought out loud.

Nurse Ann-Britt shook her head with a worried expression. Sjöberg changed tack.

'She doesn't read? I didn't see any books, newspapers or a TV in her room.'

'No, she doesn't. Solveig is not interested in the outside world whatsoever. We have a TV in the residents' lounge, and sometimes we sit her there, but she never looks at the TV. Instead she always has her gaze directed at something else in the room. She takes no notice of the other residents either, or the staff for that matter. She screens herself off from everything and everyone.'

'That sounds like pure torture. She has never injured herself physically? Tried to kill herself?'

'Nothing like that, but she does not show many human reactions in general, if I may say so. The ones who injure themselves usually do it to feel that they are alive. I have a feeling that Solveig . . . perhaps does not want to feel that she is alive.'

'Yet she holds herself prisoner in her own body,' Sjöberg continued his line of reasoning. 'Refuses any type of enjoyment. Perhaps she thinks she deserves to die.'

Ann-Britt Berg threw up her hands as if to show that she could not contribute anything else. Sjöberg could not think of anything further to ask and got up stiffly from the uncomfortable little chair.

'Thanks for taking the time to talk to me,' he said, extending his hand to the nurse.

She responded to his farewell with a slightly embarrassed expression, but whether it was because she felt she had violated patient confidentiality or because she did not think she had anything substantial to offer he could not decide.

He let her return to her duties, and with the dull thud of the heavy mansion door sounding in his ears he left Solveig Eriksson and her Solberga behind him.

* * *

His nose had become so accustomed that only now and then was he overwhelmed with disgust at himself and the miserable little figure he must cut, lying on the floor in the tool shed. Bound hand and foot, his trousers soaked and sticky after five days of imprisonment in an area considerably smaller than the shed itself, limited by the length of the rope that fettered his feet to the wall.

There was not a part of his body that did not ache from the countless hours in unnatural positions, the cold, the filth, his thirst and hunger. The water he managed to lap up from the awkwardly accessible bowl was not nearly enough to quench his thirst, and the crumbs he could get from the pieces of bread on the floor were far from sufficient to satisfy his stomach. For the first few days he had managed to hold back the more troublesome bodily functions. But on the third day he had had diarrhoea, and now he could not or no longer cared to try to control his bowels, he was not sure which.

Two of his teeth had already been kicked out when he was first dumped in the little shed, though he had been unconscious when it happened. One eye was stuck shut with blood from a wound on his forehead, two fingers on one hand were broken and probably also a couple of ribs. Yet it was the biting cold that tormented him most, that made his body shake as he lay there, even though he tried to relax to save energy.

He had given up hope long ago that any passer-by would hear him or get suspicious about the shed. The only hope he had – and it was not much; the ropes sat solid, as if moulded around his wrists – was that he would manage to loosen the knots enough to slip out of his bonds. That was the little straw he clutched at as he again started to work the rope, despite the intense pain these small movements caused him. He pulled and stretched, ten times, twenty . . . *Twenty minutes later he still had not come back to the car. She must have wondered where he had got to, would not understand how it could take him so long at the cobbler's, but perhaps she assumed there was a long queue or that he had met some acquaintance that out of politeness he could not rush away from without talking for a while first.*

Actually he had been one of only two customers in the shop, but the other — a very pregnant woman in her mid-thirties — had suddenly fainted, and he had sat on the floor with her head in his lap, giving out orders. First he got the shaken cobbler to call for an ambulance, then he managed to get him to bring towels and a jug of water. He dabbed water on the woman's pale face and tried as far as possible to clean the wound she had got on the back of her head. All the while he tried to talk reassuringly to her and the semi-hysterical cobbler, whom he had stationed at the door to keep curious passers-by out of the shop.

As they waited the heat in the car rose under the May sun, and the boys in the back seat started to become insufferable. She suggested that they should play a quiz game and that kept them distracted for a few minutes, until little Tobias lost concentration. She also told them a story, but it was not long before that also got boring for the boys. Then she caught sight of a kiosk a hundred metres further on, where the river curved, and it struck her that it was Saturday after all and that she could spoil the boys with something sweet while they were waiting.

'I know!' she said, turning towards the back seat. 'Let's drive over to the kiosk up there and each get an ice cream!'

'Yes, let's do that!' the boys answered with one voice.

'But I want a lollipop instead,' said Andreas.

She was happy with this suggestion, because lollipops would do less damage to the upholstery of the car than ice cream, she knew that, and she did not feel ready to let these little urchins loose right next to the river.

'Me too,' said Tobias, 'and I can drive the car that short way.'

'That's out of the question, Tobias, but you can each have a lollipop.'

'Can you drive the car then, Lady Girl?' asked Tobias, noticeable doubt in his voice.

'Of course, little man. I'm actually the best driver in the family. But you're not allowed to tell anyone I said that,' she added with her finger secretively to her lips.

The boys exchanged looks and started giggling, whether in delight at the confidence itself or complicity finding her statement absurd she could not decide, but in any event they sat quietly and watched large-eyed while she climbed over to the driver's seat. She turned the ignition key and released the handbrake while the little boys expectantly studied her every move. She felt their eyes on her back and suddenly became almost nervous under their watchful gaze. Then she decisively shook off her discomfort and drove the short distance up to the kiosk, backing down by the side of the little shop so that she stopped facing towards the street, and put on the handbrake.

'You could drive the car!' Tobias exclaimed in an impressed tone of voice.

Her gaze met his in the rear-view mirror and his small green eyes glistened eagerly above his freckles.

'May we go in with you and choose?' Andreas asked.

'No, stay in the car. What would you like?'

She turned towards them.

'I want a big lollipop,' Andreas replied.

'I want a red lollipop,' said Tobias.

'A big lollipop and a red one,' she repeated. 'Does it matter what colour the big lollipop is, Andreas?'

'Just not liquorice.'

173

'My red lollipop should be big too,' said Tobias. 'Otherwise a little one is fine.'

'Just so long as it's red,' she said with a laugh. 'I think I understand.'

She opened the car door and stepped out into the spring sunshine. There was a lovely breeze from the river, and the sweet aroma from a flowering hedge on the other side of the street struck her.

'Behave yourselves, boys. Don't kill each other, because then there won't be any lollipops.'

With a smile and a wink she closed the car door.

*   *   *

Johan Bråsjö, who had just turned ten, had his first bus pass. Ever since the start of term in January he had been allowed to walk to school without a grown-up. Even though Mum or Dad still had to walk with Sanna, who was in the first grade, at about the same time, he would slip out just before them, ring the doorbell of his best friend Max in the building next door and together they enjoyed the newfound privilege of moving freely through the city streets. His mum later revealed that she had sneaked after them a few times in the beginning, to check that they crossed the streets responsibly.

After hard pressure and references to this good behaviour in traffic he also finally managed to get permission to go to and from his guitar lessons on his own. So now, with his instrument on his back and in the company of Ivan, a friend from another class, every Tuesday afternoon he boarded the number 4 bus at Skanstull, showed his coveted bus pass and rode the whole way to Gärdesskolan in Östermalm, where the lessons were held.

Today was Thursday, but the boys were on the bus anyway. Johan had been allowed to go home with Ivan after school. No one was at home at Ivan's and after some resistance Johan let himself be talked into going to the cinema at Hötorget at Ivan's expense. Johan had a strong feeling that his parents wouldn't like this, but on the other hand they did not need to find out about it. Now they were on their way home after the film and Johan started to feel a bit calmer as they approached those parts of Stockholm where he had permission to be.

'You were a little scared, I could tell,' said Ivan.

'Not scared exactly, but the film was exciting,' Johan replied. 'Really exciting. Thanks for the popcorn. And the film.'

'It's cool. It wasn't my money anyway.'

'It wasn't?'

'No, it was Mum's money.'

Johan looked worriedly up at his considerably taller friend.

'That is, I get to take money from Mum. I didn't nick it, if that's what you were thinking.'

'I guess I was,' said Johan, relieved. 'I only get a weekly allowance.'

'Actually I have an allowance too,' Ivan explained. 'Or I did have before. But Mum always forgot to give it to me, so now I take money when I need it instead.'

'Mmm.'

Johan did not feel entirely satisfied with this answer, but chose to drop the subject and looked absent-mindedly at the passengers in front of them on the bus. Suddenly he caught sight of a familiar back a few seats in front of them.

'Check it out, Ivan, there's the guy who's ahead of us at guitar!'

'You don't need to yell,' Ivan hissed, sinking down a little in the seat.

'I'm not yelling, am I?' Johan defended himself. 'I'm whispering. Are you scared of him or what?'

'No, are you?'

Johan thought that Ivan's eyes did look a little afraid, but chose not to comment on that.

'No, but he looks scary. Don't you think so?'

'Yes, he's ugly as hell,' said Ivan with his hand in front of his mouth so that no one but Johan would hear him.

'He's not exactly ugly. He's more . . . like, big. And old.'

'But then what's he doing at guitar lessons?' Ivan exclaimed. 'Such an old dude.'

'He's not exactly ancient. Maybe he just wants to learn to play the guitar?' Johan suggested jokingly, and received a look that clearly showed that Ivan was not in the mood for sarcasm right now.

'Everyone else there is, like, kids and teenagers,' Ivan said dismissively. 'He's a grown-up.'

Evidently Ivan meant that this made the man in front of them a loser, but Johan happened to think of his Uncle Danny and held his ground.

'My uncle takes guitar lessons. There's nothing strange about that. Who says you can only learn when you're a kid?'

Ivan looked indifferently out of the window. Johan tried to recapture his interest.

'But he is scary, he really is. He never says hello. He

doesn't even notice us, even though we sit there outside waiting every Tuesday. weird.'

Ivan's eyes flashed as he turned back towards Johan.

'And he's tall as hell. He could strangle us both, one in each hand.'

Johan looked at the big man and imagined himself and Ivan hanging from his coarse fists, their feet kicking in the air.

The bus braked and it was time for them to get off. The guitar man got up too and a woman holding a little child by the hand slipped in between them and him. As they passed the place where he had been sitting, Johan happened to look down at the seat and noticed that the man had left a pair of gloves behind. He snatched them up in passing and called spontaneously after him, over the head of the child.

'Hey, you forgot your gloves!'

The man was already getting off the bus and did not react, but the woman with the child turned towards him with a puzzled look, Ivan likewise. Johan responded to the woman's look with a shrug. To Ivan he said, 'He forgot his gloves. I only wanted –'

'Cool,' said Ivan. 'Then we have a hold over him.'

'A hold?'

'Yeah, we'll follow him.'

'Why?'

'To see what kind of shady character he is. Like detectives!'

'But if he discovers us –'

'Then we'll give him the gloves!'

With enthusiasm mixed with terror Johan accepted this suggestion and they started tailing their unknowing target.

In the throng at Skanstull they kept close, but when the guitar man slipped into the ICA Ringen store they did not dare follow. They did not have to wait very long however; after a couple of minutes he came out again, now with a plastic bag in his hand.

Over at Tjurberget fewer people were moving about and the boys had to keep a considerable distance from the object of their detective game. They followed him a long way on Ringvägen, past Rosenlund Hospital, and when he eventually made his way across the street and down into Tantolunden they kept so far back that, after he had turned in among the allotments, they had to run so as not to lose him. Once in among the hotchpotch of small cabins and cultivated plots it was easier to follow him. Most of the cottages were closed up for the season and in the eagerness of the hunt Johan did not hesitate to follow his friend when he climbed over a fence to hide behind the cabins and frozen piles of soil.

The man was truly both tall and well built, and more than once Johan noticed the unusually large hands hanging by his side as he walked purposefully through the deserted allotment area. Occasionally the man turned and took a few quick glances around him, as if he felt he was being followed. With pounding hearts, the boys crouched behind a rubbish bin or some bushes so as not to be discovered by the man who, as the hunt dragged on, began to seem more and more terrifying.

At last he seemed to have reached his goal. While the boys hid behind a leafless but dense low hedge three plots away, he fiddled with a padlock and then opened the decaying gate to an allotment with a ramshackle little cabin. When he had carefully closed the gate behind him and disappeared from view, they ventured to dash up to the hedge that surrounded the plot. They could not get closer than that without risking discovery.

Breathing rapidly, they crouched behind the untended bushes and tried to hear the man inside. To begin with Johan could only discern the rattle of keys, but as his heart rate calmed down he could clearly hear what was going on there just a few metres beyond the hedge. He heard a key being put in a lock and turned, a metallic sound like a padlock being opened. The creaking of a wooden floor and a door being closed. Rather a long silence. Several creaking steps. Silence again. Then an angrily hissing voice.

'And here you lie, you fucking little pig, rolling in your own dung! My God, how you shit! Maybe the food isn't good enough for you?'

Then a dull thud, like the sound when you box a punch-bag, Johan thought at first, but then imagined that it might sound like that when you kick a pig. The boys exchanged glances without saying anything. Johan shuddered.

'You won't get anything else anyway.' The hissing voice was speaking again. 'This is all I'll spend on a swine like you. No potatoes for this pig.'

A rustling sound from the plastic bag, and the noise of liquid being poured out of one container into another. Footsteps on a wooden floor. More kicks.

'It's your lucky day today. Duty calls, so I have to leave now. But when I'm finished we'll have a proper chat. Bye-bye.'

179

Johan looked in terror at Ivan.

'He's coming,' he whispered so quietly that it was barely audible. 'We have to leave.'

Ivan nodded and they made their way, half running, half tiptoeing, all the way along the slushy gravel path until it turned ninety degrees, and they heard a door closing far behind them. Then they took to their heels and ran for all they were worth on the crooked paths between the garden plots, across lawns and all the way down to the promenade at Årstaviken. Only then did they slow their pace and started walking quickly, over towards Eriksdalslunden, back among the buildings.

'What was he doing with that pig?' Johan panted, still out of breath after the run. 'Boxing workout, maybe?'

'I said he was a shady character,' Ivan replied. 'Maybe he's going to slaughter the pig and eat it up.'

'Well, it won't taste any better after he's hit it,' Johan said. 'It's fucking animal cruelty.'

Ivan looked at Johan with a slightly amused expression. Johan understood why, but pretended not to. He usually didn't swear, but this was a day when he had done many forbidden things and in any event the swear word felt justified. To further underscore his repugnance at cruelty to animals, and perhaps also mark a certain independence from his parents, he delivered another swear word.

'Bloody hell, what an idiot. I hope his hands freeze. I'm never going to give him the gloves now.'

'We have to rescue the pig,' Ivan stated.

'I'm not going back there!' said Johan.

'Why not? He's at work, he said that.'

'It sounded like he had a padlock on the door. How would we get it open?'

'Doesn't your dad have any good tools?'

Johan didn't know, but breaking into someone's house was . . . burglary, wasn't it? Then he remembered that he had seen on the news that cruelty to animals was also a crime.

'It's against the law to mistreat animals,' he said. 'We can report him to the police.'

'We don't know what his name is.'

'No, but if we go to the police they can rescue the pig anyway.'

'No way am I going to the cops. You can forget that.'

Johan looked questioningly at Ivan, not really understanding what he might mean by that.

'Are they after you or something?'

'Very possibly,' Ivan answered mysteriously, with a shrug.

He didn't elaborate further and the conversation died out. At Skanstull the boys separated, and the closer to his home on Åsögatan Johan got, the more he felt his bad conscience. It was dawning on him that his parents would probably be extremely disappointed in him if they found out what he had done, and he would not be surprised if they took away his bus pass. They might even decide that he could no longer go to and from school on his own, seeing as he had broken their agreement. He promised himself that he would behave himself in the future, and that being so, he convinced himself that it was not really necessary to reveal what he had been up to. But then he could not tell them about the mistreated pig either. And what would happen to it then? Well, anyway, it would surely get eaten sooner or later. Strengthened by having made this decision, he jogged up the steps to the apartment, where his dad and little sister were probably waiting for him with dinner.

But just as he was about to turn the door handle he had a change of heart. He had done some stupid things today, he really had. All the more reason to end the day with a good deed.

* * *

Having determined that morning that Einar Eriksson had not fled the country by any traceable mode of transport, Hamad had spent the afternoon thus far going through Einar's computer and all his papers. He had learned nothing from these activities that might be of use to the investigation. Eriksson was not up to anything dodgy on his computer: he was not interested in child pornography, and he had not sent or received any email that might arouse any suspicion whatsoever. He did not seem to be involved in any lone investigations or old closed cases, and there was no reason to think that Eriksson, any more than any other detective in the unit, could be considered a target for vengeful criminals or crime victims.

Hamad had to force himself to concentrate to finish the job. He was thorough, but it took longer than it should have. Now and then he drifted off into his own thoughts, and had to shake himself back to life to get the fruitless chore done. He was finally back in his own office, browsing through old appointment diaries he had saved for some reason in a desk drawer.

There were two dates that interested him in particular. The first he would not forget any time soon: it was the date when he and Lina had definitively decided to separate. After a few weeks' consideration on both sides, that evening they had sat down at the kitchen table and calmly and collectedly set out their views on things: how it should have been and what they should do now. It had been intense and sorrowful, but without drama, and they had been in agreement: life would be better for both of them if they went their separate ways. They had wished each other luck and ended the four-year relationship with a hug and tears in their eyes. It was a major failure, and this date, along with several happier dates, was now firmly engraved in his memory.

With this incident as a reference point, he could clearly remember how the evening had gone before that important conversation at the kitchen table. Likewise the night and day that followed. Despite that he checked in one of the diaries that his memory was reliable. And he was right: the date he had seen in the lower-left corner of the film in which Petra played the lead role was indeed that very special Friday in November 2006.

They had been in the middle of a serial murder investigation, and he had dragged a rather reluctant Petra from the station to the bar up at the Clarion. They drank beer and chatted. He got her to switch off from work and as usual the discussion was free and open. Both pleasant and less inspiring topics had been discussed, affectionately and with respect. And when he had left her it had not been because he wanted to, but because he had to. He had gone home to Lina to conclude a chapter in his life.

The other date was not equally obvious. It too was a Friday, but this time in September 2007, so almost a year later. The only thing in the diary was a course that he, Petra and a few others from the Hammarby Police had attended. According to the diary it was called 'Centring on Body Language', and he remembered that the basis of the whole thing was that the impression you made depended on your posture. He recalled how to Petra's annoyance Holgersson or Malmberg or somebody had got her to agree that the police commissioner was sexy. Hamad snorted when he thought about that. Sexy? Brandt didn't even believe that himself.

But later, what had happened after the course? That was the evening he had spent with Petra at the Pelican, the evening he now considered the final quivering minutes of their previously completely normal relationship. The calm before the storm. And it was that same evening that someone had sent an amateur porno film with Petra in the lead role to Pontus Örstedt. From an all-too-familiar email address.

He slammed the diary shut and sat with his head in his hands, staring listlessly out of the window. He sighed. There was an obvious connection here, but what was it really about? Try to see it from Petra's perspective, he told himself. What is she thinking? She gets a tip-off about the damned film on amator6.nu and is furious at the troll who . . . has sent it in? Or at the one who is exploiting her in the film? For this is a question of exploitation, isn't it? Reluctantly he pictured her again, with closed eyes and half-open mouth. Stoned? Unconscious? How the hell could he know, he had no idea how she might look in . . . that situation.

But still. He thought he knew her well enough to be able to dismiss the idea that she would publicize such images. Or let herself be filmed under such circumstances. Or even subject herself to exactly such circumstances. Considering that it must have hurt, and that she did not appear to react to the pain. Or to anything for that matter.

Things were most often exactly what they appeared to be, he thought. His own mantra. And what makes it inapplicable on this occasion? Nothing, naturally.

Petra looked completely gone, so presumably she was. Unconscious or high as a kite, or both. *Drugged, that is.* And being fucked in the wrong bed, in the wrong orifice and by the wrong person. Wrong, because *he* was hardly unconscious. *Raped, that is.* On top of that he had a friend with him who filmed the whole thing, so that later they could publish the shit on the Internet. *Publicly violated, that is.*

No wonder Petra Westman was furious.

So she was drugged and raped the evening they had sat and chatted in Clarion's bar. Possibly she had drawn the conclusion that Hamad was involved because he had been so conveniently on the scene just hours before. But why had this suspicion only developed almost a year after the incident itself? Yes, because it was then that the film had been shown publicly for the first time, it was then that the film had been sent to the amator6.nu site. Right after he and Petra had gone their separate ways outside the Pelican.

And it had been sent from his own email address.

The question was: how could Petra know that? That everything pointed to it being him who had sent the film? And consequently he who had filmed or raped her, or both? And how could she know that so soon after the film had been sent? No, he could not figure that one out.

But there were other, more important questions that must be answered. Who had raped Petra and sent the film to Pontus Örstedt? Who on earth could be so seemingly omniscient and even be able to divert suspicion on to a completely different person? And how could Hamad clear his name and get justice for himself and Petra?

He could do something immediately for humanity at least, it struck him: direct the attention of the police towards at least one of the bastards, of which there were far too many. They would always find something to bring him in for, right? If they did not succeed in making a procuring charge stick, he was surely involved in drug dealing, financial crimes or some other dodgy business that they could put him away for.

He picked up the phone and entered the number of an old classmate who these days worked in the City investigative branch, and tipped him off about Pontus Örstedt. And noted that revenge was sweet. Even if it was not his own, but Jenny's and Petra's.

* * *

Johan Bråsjö stepped into the imposing entrance hall of the police station at Östgötagatan 100 and tried to put on an adult face. He took off his cap as he looked around, wondering if he was in the right place. The large marble hall with the armchairs looked completely different from what he had imagined. On TV there were usually noisy offices with processions of criminals being taken back and forth between interview rooms and holding cells. Here it was calm and quiet and there was not a crook to be seen.

With forced determination, he stepped up to the reception desk, where two pairs of curious eyes met his. He did not know which of the women behind the rather high counter, both with equally friendly smiles, he should turn to.

'Hi,' the one with glistening pink lips said.

She had light curly hair and kind blue eyes.

'Hi,' said Johan. 'I would like to report a crime.'

'How clever of you to come here,' said the other woman.

She also looked nice, slightly heavy-set with brown hair tied in a ponytail.

'What's your name?'

'Johan,' he answered, but regretted it at once.

Well, no harm done. He was not the only boy called Johan and they would get no more information out of him about who he was. And the woman probably understood what he was thinking, because she seemed content with his first name.

'So what's happened to you, little fellow?'

True, he was not one of the tallest in his class, but 'little fellow'? Really? He wasn't a preschooler; he must get them to take him seriously.

'Nothing. But I happened to walk past when a man was mistreating a pig. Beating the crap out of it.'

'Is that so?' the blonde receptionist exclaimed.

'Did you see him do it?' the brunette asked, looking serious.

'I only heard it,' Johan replied. 'A friend and I saw when he went into the shack – it was like a woodshed or something – and then he said nasty things and kicked the pig.'

The two women looked at each other.

'How strange. Tell us everything from the beginning,' the dark-haired one asked.

Johan gave a detailed account of what had happened, but as luck would have it the women never asked him how he and Ivan had come to be outside that shed.

'That's the worst thing I've ever heard!' said the blonde woman.

'Some people don't manage to take care of their animals,' said the brunette. 'But this sounds like one of the worst. What a little hero you are, Johan, coming to the police!'

She leaned over and before he knew what was happening she had tousled his hair. He wanted the ground to swallow him up, but the only thing to do was endure it – for the pig's sake. And when she was finished the other woman wanted to do the same. But he saw it coming: she was just about to stroke him across the cheek when he took a step back, out of reach.

'And could you find your way there again? Or perhaps you remember the address?' the brown-haired one continued.

'The Ugly Duckling,' Johan replied, as the blonde called to an older man who had just come in the door.

'Daddy, come and hear this! This boy wants to make a police report; you have to help him!'

The man came up to the reception desk and for a few terrifying moments Johan thought he too might start hair-tousling or hugging. But the man kept his hands in his coat pockets and looked at him with friendly but tired eyes.

'What's this about?' he asked, but before Johan managed to open his mouth the receptionists had taken over.

The man, evidently a policeman, looked even more tired when the two women began babbling away at the same time, and he started to move away before they were finished. He seemed at most moderately interested – if he had even understood what they were saying. Even so, he tried to be a little encouraging.

'Well done, kid. Take all the information down, Lotten: name, address, telephone number and so on, and we'll look at it when we have a chance. I have to rush.'

Give them his telephone number? Not likely. They would call his parents. Besides a hefty scolding he would also lose his bus pass and his freedom, and perhaps not even get to walk home from school alone in the afternoons. No, he had already learned a lesson; that would have to be enough. He turned away from the reception desk and bolted out into the cloudy grey late-winter afternoon.

'Wait, Johan! Don't go!' was the last thing he heard before the door closed behind him.

* * *

When Sjöberg had checked into the hotel in Arboga and thrown his suitcase on to the little armchair in one corner of his room, he sat on the edge of the bed and took out his mobile. He called Eniro and enquired what church parishes there were in the Arboga area. He noted names and numbers and asked the voice on the other end of the line to connect him to the last one mentioned.

'I'm searching for two individuals who have at one time possibly lived in your parish,' Sjöberg explained. 'Can you help me search in the parish registers?'

'Is this personal?'

'It's personal. It concerns my paternal grandfather and grandmother, John and Signe Sjöberg. John Sjöberg is said to have been born on 20 April 1911, Signe, maiden name Gabrielsson, on 11 January 1913.'

'Just one moment and I'll look,' said the woman who had answered.

'Thanks.'

After a few minutes she was back, but could only tell him that he must have enquired at the wrong parish. Sjöberg entered another of the numbers on his list and presented his request again.

'Are you doing genealogy?' the lady at the Arboga-bygden parish wanted to know.

'Yes, you might say that,' Sjöberg replied. 'I actually only want to know when my grandparents died and where they lived.'

'Right, then let's see what we can find.'

Sjöberg harboured faint hopes of being able to trace his grandparents so easily, but she was back right away and this time with positive news.

'I have them here,' she said, and Sjöberg felt his pulse rising. 'Let's see now, these are not exactly computer printouts ... John Emanuel Sjöberg, born on 20 April 1911, at Soldier's Croft in Björskogsnäs.'

Soldier's Croft, thought Sjöberg. The kids would like that.

'Married Signe Julia Maria Gabrielsson in May 1932. In 1933 they had a son, Christian Gunnar Sjöberg; that must be your father then?'

'That's correct,' Sjöberg confirmed.

'John and Signe were registered at Soldier's Croft until 1954, when they moved to Arboga.'

'Did Christian stay living at the cottage?' Sjöberg asked.

'Let's see, I have to change books . . .'

He could hear her turning pages in the background and imagined, without having any clear idea, that the parish registers were very large and dusty, with hard covers.

'He did. Until 1961, when he died. Oh, you were only three years old then; it must have been hard.'

'Well, yes, you might say so,' muttered Sjöberg, who hardly remembered having had a father at all. 'And when did John and Signe die?'

'John died in 1967 . . .'

There was silence on the line.

'And Signe?' Sjöberg said at last.

'No, I can't find any entry about that.'

'And what could that mean?'

'Well . . . It could be that someone has been careless, naturally. Or that she died after 1 July 1991, when everything was transferred to computer registries, but you ought to have known about it in that case. You'll have to enquire at the census office to find the date. Or she may still be alive.'

Sjöberg did not think it was necessary to tell this helpful woman that in his capacity as a police officer he already knew the process, and instead he thanked her for her help and hung up. 'Soldier's Croft,' he repeated to himself; so had he lived there during the first three years of his life. It was strange that he had no memories at all from that period, but on the other hand he had never had much help from his mother to remember. What most surprised him still was that his mother did not want to acknowledge the property, that she consistently refused to talk about it. What in the world could be the reason for that? And why had they moved from the parental farm to an apartment in Stockholm? Because his father had got sick, naturally. Perhaps he had needed advanced care that was only available in the capital.

Suddenly it struck him that his grandfather John had not died until 1967. Sjöberg had been nine years old then. He ought to have some memories of him at least. He had no memories of his grandmother either; how come? He could not recall either of them being mentioned while he was growing up, nor had his mother told him anything later when as an adult he had tried to find out about his family history. Sjöberg became increasingly convinced that there was something fishy about this. Something must have happened to cause his mother and his paternal grandparents to have no contact. And in that case, on which side had his father stood? Or had the split arisen after or in connection with his death?

Sjöberg glanced at his watch. It was five minutes to five.

There was no time to lose: he had to call the census office before they closed for the day. It would be just as well to gather all the information he could before he confronted his mother in earnest with this strange story. He called Information again and asked to be connected to the census office.

'My name is Conny Sjöberg. I would like information concerning my paternal grandmother, Signe Julia Maria Sjöberg, born Gabrielsson on 11 January 1913.'

'Yes, and what is it you want to know?'

The female voice on the telephone sounded uninterested and a bit snooty.

'I want to know when she died,' said Sjöberg.

'Don't you already know that, if she is your grandmother?'

'Evidently not, because I'm asking you,' Sjöberg answered with irritation.

'Unfortunately we can't give out such information.'

Sjöberg thought he could hear a shade of satisfaction in her reply. He put on his most authoritative voice and made a fresh attempt.

'I'm a detective inspector with the Hammarby Police in Stockholm, Conny Sjöberg. Will you please call me back immediately. The matter is urgent.'

Suddenly the attitude on the other end changed.

'Conny Sjöberg, Hammarby Police. I'll get back to you right away.'

Sjöberg smiled to himself while he waited. Actually he had no authorization to act this way; the matter was personal, after all, and he should not misuse his position in the police for the pleasure of taking a faceless bureaucrat at the census office down a peg. But who would ever catch him at it? Not her anyway. The phone in his hand shook and let out a shrill signal.

'Conny Sjöberg,' he answered curtly.

'Hi, Conny, it's Jenny.'

'Hi, Jenny! Listen, I can't talk to you right now because I'm waiting for an urgent call. We can talk a little later, can't we? I'll call this evening.'

'Okay. Bye now.'

'Bye.'

He clicked off the call and after another two minutes the woman at the census office called back. It was now past five and for a while he had thought she would wait until the next business day to punish him for his brusque manner. But he had not misjudged her respect for 'the uniform' and here she was again with a completely different tone of voice from before.

'Yes, I'm calling back from the census registry. What was it you wanted help with, sir?'

Apparently they were no longer on informal terms. He struck his most cordial tone, thinking to himself that he sounded like an old provincial governor, as he presented his request again.

'Do you have her last four digits?' the woman asked.

Sjöberg rolled his eyes.

'No, I don't. I think she has been dead a very long time, so she's probably not in the registers at all. But if you could just do a search in the computer for her name and date of birth, young lady, I can get that confirmed. You have a search function, don't you?'

She was, as Sjöberg suspected, insensitive to irony and did as she was told.

'Yes, here she is, definitely.'

Sjöberg frowned. This was not what he had expected.

'Signe Julia Maria Sjöberg, born Gabrielsson, 130111–1841, Birgittagatan 6, Arboga.'

'And she was registered there until . . .?'

'Yes, she's registered there. She's still alive.'

Sjöberg could not get a word out. He sat as if petrified on the edge of the bed, still wearing his shoes and winter jacket, and felt like an idiot.

'Congratulations,' said the woman on the phone. 'Congratulations on your newfound grandmother!'

* * *

Hamad had chased around town on his own for several hours. When he had visited Vida and Göran Johansson at their respective workplaces and shown them a photograph of Einar Eriksson, there had been no reaction. Neither of them had ever met or seen Eriksson. But several of Catherine Larsson's neighbours on Trålgränd recognized Eriksson as the man who was occasionally seen in the stairwell, sometimes alone, sometimes with the children. He had not been seen however in the days before or on the night of the murder.

Now Hamad was going to meet Christer Larsson for the first time, and with him he had a sulky Westman, who had had to leave Sandén to tackle alone the last item on their list for the day: Eriksson's car. After an apathetic hello from Westman outside Larsson's building, Hamad decided to temporarily turn off the personal and concentrate on the task in hand. Westman had not met the executed children's father, Catherine Larsson's husband, either, and they were both tense with expectation as they followed him into his home.

'You have a nice place here,' Westman said, in an attempt to get the conversation going.

Christer Larsson muttered something inaudible in reply, without meeting her gaze. He sat in his armchair with his hands laced together and loosely hanging between his knees, his eyes fixed on the rug in front of him. His hands were unusually coarse, but the nails were well tended. His greying hair was clean and recently cut, but he did not seem to have shaved for some time. The little apartment was tidy and the potted plants on the living-room windowsill seemed to be thriving.

'Do you sail?' Hamad asked, catching sight of a framed photograph on the wall of a sailing boat, of a type unknown to him, which with billowing spinnaker was ploughing through an azure-blue sea in radiant sunshine.

'I did at one time,' Larsson answered in a low voice without looking up.

He spoke very slowly and the two police officers exchanged glances before Hamad started speaking again.

'We are truly sorry about what happened. It must be hard for you?'

This elicited a shrug of the shoulders, nothing more.

'You must be feeling awful right now?' Westman clarified, to get him to talk.

'You get what you deserve.'

His gaze was still aimed down at the rug. He straightened the fingers of one hand and lightly cracked the knuckles with the other.

'What do you mean?' asked Hamad.

Instinctively he wanted to develop the question, but he restrained himself and tried to be patient. After a period of silence Larsson answered.

'An old bore like me. They were better off without me.'

'And what about you? Haven't you missed them?'

'Well . . .'

Silence.

'Not enough.'

'Do you have a bad conscience because you didn't stay involved with your family?' Westman attempted.

Suddenly Christer Larsson looked up and his eyes met hers. In a drawling voice but with a razor-sharp gaze he answered, 'Guilt is a heavy chain that rattles behind you wherever you go. It's part of your body. Finally you don't notice it any longer.'

'What do you mean by that?'

'Nothing other than what I said.'

Hamad made an attempt to interpret Larsson's words.

'You feel guilt because you've been a bad father?'

Christer Larsson turned his eyes away from Westman and looked out of the window.

'I have been a very bad father.'

Hamad expected that something would follow this, but nothing did. He was having difficulty with the slow tempo of the conversation and wanted to pick up the pace.

'Such a bad father that you killed the children?'

'Not in the legal sense.'

'Did you or did you not murder your wife and your children?' Hamad asked with new sharpness in his voice.

'I haven't murdered anyone,' Christer Larsson replied.

Westman changed tack.

'We now know that Catherine had a new man in her life. He was the one who bought the apartment for her.'

Larsson did not react, but still sat with his eyes morosely lingering on some indeterminable thing outside the window.

'He called himself Erik. Does that sound familiar?'

A hint of a shake of the head.

'You haven't heard Catherine mention a man called Erik?' she tried again.

'No.'

Hamad took over.

'But actually his name is not Erik. His real name is Eriksson. Einar Eriksson.'

Christer Larsson turned slowly towards him and in his eyes there was now something new, something that neither of the two police officers was able to interpret. Hamad thought he sensed surprise, perhaps worry, in Larsson's eyes, while Westman would later say that she saw a moment of passion. But it disappeared as quickly as it had come and immediately the brown eyes looked just as mournfully tired as before. But for a fraction of a second a different Christer Larsson had been discernible. Still a tall, muscular man with coarse fists, but now with a flame burning behind the indifferent facade. And that combination, Hamad imagined, could be disastrous if the circumstances were right.

'I have a picture of him here that I meant to show you,' said Westman. 'To see if you recognize him.'

She got up from the sofa bed where she and Hamad had sat down and went over to the armchair.

'Do you suspect him of the murders?' asked Christer Larsson.

'We're not ruling anything out,' Westman replied.

Larsson straightened up in the chair and looked at the photograph in Westman's hand. Hamad could see from his seat on the couch that Larsson squinted and moved back a little, as the far-sighted do, to be able to see the picture more sharply. It was completely quiet in the room for several seconds. Then something quite unexpected happened. Christer Larsson leaped up from the chair and Westman stepped to one side and stood as if petrified with the photograph in her hand, observing this phlegmatic man's suddenly flaring emotional outburst.

'You bastard! Have you done it again, you sick bastard? As if you hadn't done enough! What the hell is going on in your stunted little fucking . . . ? Ahhh . . .'

Then there were no longer any words; only grunts and distressed moans came out of his mouth. He rushed over to the wall beside the window and pounded his head against it again and again with full force. The picture of the sailing boat fell to the floor and the glass shattered into a thousand pieces, but Christer Larsson did not bother about that and even stepped with one foot on the broken glass as he made his way over to the opposite side of the room and rammed his clenched fist right into the wall.

Hamad got up from the couch and took a couple of

determined steps towards the frantic man. He tried to make himself heard, saying, 'There now, let's calm down,' but his words had no effect. Westman rushed over to Christer Larsson and tried to hold on to him around his waist, but without even noticing her Larsson stepped quickly away, spinning around the room, incapable of finding expression for his tumultuous thoughts. Then he suddenly fell sideways, making no attempt to put out his hands to break his fall. His head struck the floor with a nasty crack, and the two police officers saw the tension in all his limbs instantly disappear. He remained lying quietly on his side, with his arm at such an unnatural angle that it must surely be broken. His eyes were wide open, and he was still breathing hard. Hamad sank down in dismay at his side and stroked a hand over Larsson's forehead.

'We have to turn him,' he said. 'Take his feet.'

While Hamad linked his hands around Christer Larsson's upper body Westman took hold of his ankles. The burly man made no resistance and they managed to place him gently on his back without causing further injury to the broken arm.

'What's the matter with you?' asked Hamad, gently touching his hand to the side of the face that had taken the heavy fall, but Christer Larsson showed no signs of consciousness besides the open eyes and breathing.

He did not even react when Hamad carefully raised the injured arm.

'We have to . . . do something. Place a pillow under his neck and fetch a towel and cold water. I'll call an ambulance,' said Westman.

When the ambulance arrived a short time later Christer

Larsson still showed no signs of awareness, but strangely enough he seemed almost at peace lying there on the living-room floor.

* * *

Christer Larsson's breakdown had been trying and Hamad had ridden along in the ambulance to give his account of what had happened. Afterwards he needed to clear his mind, so once back at the police station he decided to go and work out. After a fairly hard session on the machines he went into the boxing room next door to do some stretches on the mat. Like the gym section, this room too had glass walls, in line with the prevailing fashion. Hamad actually preferred to work out in peace, without being put on show for curious passers-by, but apparently you had to be a display object while you tormented your poor body with exercise.

Just as he was about to enter the room he spotted Westman in boxing gloves on the other side of the glass, shiny with sweat and putting her all into thumping a punchbag. He stopped with his hand on the door handle, but convinced himself not to let another person's demons determine his own actions. Perhaps this might even be a good time to try a little strategic rapprochement? He changed his mind about stretching, opened the door and went in.

'Hi,' he said, not expecting a reply and not getting one.

Hamad tossed aside his water bottle and towel in a corner, while Westman seemed to get a burst of energy and pounded on the poor bag even faster. He went over to the equipment alcove and took out of a pair of practice gloves that he put on. He took a deep breath, and then he plucked up courage and went over to Westman.

'Come on, lady. Let the bag recover and box a little with me instead.'

It seemed to be a marketable proposal; he barely had time to get his gloves up in front of him before the blows started raining down. It was crucial to keep his feet going to counter the hits and meet them with just enough resistance. He was about to back off and ask her to calm down when he managed to get into a rhythm, and with that get his balance too, just in time to halt the words on the tip of his tongue. Sweat was spraying off Westman as she plugged away; her eyes were dark as night and had still not met his for a moment. If anything, she seemed to be looking for gaps in his technique, gaps between, under, over or to the side of the gloves where she could get in a hit against his body instead.

He had never seen her so full of energy, so full of . . . yes, it must be hate, that blackness in her eyes. This was not an exercise session for her; she was hitting to hurt. And when that realization suddenly occurred to Hamad he no longer wanted to be part of it. He probably had a chance against her, even though she had proper gloves and he only had clumsy workout equipment; he was a head taller and no doubt considerably stronger. But he lacked the energy and above all the will for this sick spectacle. She seemed prepared to beat him to death, and he did not want to be beaten to death, much less hit back. He had to put a stop to this relentless maniac who was pounding on him like a frenzied woodpecker.

'What are you up to, Petra? Can't you calm down a little?'

'What am *I* up to? You're out of your fucking mind!'

During this exchange he lost concentration for a moment, she got a clear hit on the cheek and it was followed by another to the stomach.

'Lay off now, damn it, can't we talk about this instead?' he attempted while he folded his arms up to protect his head.

With unusual doggedness she continued to hit him, first two quick blows to the side and then one across the neck.

'I know what you think,' he whimpered, 'but you're completely on the wrong track!'

She answered with several blows to the head. In the midst of the panting and puffing, kicks, blows and quick feather-light steps on the mat he could suddenly make out the sound of the door being opened, and at the same time Bach's *Badinerie* started up on someone's mobile from the same direction. He hoped that this new arrival would stop Westman's assault, but she continued to pound on him with undiminished strength for another minute or two, the time it took for his rescuers to grasp what was happening, make their way over to the mat, get hold of Westman's slippery wet arms from behind and pull her away from him, where he now lay curled up on the mat in a foetal position.

When he had recovered somewhat he looked up to see Holgersson leaning over him, with a self-important expression, sponging his face with a damp towel. Hamad wanted to get an overview of the situation and his clouded gaze ranged across the room. By the door stood Roland Brandt, the police commissioner, looking ruefully at Hamad with his mobile in his hand. And in the far corner of the room he finally caught sight of Petra, and that image would linger in his mind for a long time to come.

With a satisfied and somewhat cheeky smile on her face she stood – still with the boxing gloves on – leaning back as if in a boxing-ring corner. Leaning over her, with a hand on the wall on either side of her face, the deputy police chief, Gunnar Malmberg, was talking in a low voice. Evidently it had been him who had come in and freed Hamad from the irritable Amazon, and now presumably he was questioning her about what had happened and discreetly making her see reason.

Hamad did not know if he lay there for a matter of seconds or minutes, with the thoughts whirling in his head, but the peculiar atmosphere was relieved by Malmberg's phone ringing. An extremely familiar tune, which Hamad in his foggy condition could not put a name to, sounded across the room and somehow brought everything back to something like normality. Holgersson reached out his hand and pulled Hamad to his feet. Brandt shook his head, tapped his thumb on his own phone, brought it to his ear and left the room. Malmberg stepped aside to let Petra, still smiling, slip past him. She gave Hamad an expressionless look as she passed him on her way out. Holgersson gave him a thump on the back and he too left the room. Hamad staggered over to pick up his towel and water bottle, while Malmberg answered his phone.

'Yes? . . . I see . . . Yes . . . No, that I don't know.'

Their eyes met as Hamad turned around at the door, but Malmberg's thoughts were elsewhere.

'Talk to Lu– or that new girl. Jenny . . . Sure. No problem.'

Hamad made an effort anyway to seem grateful and nodded at Malmberg before he headed off towards the changing room.

He sat for fifteen minutes in the sauna to soften up his stiff, tender body, took a long shower and despite everything felt in decent physical shape when he went back up to the office to work for a while longer. It seemed as if he had escaped a concussion, and a few bruises he could put up with. But his mental state was not so good. That he had made himself ridiculous in front of the police commissioner and his coterie was bad enough, but how could he sort things out with Petra? How could they continue to work together when she was obviously prepared to beat him to a pulp when the opportunity arose?

He did not expect an apology – and didn't need one either, for that matter – but he had to get a chance to talk to her, get her to trust him again. And as soon as possible; they were caught up in a complicated investigation, and that needed everyone to do their best and not to pull in different directions. Perhaps it would be a good idea to get help from Sjöberg, as a kind of intermediary? But no, his boss had enough worries as it was, with one of his own officers a prime suspect in a triple murder and Sandén working part-time besides. He and Westman ought to be able to resolve their own private difficulties, in a professional and mature fashion – which Westman had actually shown herself incapable of. She'd treated him like a punchbag. He couldn't deny that he was starting to feel a little upset.

In that frame of mind he reached the marble landing between the reception level and the stairs up to his own corridor.

'Jamal, come here. You've got to hear this!'

Lotten's voice echoed across to him, and that if anything would usually have put him in a better mood. But it didn't this time; he wanted to get up to his office and get to work on what felt most urgent.

'Sorry, but I don't have time right now. We'll deal with it tomorrow.'

'But it's important,' Jenny chimed in. 'There was a little boy here who told us an awful story about animal cruelty!'

'Prepare a report then, but you'll have to ask someone who doesn't have quite as much to do as me right now.'

'The Ugly Duckling – that sounds like a café or something. Do you know where it is?' asked Lotten.

He shook his head, starting to move away.

'A pig,' she tried again. 'There was some idiot who was kicking a pig to death. We can't just let that sort of thing go on, can we? It's a living creature, for crying out loud!'

Then suddenly her tone changed to one – so typical for Lotten, and in this situation extremely irritating – of a grown-up coddling a child.

'But honey, what have you been doing? Your face is completely red!'

It had not occurred to Hamad that what he had just been through would be apparent on his face. He had only dragged a hand through his hair after his shower and not looked in the mirror.

'A pig kicked to death – that's roughly the way I feel right now,' he muttered, but not so loudly that it reached Lotten's ears.

'What happened?' she went on, but Hamad recovered quickly.

'I've been . . . in the sauna,' he replied, making his way up the stairs.

He had barely made it into his office before Malmberg was there, knocking on the doorframe. Damn it, the fight had really stirred things up.

'Come in,' he said, sighing inwardly as he sat down at the desk and showed his visitor to a chair.

Malmberg ominously pulled the door shut behind him, took a gulp of the Ramlösa he had with him and sat down.

'Well now, that was not a pleasant experience,' he noted with a look that clearly demanded something from Hamad.

Presumably an explanation, but Hamad had no intention of giving him one. Not an honest one in any event. He felt disrobed, somehow childish under the chief's scrutinizing gaze.

'No, not for me either,' he answered with a wry smile.

Say as little as possible, he told himself. The less said, the less that can be refuted. Malmberg finished the last of his mineral water and set the bottle aside on the desk.

'You look a bit worse for wear. Are you sure everything is okay?'

Instinctively Hamad's hand flew up to what he hoped was so far only redness on his cheek.

'It's cool. I was just taking a sauna.'

'What really happened?'

'Oh, we were working out. But she's such a competitive person, Westman, she went at it a little hard. It got a little out of hand, you might say.'

He tried another smile.

'Yes, you can safely say that,' said Malmberg.

Hamad had hoped for a laugh there, but Malmberg was deadly serious.

'And you're not a competitive person yourself?'

'No,' Hamad lied, but his competitiveness had nothing to do with it.

'And what is your attitude to this assault? For we must consider it an assault, mustn't we?'

Is that what Malmberg wanted it to be? Or was he subjecting Hamad to some kind of loyalty test? The question was easily answered in any event. It was Hamad's turn to be deadly serious.

'Hardly. As I said, a boxing workout got a little out of control. It's already forgotten.'

'No report?'

'Report? Are you joking?'

'Does it look like I'm joking?'

'I would never dream of reporting a colleague.'

Hamad lied again. Because of course he would not hesitate to report a corrupt cop or a cop who in some other criminal way abused his position. This, however, was something quite different.

'Not even if it turns out that you have incurred some form of injury?'

'In that case I would see it as an accident on the job,' Hamad answered without the hint of a smile.

'How do you think it will be for the two of you working together after this?' Malmberg continued stubbornly.

'It's going to be just fine,' Hamad replied without the slightest hesitation. 'As it always has been. And work always comes first,' he added, out of some kind of hazily conceived sense of solidarity, of the team as a whole.

Or was it really mostly for Petra's sake? And why should it be more important to emphasize her professionalism in particular? Because she was a woman, it struck him. She ended up under the management's magnifying glass more often than the rest of them for just that reason. And considering how much he loathed being there himself . . .

'Westman is a shining example of that. She is enormously focused and professional,' he maintained, and suddenly felt quite pleased with how he was handling this interrogation, weaving between landmines surprisingly agilely.

'So how will we proceed?'

'We' sounded bad to Hamad's ears. Malmberg and the rest of the mafia up there on the management level must be shaken off as soon as possible, so that he and Petra could resolve this between themselves.

'I'll talk to her. Everything will be worked out next time we meet, that I can promise.'

'We have to hope so. But I still haven't had any explanation for what happened,' said Malmberg in a voice like dry leaves.

Tenacious as a terrier, thought Hamad, and hesitated

for a moment before he answered. Then he smiled broadly and turned his palms up in a resigned gesture.

'Well, what can I say? You know how it is with women. PMT.'

That did the trick. Malmberg's stony face cracked from ear to ear. Hamad had male-bonded with the deputy police commissioner, hopefully had succeeded in defusing the matter from an official perspective and was now back at square one. Malmberg left the office with a guffaw that could be heard a good way down the corridor.

Hamad stood in the window and gazed out at the twilight falling over the Hammarby canal. He felt sickened.

Thursday Evening

'Critical but stable, they said. He is breathing on his own, but his pulse was very high. At first I thought he was dead. He was staring straight ahead, but I noticed that his blink reflexes functioned. He'd stepped on broken glass so his foot was completely bloody, he'd run his fist into the wall so it must have hurt like hell and on top of that he broke one arm when he fell. And he did not react in the slightest to the pain. They say he's catatonic.'

'Catatonic – is that a temporary condition?' Sjöberg asked.

'It depends, apparently,' Westman replied. 'In this case it may have been caused by possible brain damage – from the fall or when he banged his head against the wall – or by some kind of mental shock or however you want to put it, a reaction to the photograph. They are also talking about epileptic fits; I don't know whether that can be brought on mentally or just physically. In any event he's going to get electroconvulsive therapy and is on a drip. They seem to think there is some hope that he will recover.'

'Tell me what happened.'

'But I already have.'

'Tell it again, from a psychological perspective, so to speak.'

Westman cleared her throat and tried again.

'He was just as you described. Taciturn. A little

melancholy as I interpreted it. He talked in a drawl; I can understand how it must have been unbearable for Jens. He did not comment on his wife's and children's deaths at all. It was as if they did not really concern him. Or as if he didn't think it concerned him, if you know what I mean?'

'As if he had waived his right to mourn them?'

'Exactly. And then quite unexpectedly he started talking about guilt.'

'Guilt?'

'Yes, he said something along the lines that guilt is like a shackle that you drag around, but that you get used to it.'

'In what context did he say this?' Sjöberg wondered.

'We asked him if he had a bad conscience because he hadn't taken responsibility for the children. Then he said that he'd been a bad father. He said something else strange too: that he had not killed his children in a legal sense.'

'As if all the same he believes that he is responsible for the children's deaths in some way? Morally responsible?'

'That was how I understood it.'

'That would mean that he knows something about these murders after all,' Sjöberg said thoughtfully. 'Even if he didn't commit them himself.'

'He denied that he murdered them. It was a concrete no to that question.'

'And then you showed him the photograph?'

'First we asked if he knew that Catherine had a man in her life, Erik. He did not. Then we told him that Erik was actually named Einar Eriksson and there was a flash in his eyes. I thought it seemed as if the name had struck a chord. But it passed just as quickly again.'

'Perhaps it occurred to him that there must be many people with that name?' Sjöberg suggested.

'Very possibly, or else he simply held back his reaction,' Westman speculated. 'But on the other hand he asked – before I showed him the photograph – if we suspected Einar of the murders. And of course I answered somewhat evasively, along the lines of wanting to rule out as many conceivable alternatives as possible. Well, you know.'

'But then, once he had seen the picture –'

'Then all hell broke loose. You know the rest.'

'And what do you think, Petra? Is Christer Larsson our man?'

'Absolutely not. Einar Eriksson is our man. And if Larsson wakes up out of his condition he is going to be able to tell us why. *Then* he might be prepared to commit murder; that's the impression I got.'

'Murder Einar, you mean?'

'Exactly.'

'Maybe he's already done that.'

'Then how do you explain his reaction to the photo, Conny?'

'Perhaps Christer Larsson is a skilled actor.'

'You don't believe that yourself,' Westman refuted him, and he had to agree with her on that point.

Sjöberg briefly accounted for his day and his meetings with Ingegärd Rydin, Solveig Eriksson and Ann-Britt Berg. Westman told him about their fruitless attempts in the little apartment on Eriksdalsgatan to find the reason for Einar Eriksson's disappearance. The neighbours in the building had not contributed anything of value either.

'Now I'm going down into town to partake of a steak

with Béarnaise sauce and a pint of beer,' Sjöberg concluded the conversation.

This wasn't quite true, however, because as soon as he hung up he stretched out on the bed with his hands behind his head and started thinking about the incident with Christer Larsson. It was too bad he hadn't been there. Westman had provided a vivid and extremely thorough description of the course of events, but he would have given a lot to have seen Larsson's reactions with his own eyes.

But it did open up new paths in the investigation. Christer Larsson and Einar Eriksson had a shared past, that was obvious. And he himself was now in Arboga, the town where Erik Eriksson had served as a policeman during the early years of his career. The town where Christer Larsson and Ingegärd Rydin had lived together during the same period. There was some ancient history behind the brutal murders of Catherine Larsson and her two children, Sjöberg was becoming more and more convinced of that. Unfortunately it was already too late for him to get to the bottom of it today, but tomorrow he would root about in Einar Eriksson's past in the locality.

He was roused from his musings by Åsa calling.

'I've been out to look at that piece of property,' Sjöberg told her.

'Property?'

'Don't you remember that I found a title deed at my mother's place? I made enquiries and it turned out to be in this area, outside Arboga. So I took the opportunity to drive out and look at it, since I was here anyway.'

'So, what sort of place is it? How did she acquire it?' Åsa asked.

'Wait and you'll hear,' said Sjöberg, giving a thorough account of the condition of the property and his high-flown plans for it.

'But Conny, it's not ours,' Åsa objected.

'It's going to be ours. It's Mother's land, but she is obviously not the least bit interested in it. It's really nice; you would love it. It's called Soldier's Croft – great name.'

'But why hasn't she ever mentioned it?'

'I've made some investigations and you have no idea what I discovered. For one thing, I lived there during the first years of my life.'

'But I thought you were born in Stockholm?'

'I was born in Stockholm, but there must have been a special reason for that. Risky pregnancy, difficult delivery or maybe just that Mother happened to be in Stockholm when I was born – I have no idea. Anyway, my paternal grandmother and grandfather lived at Soldier's Croft roughly until Mother and Father got married, then we took over the place. We lived there until Father got sick and we moved to Stockholm. It's my childhood home – of course we should fix it up!'

'That sounds quite amazing! But why in the world hasn't she ever said anything?'

'I think there's something fishy there. Presumably Mother has no positive feelings about the place. You see, it turns out that my grandfather died in 1967, when I was nine years old. I can't remember ever having met him, or him or my grandmother ever being mentioned in our home. That must mean that Mother didn't get along with them, don't you think?'

'While your father was alive they must have got along, because your parents got to take over the cottage.'

'Yes, but some time during those years there must have been a serious falling-out between them.'

'And your grandmother, was she already dead when you were born?'

'Grandmother is alive.'

'Are you joking?'

'It's true. She's ninety-five years old, but she is still alive.'

'Unbelievable! And you've never met her?'

'In any event not since I was very small. I thought she'd been dead for half a century.'

'But you must visit her!'

'I'm going there tomorrow. I found out where she lives, so I'll go there first thing tomorrow.'

'What a story! Have you spoken to Eivor?'

'I called her this morning from Soldier's Croft and told her I was there. She made no comment. That was before I discovered that my grandmother is alive. I'll visit Mother over the weekend and take her to task. Damn it, we ought to be able to talk about things.'

'Well, I'll eat my hat!'

Åsa was a treasure trove of folksy old expressions her grandmother always used.

'Hug the kids for me,' said Sjöberg. 'I'll be back tomorrow night. I love you.'

'It's mutual. Hugs.'

When he had finished the overcooked piece of meat with its standard trimmings and started his second and –

considering his schedule the next day – last beer for the evening, Sjöberg called Sandén.

'The night life in Arboga seems to be world class. Are you at a disco or . . . ?'

'Not really,' Sjöberg replied, 'but there is quite a racket in this greasy spoon. I've just eaten something that will have to be considered dinner.'

'Oh dear, it's hard to be a police inspector. Listen, I found Einar's passport. It was in the glove compartment.'

'Good. But that doesn't change anything. I've never doubted that he's still in the country.'

'And then I put Bella on Eriksson's car.'

'I see. Was there anything in particular?' Sjöberg asked.

'Someone has sat on the passenger side,' Sandén answered. 'I thought it might be interesting to know who.'

'Shoeprints?'

'In the best case. There was a little gravel and stuff.'

It struck Sjöberg that he ought to have asked Ann-Britt Berg if she happened to remember what kind of shoes Einar had worn on his visit to Solberga on Saturday. Of course it was highly unlikely that she would have noticed, but anyway he took out his notebook from the pocket of his jacket, which was hanging behind him on the back of the chair, and made a little note about it while still on the phone to Sandén.

'It may have been Einar who sat there,' Sjöberg suggested.

'You're still clinging to your conspiracy theories,' Sandén said with a laugh. 'You think he could have been taken away in his own car?'

'Why not?' Sjöberg answered seriously. 'And if that's

the case I don't want to think about how he's doing right now.'

'But by who, Conny?'

'By Christer Larsson perhaps. He apparently has a bone to pick with Einar.'

'Yes, that was a dreadful story. But that man hardly seems to be in a condition to –'

'We know nothing about it,' Sjöberg interrupted. 'He seems to have some pent-up rage inside him.'

'If Eriksson murdered his wife and kids, of course he'll be angry.'

'I wish I'd been there,' Sjöberg said with a sigh, taking a sip of beer. 'I'm not at all satisfied with this second-hand information. I can't piece it together.'

'We'll have to see what tomorrow holds in store,' Sandén said philosophically.

'Well, not tennis anyway,' said Sjöberg, referring to the matches he and Sandén played every Friday morning at seven o'clock.

'No, I suspected that. Seeing as you're at the disco instead of getting some rest. Chalk one up to me.'

'You can't do that!'

'Walkover, damn it! It's a result reflecting that the mentally weaker player has made excuses to avoid playing the match. What is it you're going to do tomorrow?'

'First I'm going to visit my grandmother.'

'You see!' said Sandén triumphantly. 'Talk about a poor reason to miss a tennis match. By the way, I didn't know you had a grandmother.'

'I didn't either, actually,' said Sjöberg.

'I beg your pardon?'

'I discovered it a couple of hours ago. She lives here in Arboga, so I thought I would take the opportunity to visit her since I happen to be here.'

'And this knowledge you just stumbled across, in the middle of the intensive hunt for Einar Eriksson?'

'Something like that. I'll tell you when I see you. Then I thought I would drop by the police station here and ask a few questions about Einar. He worked there about thirty years ago.'

'That sounds more substantial,' said Sandén, teasing still.

'That remains to be seen. See you tomorrow.'

'My regards to your grandmother.'

Early Friday Morning

The lawn under his bare feet was cold and wet from the night dew. He did not dare look up towards the house. His head felt so frightfully heavy that he was hardly able to lift it. With an enormous effort he finally managed to turn his face up towards the light, towards the window. His cheeks were burning, despite the coolness of the night, as he let his head fall backwards, between his tense shoulders. He must also dare to open his eyes, but somehow he could not make himself look at her. He swayed in the darkness, about to lose his balance, and his eyes involuntarily opened. There she stood in the window on the upper floor – Margit, rosy and inviting, with her amazing blazing red hair like a backdrop for her soft face. She was dancing for him, only a few tentative steps, with a questioning look on her face: Will you dance with me? He answered by extending his hands towards her, but the unnatural weight of his head restrained him, pulled him backwards, and everything turned black before his eyes as he fell heavily through the dark August night.

He sat up in bed with a stifled scream. It had happened to him so many times before that even in his sleep he could prevent himself from screaming out loud. The bedding was soaked and he drew the back of his hand across his forehead and dried it off on the cover. Then he started to feel cold. He threw his arms around his bare upper body and sat shaking with cold and tension, unable to suppress a drawn-out whimper. It was more than a week since he had last been woken by the dream, but this time it had felt more real than ever. After a few minutes, when he no longer felt the pounding of his heart in his temples, he turned on the lamp fixed to the wall behind him, reached for his phone on the bedside table and entered Margit Olofsson's mobile number.

'Conny, what are you doing up at this hour?'

'What time is it?'

'It's after three. What's the matter with you? You sound out of breath.'

'I suddenly got so worried.'

'About me?'

'Are you at work?'

'Otherwise I wouldn't have picked up. Where are you?'

'I'm . . . on a business trip. Forgive me for calling.'

'You can call whenever you want. I miss you.'

'I miss you too. I got worried —'

'I'm at work, Conny. There's nothing to be worried about.'

'That's good. Forgive me . . . I'll be in touch.'

He ended the call and crept under the covers with the phone still in his hand. He did not know why he had called her. A sudden impulse, some kind of acute longing for . . . for what? He squeezed his eyelids together and tried to shut out the unpleasantness of the dream, all the unanswered questions.

He wanted everything to be back to normal again, wished he had never met Margit, or that he at least had backbone enough to break off the relationship. He did not love Margit, he loved Åsa, but there was something about Margit that he needed, and he could not put his finger on what it was. He had to end it, he knew that, but then he would keep on going, making the wrong choices. What the reaction would be at home if he told them about his affair he dared not think. He had seen Margit four times since September; it was only a matter of four times. But four times was not a casual fling, it was a relationship. A sick, destructive relationship that could only lead . . . to hell.

They only ever saw each other on his initiative – she never called, never sought him out. That was how he wanted it and she seemed to read his thoughts, because they had never discussed it. Even this was something he was ashamed of. He was exploiting Margit for his own needs, whatever they may be. And that was not the sort of man he wanted to be, a man who exploits women – people – for his own satisfaction. That was not who he really was, never had been. But the damned dream had drawn something rotten out in him, something that evidently had been inside him all along but that he did not recognize. He thought he had become alienated from himself, become colder, less empathetic.

With a jerk he was wakened from his brooding or his sleep, he did not know which. It was the mobile, still in his hand under the covers, that was ringing. The lamp was still on; he cast a glance at the clock radio on the bedside table. The time was three-thirty.

'Hi, Conny, it's Jenny.'

That's right, Jenny had called him earlier and he had

promised to call her back. But he had forgotten that and now he'd got his punishment in the small hours. Sjöberg had known the Sandén girls since they were born. He definitely did not see himself as some kind of reserve dad, because they didn't need one, but he was without a doubt the adult person that Jenny knew best besides her parents. But he could not figure out what business she could have in the middle of the night; nothing like this had ever happened before.

'But my dear, what are you doing up at this hour? Don't you have to get up for work tomorrow?'

'Yes, but I can't sleep.'

'Have you slept at all?'

'Maybe a little, but I don't think so.'

'Poor thing. So what's on your mind? Has something happened?'

'Isn't cruelty to animals against the law?'

Sjöberg smiled, realizing what this was about. Micke and especially Lotten had turned Jenny's head. Since she had become the owner of little Blaisy she had become mad about dogs, and she soaked up her collegues' craziness like a sponge.

'Yes, it can be a punishable offence. But that depends of course on what kind of animal it is and what has been done to it,' he answered factually.

'There was a little boy at the station today and he told such an awful story.'

'Oh dear. Have you told your dad?'

'Yes, but he didn't care. Or didn't have time,' she corrected herself. 'There was a man who had a pig locked up and it was lying in its own dung.'

'Pigs usually do that.'

'But he yelled at it and kicked it hard as anything.'

'And the boy saw this?'

'No, but he and a friend were hiding nearby and heard the whole thing. Isn't it strange to keep a pig in the city?'

'It's probably not that common, but I don't think it's illegal exactly. By the way, maybe it wasn't an ordinary pig but one of those Vietnamese potbellied pigs. They're popular these days.'

'He kicked it really hard anyway, lots of times. And it didn't get proper food either, no potatoes or anything.'

'How do you know that?' asked Sjöberg.

'The man was laughing at the pig because it had got sick from the food.'

'But potatoes?' said Sjöberg, surprised. 'Where did you get that from?'

'Oh, I don't know,' said Jenny. 'It was the boy who said it.'

Sjöberg could not help smiling a little.

'He'll have to make sure he stays away from that man. He seems to be an unpleasant character.'

'But we have to rescue the pig, Conny! If cruelty to animals is a crime and you're a policeman, then you have to be able to do something, don't you?'

'I see, you're actually phoning to report a crime?' said Sjöberg, mildly amused.

'Yes, because Daddy wouldn't help me and Jamal wouldn't either.'

'They have a lot to do right now.'

'But it's important. Lotten thinks so too.'

'Hmm, I can imagine. Let's do this, Jenny, we'll file an official report when I get back. But now let's both sleep. Okay?'

'Okay,' Jenny answered, and he heard her yawn. 'Good night then.'

'Good night, my dear. Sleep well.'

Friday Morning

So Conny Sjöberg, at nearly fifty, found himself for the first time face to face with his paternal grandmother. He immediately recognized the high cheekbones and the narrow, long bridge of the nose from the image he saw in the mirror. Signe Sjöberg was a woman with her head held high, standing up straight in the doorway, wearing a simple but elegant dress and court shoes with heels. She looked suspiciously at him with intense blue eyes from behind a pair of steel-rimmed glasses.

'What can I do for you?' she wanted to know when Sjöberg, preoccupied with studying her facial features, did not say anything.

'My name is Conny Sjöberg, and I think' – he was convinced at that moment of the family relationship – 'that you are my grandmother.'

She stared at him without revealing what she was thinking.

'May I come in, so we can talk?'

She examined him critically up and down, and seeming to approve his exterior she backed up a little to let him into the apartment. Sjöberg felt awkward standing there in her little hallway, with his hands clasped in front of him like a shy schoolboy. After closing the outside door she turned her back to him and walked quickly for a ninety-five-year-old into the living room. One of the chairs at the dining table was already pulled out and she sat down on it. On the table was an open newspaper and alongside it a pencil and a rubber. Sjöberg drew the conclusion that he had interrupted her in the middle of the daily crossword puzzle, which he knew from his own experience could be quite irritating. Something hereditary perhaps? He pulled out a chair and he too sat down.

She studied his movements with clear scepticism. The atmosphere in the little apartment was saturated with antipathy and he was determined to find out why.

'Is it true that you are my grandmother?' Sjöberg opened, with a friendly smile.

She hesitated a little before replying, but then said curtly, in a sharper tone than he had expected, 'It's not inconceivable.'

'If you'll excuse my saying so, you don't seem to be especially happy to see me,' Sjöberg suggested.

'Should I be?'

Sjöberg laughed, feeling that he was being dragged into some kind of psychological power play, the reasons behind which he did not grasp. He decided to try to avoid any strife and put his cards on the table.

'I've grown up believing that my grandmother and grandfather died before I was born. Yesterday I discovered that my grandfather died when I was nine years old but that you are still alive. As you can imagine, I was extremely surprised by that discovery, but above all I was happy to suddenly have been given a grandmother. It doesn't feel like you are equally happy to see me.'

She did not say anything, simply stared at him with icy-cold eyes. At first glance he had been positively surprised at her vitality and the clearness of her gaze, but now he began to think it would have been easier if she had been more confused.

'Could you explain to me why?' Sjöberg continued.

'Your mother can explain that to you.'

Is it us versus them now? thought Sjöberg. How much could he say about his mother without being disloyal?

'She's not the talkative sort. Believe me, I've tried to ask questions about this and that, but she avoids talking about what's in the past. But you should know that she has never said a bad word about you or my grandfather.'

'I should think not. We have never done her any harm,' his grandmother replied.

Her blue eyes stared right into his. She stood by what she said and Sjöberg had great difficulty not averting his gaze.

'But you think that she has done something to you? To both of you? Then in that case I would like to know what.'

'She killed my son,' Signe Sjöberg answered in a firm voice.

Sjöberg turned completely cold inside. What could she mean? But he maintained his factual tone as he continued to coax his grandmother into revealing the missing pieces of the puzzle of his life.

'Can you expand on that, please? I have no idea what you are trying to say.'

'I'm not trying to say anything. You are the one who is trying to force me to talk about things that should have been forgotten long ago.'

'Should have been forgotten? I have a feeling that you are the one who refuses to forget, Grandmother.'

She winced at the last word. Apparently she did not appreciate his choice of address.

'I thought that Dad got sick,' Sjöberg continued. 'I recall that he was in the hospital for a long time before he died. I never got to visit him, so I've never understood what illness he suffered from.'

'Illness!' she exclaimed. 'It was no illness; he was in intensive care with severe burns for months before it ended.'

'Burns?' said Sjöberg with a shudder. 'Please, tell me what happened.'

'Your mother ought to have done that. Why should I have to sit here and dwell on the past?'

'Because I'm asking you,' said Sjöberg, showing his open palms as if to underscore that he had no hidden agenda. 'Because your son was my father. Because I have the right to know.'

'You and your mother have forfeited your rights. I don't owe you anything.'

Not for a single moment did she take her eyes off him. Signe Sjöberg seemed to be a strong person, someone you would rather have with you than against you. But Sjöberg found it easier to deal with this type of person than with the repressed, evasive type, like his mother. He decided to appeal to her common sense and steeled himself against her frosty scrutiny.

'I was three years old. I understand that I was involved in the crime that was committed against Dad, but actually I have no memories at all from that age. So I feel no guilt. It seems to me that the question of guilt is extremely important to you, so for that reason I ask you again: what happened?'

Her eyes gave no clue to what she might be thinking, but Sjöberg noticed how her lips tensed. He waited in silence until finally she spoke.

'The house caught fire. All of you were sleeping in the same room, but she woke up and took you with her down to the garden. Only you. She left Christian behind in the flames. The men managed at last to pull him out, but it was already too late. He got to live a few more months, but what kind of life was that?'

No tears, and the gaze as well as the voice was firm, but the whole room was permeated by bitterness, all directed at his mother. And obviously at him too. Because he'd had the luck to escape from a fire when he had just turned three, because his mother had helped her little son out of the burning house first and not her husband. Sjöberg felt a lump growing in his throat. So this was his mother's lot; after having lost her husband and her home, she assumed the guilt for the irreplaceable loss and was rejected besides by her in-laws.

Sjöberg felt an urgent need to get out of there; he could not bear to sit there with this inhuman statue of a grandmother and be the scapegoat of her absurd accusations. But on the surface he maintained his friendly calm as he got up from the chair.

'I'm sorry it turned out the way it did,' he said. 'I assume we won't meet again. Take care, Grandmother.'

She looked back at him with her inscrutable gaze, and he lingered there for a few seconds before he calmly turned and left.

* * *

Westman was already in her office when Hamad passed her door at nine. He thought he had built up enough self-confidence last night and this morning to go in to her with authority, and get out what he wanted to say. But at the same time he cursed himself for not having dealt with it earlier. Which would, in fact, have been difficult because then he had not had the slightest idea what the problem was. But still, it never hurt to clear the air. If the relationship meant anything.

He tore off his jacket and tossed it on his desk, strode back to Westman's office and walked in without knocking. She looked up at him from her seat at the desk with a blank look. He pulled the door shut and sat down in the visitor's chair without asking for permission. Leaning back with his hands on the armrests and his legs crossed, he looked at her contemplatively. Her expression was completely neutral.

'We have to talk,' he said.

'I see.'

Contempt.

'I repeat: I know what you think, but you're on the wrong track. For my sake and for your sake and the team's, we have to work this out.'

'The team's?'

'The management mob is threatening a split if we can't cooperate.'

'Oh, I'm so scared. I'm sure I'm the one who will have to go.'

Sarcasm. How could she be so sure that he was the one in a precarious position and not her?

'And you have no fucking idea what I think,' she added.

He steeled himself, tried to look confident, although he knew his hands would shake like an old wino's if he ventured to release his grip on the armrests.

'Okay then. You think I spend my nights drugging and raping women. And that I film that shit too.'

He tried to sound impersonal, but his cheeks were burning and it was not impossible that his voice was trembling a tiny bit too. He was afraid that she would have another outburst, wallop him again. But she stayed in her chair. Simply raised one eyebrow and smiled condescendingly.

'Do I think that? I think that proves it's true. I take that as a confession.'

'Don't. I can prove I'm innocent.'

'Yes, exactly. It seems highly probable that you would know all about it if you aren't involved. It's the talk of the town, I understand.'

More sarcasm.

'When I left you at the Clarion that Friday in November 2006 I went home and got a divorce from Lina. We sat and talked for almost the whole night. The next morning we divided up our things and then I drove her home to her parents'. You can call her and check.'

Westman listened. Still without visible interest, but she did not interrupt.

'After that body-language course, when we parted outside the Pelican, Bella picked me up in her car. We drove to her place and I stayed the night. We had a relationship for a while. That has nothing to do with you or anyone else, but I'm telling you because I have to. Ask her and you'll see.'

He saw something new in Westman's eyes, something that had not been there before. She still said nothing, but she was thinking. Hamad believed he had some idea of what was going on in her mind. If he was innocent after all, how could he know what dates had any significance in this mess?

'I found some shit on the computer,' he clarified.

A white lie; he did not think she needed to know that he was not the only one who had seen the unpleasant, humiliating images.

'Not until the other day. I didn't look that carefully, didn't want to see. But I saw enough to understand what had happened. And the date was in one corner.'

Westman frowned, suspicious now.

'And the other date, where did you get that from?'

So she had asked. He would not be able to keep the truth from her, that other people had seen that film. But there was hope. He had managed to make her curious.

'Someone sent those images from my email address.'

'The images?'

'The film.'

'Was it a film? Not just an image?'

'It was a film clip. As I said, I didn't look all that carefully.'

'You're lying,' Westman stated firmly. 'I found an image on your computer, not a film. And I deleted it. And if something had been sent from your computer then the traces were wiped out. The image was sent from my email address.'

'You've been into my computer?'

'I had to confirm that it was you.'

Suddenly they had a dialogue. They could set factual argument against factual argument, and that was a good start.

'But it wasn't,' said Hamad.

'What you're saying doesn't add up.'

'Listen to me, Petra. Someone has sent an image from your computer and a film from mine. So on my computer there are no traces, except that the image that was sent from your email is there, but you've deleted it. You're right. But I found out from the addressee that the film was sent from my email address. I wanted to spare you, thought you'd be better off not knowing.'

'Not knowing what?'

'That others besides me have seen the film.'

'And who was the film sent to?' Westman wanted to know.

She looked more sad than angry now. He felt that he was near to achieving his goal, and started to relax. His hard-clenched jaw muscles softened, the pressure he'd felt for six months at his temples eased. Most of all he wanted to give her a big hug – she seemed to need it.

'I'm not going to tell you. But don't worry, he no longer has it. Trust me. Do you trust me?'

Westman studied him thoughtfully for several seconds. She had collapsed in her chair, deflated.

'So how did you find out that this person had the film?' she asked with an almost mournful expression on her face. 'And that it came from you?'

'Detective work,' Hamad said with a smile. 'I'm a police officer, as perhaps you are aware.'

'Was it Conny?'

He shook his head, surprised.

'Hadar?'

This was even more of a surprise. Was he the only one who didn't know what this was all about?

But now he could not hold himself back any more. He had longed for this moment for months, though never so clearly as now. He got up and went around the desk, carefully pulled her out of the chair and put his arms around her.

'I've wanted to do that for a long time,' he whispered into her hair. 'Now you have to tell me what happened to you.'

He felt her relax and adjust her head against his shoulder.

'I trust you,' she sighed.

And she told him.

When he left her an hour or so later, it was with mixed emotions. Enormous relief at having been allowed to come in from the cold. Firm resolve where closing in on the Other Man, as Petra called him, was concerned. And a bitter taste in his mouth in the aftermath of the longed-for confidence. Petra, with a big smile, had let it slip that she had actually managed to make things happen on the love front once recently. But that it would not be anything, *could* not be anything more. He wondered why. 'Could not' usually meant the person was already taken, and he did not like that. Or perhaps it was the case that he didn't like the idea of her being with anyone at all.

She had laughed the whole thing off, unconcerned. He regretted having asked.

* * *

On the sixth day his courage started to fail. He now felt so weak that he stopped worrying about time and no longer cared when he should sleep and when he should be awake. He could not be certain either if his sleep really was sleep, because he glided in and out of a kind of trance-like state that might be unconsciousness. Now he no longer cared as much about the cold, which he interpreted as the beginning of the end. He did not abandon his one slight hope however; stubbornly he kept stretching the rope around his wrists with brief little jerks whenever he was able to summon enough energy.

The little pile of bread pieces had been replenished the day before, but even though his stomach ached with hunger he could not make himself eat. His mouth was not hungry. Besides he was put off by the elaborate and painful procedure he had to go through to get to the bread and take in some of the crumbs. He had placed himself beside the water bowl on the other hand, and now and then he forced himself to lap up a few drops. He lay motionless, with aching, numb limbs, changing position only when it was absolutely necessary.

Thoughts and dreams alternated, flowed together and sometimes he woke up in total confusion, not knowing where he was. His thoughts and memories as well as the insistent reality tormented him, more than the continuous aches. In his dreams he could occasionally be freed from the suffering that was now his whole existence. But during the waking moments there were no dreams. Only a painful, drawn-out understanding that life was again sneering in his face, with its constantly recurring reminders of the guilt he bore and the guilt he would bear in the future. And then all the memories pursued him, memories from the life he had lived. The pitiful, meaningless little life he had lost to *a day in May long ago, when the aroma of freshly cut grass filled his nostrils, the aroma of soil where new life would sprout, the aroma of the blossoming hedge on the other side of the street. A day in May when the sun shone from a clear blue sky and the wind stirred a playfully rippling river and ruffled his wife's blonde hair as she stood in line at the kiosk where she thought she would soon be buying two lollipops, but where she would lose all her words.*

A few grey sparrows sat under the rubbish bin right in front of her and pecked up the crumbs from an ice-cream cone. With small hopping steps they moved around the desirable spoils and when she cast a glance over towards the car she saw that there was movement there too. One of the boys, presumably the younger one, Tobias, had stood up and she thought it looked as though he was about to climb between the seats up to the driver's spot. She glanced at her watch and thought that by now Einar must be on his way back. At the same time the customer in front of her had finished his purchase and it was her turn.

'Do you have any lollipops?' she asked the man behind the counter, looking again towards the car, where to her relief she could see the boy not in the driver's seat but hanging between the seats, with his face pointing downwards, hopefully in the process of sitting down again in the back seat.

'Sure,' the kiosk-owner answered, holding out a container for her to choose from lollipops of several different colours and sizes. For

some reason she pulled out a black one and, still holding it, took a few hesitant steps in the direction of the slowly rolling car and then started running, first with small worried steps and then with big clumsy strides in her heeled shoes towards the car that was now rolling rapidly backwards in the direction of the glistening water.

Before the back wheels went over the edge she was at the car, trying to tear open the door to the passenger's side, but fumbled it when the car slipped away from her. She screamed, and her eyes, filled with terror, met the astonished wide-open eyes of one of the boys — she would never remember which — from the back seat, just as the car tipped and with unexpected speed disappeared from the stone-paved promenade she stood on and fell through the clear air down into the black water with a heavy and audible splash. As if paralysed, she stood for a moment and watched the car quickly fill with water through the half-rolled-down window on the driver's side. With a piercing scream, she threw herself into the ice-cold, rushing water and, taking a deep breath, disappeared below the surface, just as he arrived on the scene. During her struggle against impossible forces, soon helped by himself and two passers-by, the car was pulled deeper and deeper down to the bottom, to settle at a depth that the poorly equipped and severely strained figures struggling in the swift water could not cope with.

With desperate, exhausted, panting hints of screams, they finally let themselves be hoisted up on to the ground that would never again feel firm under their feet. In the water now only the black lollipop was seen, peacefully bobbing by the edge of the pier.

* * *

With pounding heart, and feeling so angry that his ears had turned red, Sjöberg got into the car and tried to calm his breathing. Just as his entire being recoiled from that bitter, self-obsessed creature who was supposed to be his grandmother, he also felt a ray of warmth inside him. And as he sat there, leaning over the steering wheel with the engine not yet turned on, trying to think, he noticed how that feeling of warmth began to take over and at last all the anger against the emotionally cold grandmother was transformed into a kind of admiration for his mother.

Suddenly he visualized his mother as she must have looked when she was young, before she became a widow. With the help of old photographs he had seen he created a new picture of his young mother: the picture of a young woman full of life with a warm smile. The image of a different woman from the one he knew, strong and secure with her life ahead of her, happily married, living in a cottage in the country and with her little son in her arms. A woman whose life was one day shattered by a fire that left her alone in an inhospitable suburb in a strange city with three heavy burdens: the little son she would have to bring up alone, the sorrow after her life partner had tragically perished, and the great guilt that her in-laws placed on her.

The silence, the secrecy, it had all been only for his sake, to spare him from the indescribable: the grief for his father and the memories of the fire. That was not the way people dealt with catastrophe today, but it was her way, to help her son grow up into an independent and well-balanced person. And she had succeeded, if you overlooked what had recently been going on in his head, his temporary mental meltdown – but that was the sort of thing that affected everyone. Midlife crisis perhaps? If there was such a thing.

Sjöberg sighed and turned the key in the ignition. A new page had been written in the story of his mother. Of himself. And he would do what he could to turn his new knowledge into something positive in his relationship with her. But that would have to wait for the time being. Right now he was going to touch down in Einar Eriksson's old reality.

For the second time during his visit to Arboga Sjöberg found himself in a reception area, asking to see the employee who had been there longest. The uniformed youngster he spoke to referred him to a room at the far end of a corridor on the fourth floor.

The room was shared by two police inspectors, Möller and Edin, both in their sixties. Möller was a tall, sinewy fellow who spoke a distinct Skåne dialect, while Edin was of medium height, broad-shouldered and completely bald. Sjöberg introduced himself and was invited to sit down in one of the two visitor's chairs against the wall by the door. Möller offered him something to drink and disappeared from the room, while Edin rolled his chair over to Sjöberg. They exchanged a few words about the noisy renovation work a few offices away and the water damage that had caused it. Once Möller had placed a plate of fruit and some bottles of Ramlösa on the little table between the armchairs and sat down himself, Sjöberg outlined his errand.

'I'm working on a case where a woman and her two small children were found in their home with their throats cut. Perhaps you've heard about it?'

Both the police inspectors had.

'Two men who figure in this investigation have their roots in Arboga and the reason I'm here in town is that I have been questioning their relatives. The interviews did not produce much, for a number of reasons, but one of these two men once served as a policeman here, so it struck me that perhaps you might have something to contribute. You both would have been working here already in the early seventies?'

'That's correct,' said Edin, and Möller nodded in agreement.

'Is he suspected of the murders?' Möller asked in his broad accent.

'No,' answered Sjöberg, giving a doctored version of the truth. 'But he has a central role in this case and now he's missing.'

'And the other man, has he vanished too?' asked Edin.

'No, but he's in hospital and in no condition to help us.'

'So what's his name, the policeman?' asked Möller.

'He worked here between 1975 and 1980, Einar Eriksson.'

The two police inspectors exchanged a glance which Sjöberg could not interpret.

'Do you remember him?' he asked.

Edin leaned forward and with his elbows supported on his knees he put his hands in front of his mouth and nodded seriously. Möller leaned back in the armchair and took a deep breath before he answered.

'We knew him very well. It's terrible, what happened. It was hard on Einar.'

'Poor devil,' Edin added, shaking his head mournfully.

Sjöberg furrowed his brow in surprise. Were they referring to something he was expected to know about?

'Now I'm not following. What was it that happened to Einar?' he asked.

'Excuse me, I thought you knew,' said Möller. 'Well, where should we begin?'

'In brief, it was like this,' Edin explained. 'Einar and his wife, Solveig, were asked to mind their neighbours' children. They were two small boys, about three and five years old. The kids were supposed to be dropped off at the mother's workplace – she worked at a beauty salon in town. On the way there Einar, who was the one driving the car to start with, stopped to run an errand. It dragged on a little, so Solveig took over the wheel and drove up to the kiosk down by the river, to buy sweets for the boys. She parked the car alongside the kiosk, with the front towards the street and the back towards the water. At that time there was no guardrail there by the river and there was a slight incline. While she was buying the sweets the car started to roll and . . .'

Edin stopped and looked urgently at his colleague. Sjöberg sat with every muscle in his body tensed, waiting apprehensively for the rest of the story, even if he thought he could guess how it would end. Möller took over.

'Solveig ran up to the car to try to prevent the catastrophe. But she didn't succeed, and the car backed over the edge. One window was rolled down, so the car quickly filled with water and went to the bottom. With the kids and everything. She threw herself into the water and tried to get the doors open. Einar arrived then and he tried too. And a few others. But you know, it's hard when the whole car is under. And then it was probably no fun to have to confess face to face to those poor neighbours. Oh, good Lord, what a tragedy it was.'

Sjöberg was dazed. For thirty years Einar had borne this: the memories, the anxiety, all the feelings of guilt such an event must carry with it. What a burden.

'Was she punished, Solveig?'

Edin laughed, a brief, toneless laugh.

'Oh, she was punished. But not in the legal sense.'

'Not in the legal sense' fluttered through Sjöberg's brain, but the thought didn't have time to take root.

'She was never herself again,' Edin continued sorrowfully. 'For the first few days she screamed, tried to explain, excuse herself, get forgiveness, take on the guilt, grant herself forgiveness. And then she fell silent. First she was in a hospital, for a pretty long time, I think, but then Einar put her in a home of some kind. For three years he stayed living in town. You can imagine what kind of a life he had here. There was whispering and pity and pointing. And naturally the accusations came thick and fast. But he endured it, for Solveig's sake.'

'Every day he came to work and did what he was supposed to,' Möller continued, with admiration in his voice. 'He was not the same happy man after that, but he was here and he struggled on. All his free time he spent with Solveig, at the hospital at first, and then at that home. It was three years before he gave up hope and moved to Stockholm.'

'He didn't give up hope,' Sjöberg interjected. 'He bought a townhouse for them to move into when she got well. And he still visits her every Saturday. For twelve hours he sits there with her, takes walks with her, talks to her. Her birthday, Christmas and New Year's he spends with Solveig too.'

'So Einar was punished too, and then some,' said Edin. 'And Solveig had not done anything wrong. It was one of the boys, who was car-crazy. And disobedient. He released the handbrake, although he was clearly told not to touch anything in the car. But of course she shouldn't have left them alone.'

'She could have parked a little better,' was Möller's comment. 'But what the hell, we all make little mistakes. It's just in most cases it works out okay. After the accident they set up a fence by the river, so it couldn't happen again.'

Sjöberg looked at the fruit on the table but suddenly felt no desire to eat. He was shaken by the story about Einar's and his wife's fate. Shaken, but also filled with admiration for his co-worker, who had never betrayed his Solveig.

'You mentioned another man too,' said Edin. 'What's his name?'

'His name is Christer Larsson,' Sjöberg replied.

The two police inspectors exchanged a glance again and Edin's next comment made Sjöberg's blood run cold.

'Christer Larsson was the father of the little boys.'

Thoughts were whirling in his head. He cursed his incompetence and asked himself why this thought had not occurred to him. Overwhelmed by the new information, he quickly ended the questioning and thanked his colleagues.

'I have to sort my thoughts,' he said, leaving them to their work, without having touched either the fruit or the water.

* * *

During the difficult hours that immediately followed the unthinkable catastrophe, and with his beloved wife in the hospital, he had taken upon himself the dreadful task of visiting the beauty salon. He had stood by the mother's side, sometimes with his arm around her shoulders, and watched the divers searching for the children's bodies. Only when Christer eventually arrived, escorted by a pair of uniformed police officers, had the split begun.

In the dark labyrinth of sorrow all four of them had wandered, but not together. No one apart from himself had felt up to seeing Solveig. She screamed in desperation and explained again and again in an increasingly cracked voice how the accident had happened. He caressed her and tried to console her, shared the guilt with her, but as time passed her desire to share anything with him disappeared. At last she gave up her desperate attempts to cling to the life that had been theirs, took on all the guilt alone and closed up. No words could give her absolution before the sternest of judges – herself – so she fell silent.

The guilt Ingegärd did not spit out in frothing tirades over Einar she transferred to Christer. It was Christer to whom she had given responsibility for the children when she went to work. It was Christer who had nonchalantly turned the children over to Einar – someone who had no experience with children, who without a thought had left the boys in the middle of the street in a boiling-hot car, along with an even less conscientious woman, a woman with no intuition, a woman who did not know that children are thoughtless, unpredictable.

Christer tried desperately to free himself from the burden that had been placed on him by passing it on to Einar, and this took the form of a hissing torrent of invective about shattered trust, treachery and selfishness, which later changed to vulgar accusations concerning his choice of wife and graphic descriptions of her negligent character.

At last there was silence. At last all four of them had moved so far from each other that there was no longer anything that could be said. Every single one of them chose their own solitude. Ingegärd and Christer could not live with the silence in the apartment, and neither of them could bear to be in the presence of the one who most reminded them of the children they missed. They packed up their things and moved to separate places. He himself remained in his and Solveig's apartment for another three years. Three years of reproaches from himself and others, only the hope that he could help her back to a normal life keeping him going.

When three years had passed he gave up. He could no longer endure the long looks that followed him on the street or the memories that pursued him wherever he went. So he moved to the noise and anonymity of the big city. He bought a townhouse for himself and Solveig, refusing to abandon the dream of a life together with the wonderful woman he had once known.

Until one day he met Kate. An Asian woman alone in a circle of shaved heads and black bomber jackets, cowardly little jerks who took to their heels as soon as he raised his voice. He did not even need to show his police identification to make them scatter. But Kate was shaken. He put his arm around her paternally and treated her to a soft drink and a cookie at a café nearby. She asked what his name was and he answered Eriksson. Perhaps she had not understood, perhaps it sounded awkward or just boring. She called him Erik and that didn't matter. He liked it. They talked about her life in this inhospitable country, about her homesickness for the Philippines, but also about the advantages of Sweden and about her small children, who were doing so well here.

By and by she showed him a photograph of herself with her family, and his heart skipped a beat when it turned out to be Christer she was married to. It felt as if someone had struck him with a bat across the stomach, and everything came back to him with renewed force: the terror, sorrow, guilt.

He tried to stop her; he did not want to encroach on Christer's territory, did not want to awaken old emotions, either in himself or in Christer. But Kate, in her charmingly forward and open way, could not be stopped. She had met a person who listened to her, a person who had noticed a little lost, homesick Filipina among the broad backs in Björn's Garden, so she opened the floodgates and told him a story of depression and inaccessibility, about nightmares, estrangement and mood swings. And he understood – no one could understand better than him what Christer was like to live with – and he gave her the support she so desperately needed to carry on.

They continued to meet. She did not want to let him go and he could not release her, thought that maybe Providence had had something special in mind when their paths crossed. When she and Christer at last decided to go their separate ways and she told him, relieved but with a glimmer of fear in her dark eyes, that she and the children would move to an apartment in Fittja, the reason they had met became clear to him. It was time to give up his dream of a normal family life in the townhouse in Huddinge. He had been given a new chance to do his share, to pay off a little of the great debt he owed *to Christer Larsson. He offered her a considerably more agreeable solution for everyone involved.*

He worked hard and there was not much left over for himself, but nothing could give him greater pleasure than being close to those brown-eyed, silken-haired little rascals, and seeing their happiness among their playmates at preschool and in the light, pleasant apartment with a view of the water. This was the closest to happiness he could come and for the first time in a very long while he felt he had a purpose in life.

In Kate he had also found a friend. Their relationship made no demands and her unforced manner invited openness and laughter. He was a little ashamed however about the secrecy he imposed on her. But she accepted without asking any questions the fact that he did not give out his telephone number and could not reveal his identity. For her, a first name, their friendship and the love he offered her children was enough. That was how it had to be, for more than anything he was watching out for Christer.

* * *

Sjöberg sat in the car for a long time staring into space. He felt that they were very close to solving the case now, but still he did not understand a thing. What was it he was not seeing? Here they had a clear connection between Christer Larsson and Einar Eriksson. In Christer Larsson's eyes, Einar was responsible for the boys' deaths. It was as good a motive for murder as any. But it was a motive to murder Einar and it was far from certain that Einar was dead. And why now, more than thirty years later? Above all there was no motive for Christer Larsson to

248

cold-bloodedly murder his current wife and his children by her. Yet the murders of the two children, which had seemed at first like a chance misfortune, now seemed to make sense in the aftermath of the tragic accident long ago.

When Christer Larsson saw the photograph of Einar he fell apart. That was reasonable if that was how he had found out Einar was involved with his wife and children, especially if he had got the impression that Einar was suspected of the murders. However, that did not necessarily mean he was behind Einar's disappearance. On the other hand, Larsson's cool reaction to the news of the deaths – though possibly due to his numbness and depression since the tragedy in Arboga – could suggest that he himself was the one who had murdered his family. The phrase 'not in the legal sense' came back to Sjöberg again. Christer Larsson clearly considered himself in some way guilty of the children's deaths. Could it have been the deaths of his two sons long ago he was referring to? Presumably he blamed himself for having turned responsibility for the children over to Einar and his wife. No doubt Ingegärd Rydin had blamed him for this and many other things in the wake of the catastrophe, when the accusations came thick and fast, as Edin had put it.

Sjöberg changed perspective. What might be going on in Einar's head? This fresh information cast new light on Einar's involvement in Catherine Larsson and her children's lives. Was this about love? Could it be coincidence that the new woman in Einar's life happened to be married to his old buddy, the father of the boys who had perished while in his care? That could not be the case,

Sjöberg decided. And with his new knowledge of Einar's character it slowly occurred to Sjöberg what it was Einar had devoted himself to. It was perhaps by chance that he had met Catherine Larsson, but what Einar did subsequently had been very carefully thought out. It was not about love at all and what Catherine had said to her girlfriend was correct: she and Einar did not have that kind of relationship.

In reality it was about guilt. It was about the unbearable weight Einar had struggled with ever since the tragic accident at the Arboga River more than thirty years ago. Quite suddenly an opportunity had arisen for Einar to do something for Christer Larsson and his children. Einar had committed his life to giving Christer Larsson's living children and the woman he had chosen to have them with a tolerable life. In that way he was also doing Christer Larsson a service – even if Larsson was and must be completely unaware of it. It was Einar's way of relieving some of his heavy burden, a small joy in an otherwise sorrowful life. Einar Eriksson was a man who lived for a single thing: to atone for his crime by helping the people he had dragged down with him in the fall.

Sjöberg was now dead certain of his case: Einar Eriksson had not murdered Tom, Linn and Catherine Larsson. On the contrary, he had met with some great misfortune. In the worst case he was already dead. In any event Sjöberg did not need to call Ann-Britt Berg at Solberga to ask questions about Einar's shoes. On Saturday he had certainly had them on, but not when the murders were committed, because Einar Eriksson was no murderer. And Einar's wife wasn't either, although her punishment was far worse than that of most murderers.

His thoughts wandered to his own mother. His grandmother considered her a murderer and had rejected her, even though she had managed to rescue her son from the flames. 'All of you were sleeping in the same room,' Grandmother had said, 'but she woke up and took you with her down to the garden.' Why hadn't his father woken up when his mother did? Probably he was already asphyxiated and impossible to rouse. He was certain that his mother's intention had been to run back into the house again to drag his father out to the garden too. But she had not succeeded. For one reason or another she had not had time to get her husband out of the house before it was too late. All of you, thought Sjöberg. How many were there? On a sudden impulse he pulled his mobile out of his pocket and searched through the list of numbers called, and then once again called the Arbogabygden parish.

'We spoke yesterday,' Sjöberg explained. 'Christian Gunnar Sjöberg, born 22 August 1933 – can you please look up his information for me again?'

'Of course,' the helpful woman replied, and after a minute or so she was back. 'What is it you want to know?'

'I want to know how many members of the family there were in 1961.'

He held the phone tightly to his ear, with a strange feeling that her answer would turn everything upside down.

'Let's see now . . . Here he is . . . A proper nuclear family: mother, father and two children.'

Sjöberg felt as if his heart had stopped for a moment.

'Me and . . . ?'

'Alice Eleonor, born on 3 October 1955.'

'Dead . . . ?'

'I'll have to change books. One moment . . .'

Almost immediately she was back on the line.

'Died on 20 August 1961.'

'Now I won't disturb you any more. Thanks very much for your help,' said Sjöberg, ending the call without waiting for her reply.

This was beyond what he ever could have imagined. He'd had a sister three years older and like his father she had perished in the fire. Grandmother had not even mentioned her. Her sorrow encompassed only her son. It was reasonable to think that his mother would have tried to wake her husband and daughter and was forced to trust that they would manage to get out on their own. What could be more obvious in an emergency situation than to rescue the younger child first and hope that the older child would be able to escape?

Sjöberg tried to put himself in his mother's place in the terrible misfortune that had struck her. But there was something that put up resistance, something inside him that would not let him closer to this very distant tragedy. The new knowledge about the sister and her gruesome death was too much for him and he was suddenly no longer able to summon the energy to assimilate his new impressions. Vainly he made the decision to try to keep his personal brooding at a distance for now, to push it to one side and focus on Einar Eriksson's tragedy.

With a listlessness that he did not recognize in himself

he again tried to bring to life the thoughts of the four adults, each of whom in their own way had been hit so hard by the accident at the Arboga River long ago. How would he, in the Larsson couple's shoes, have managed to go on? Would he have had more children? That was impossible to answer. Children are not interchangeable, but perhaps a new child could have relieved their grief for the lost boys, at least at times? Christer Larsson did in time have two more children, but had that helped him? Obviously he had not bonded with the new children, so for him it had not been a successful strategy. Quite apart from the fact that he had now also lost both of these children in traumatic circumstances, becoming a parent again had not turned out well for him.

Sjöberg's own mother had also lost a child. Try as he might, he could not shake off this thought. She had a child in reserve and had been content with that. The circumstances were not the same as for a woman who had lost her only child or all of her children.

Ingegärd Rydin? In Sjöberg's scant experience of women who had lost their children, they either accepted the loss and continued without children or they hurried to try to fill the vacuum with a baby. Ingegärd Rydin had rejected a relationship and thereby also the possibility of bringing new children into the world. But could he be sure of that? It struck him that his investigation of her had been careless. He had found out her name and address, he knew she had once been married to Christer Larsson, that since the divorce she had remained unmarried. What more he knew about Ingegärd Rydin was what he had seen with his own eyes and what the two police inspectors Möller and Edin had told him. He had not made any effort to find out more, because due to her poor health he had immediately removed her from the list of suspects. He had not bothered to find out whether she'd had more children or not after the loss of her two sons. Sjöberg cursed his hasty assumptions, once again took his phone out of his pocket and entered the number of the census office. Four minutes later they called back. Eight minutes later Sjöberg had found out that Ingegärd Rydin had a son. Mikael Rydin would turn thirty at the beginning of April.

* * *

'He's not at home anyway,' said Sandén. 'He's not answering the phone or the door.'

'Where does he live?' asked Sjöberg.

'At Gärdet. In a student room. But he doesn't seem to be pursuing any studies to speak of, because he hasn't earned too many credits over the past few years.'

'What is it he's supposed to be studying?'

'This term it's Music History. Last term it was Introduction to Law.'

'If he doesn't earn enough credits, he won't get any student grant either. He must have a job.'

'He works part-time, five hours a day, Monday to Thursday, at a cleaning company.'

'A cleaning company?' Sjöberg said thoughtfully. 'Could he have come into contact with Catherine Larsson through his job?'

'It's possible,' Sandén replied. 'But they've never been

employed by the same company. We talked to several other students on his corridor. Mikael Rydin keeps to himself. He doesn't attend their parties, never eats with any of the others. He never has visitors, except for the occasional girl, much younger, who spends the night, never more than once.'

'Younger?'

'Read teenage.'

'So what does he do during the day, when he's not studying?'

'Apparently he works out a lot. No one knows how or where he works out, but he usually carries a gym bag. He plays guitar too, they say. For that matter there could be a machine gun in the guitar case. Maybe he robs banks.'

'Does he have a record?' Sjöberg asked hopefully.

'Nope.'

'Any other thoughts? Is he well liked?'

'Of course not. Apparently he barely answers when he's spoken to, but on the other hand he has never made an arse of himself either. He seems to keep a low profile, but according to his neighbours he gives a generally unsympathetic impression.'

'How long has he lived there?'

'Four years.'

'Can you live in student housing if you're not studying? I thought there was a shortage,' said Sjöberg.

'As long as he applies for and goes to classes I guess he can keep living there,' said Sandén. 'Maybe that's why he signs up for those courses. And he has actually earned some credits, but during the past year he hasn't been seen at the lectures at all. So maybe he'll be kicked out now.'

'And no clues as to who his father is?'

'Father unknown,' said Sandén drily. 'Do you think Mikael Rydin is our man?'

'Everything else has felt like a dead end. This guy opens new doors.'

'And his motive would be . . . ?'

'Well,' Sjöberg sighed, tired of endless speculation, 'I guess I'll have to stick with my revenge motive, but I don't have the energy to develop it right now. I'll have another chat with Ingegärd Rydin. There was nothing in her home or in what she said that gave any indication whatsoever that she had a son. I'll find out why. Then I'm coming home. In the meantime you can try to find this guy.'

'Sooner or later he has to show up back at his room. Then we'll bring him in for questioning.'

'Or at work,' Sjöberg suggested.

'As I said, he's off on Fridays. Are you napping, Conny?' Sandén teased.

'I must be,' Sjöberg said lamely.

He was not in a joking mood. Einar must be found and this so-called student was perhaps their best chance.

'It's not enough to sit and wait for him to show up,' said Sjöberg with fresh determination. 'Put all your energy into finding him.'

'Should we go into his room?' Sandén asked cautiously.

'Absolutely not. We have nothing on him and this has to be done right.'

'Look who's talking.'

'That was different! What I did I did out of concern for a missing colleague, not to put him away for murder.'

'According to my feeble understanding, Einar is still the

prime suspect in this case. If it's the prosecutor you're afraid of then –'

'Cut the crap,' Sjöberg interrupted him, half in jest, half in earnest. 'Question Rydin's co-workers, people at his workplace, wherever that is. Find him.'

* * *

'Who is it?' Sjöberg heard Ingegärd Rydin call from inside the apartment.

He crouched down and tried to make himself heard through the letterbox.

'Conny Sjöberg, Hammarby Police. We spoke yesterday. May I come in?'

Unable to catch her reply, he stood up and opened the door anyway. He could see her in the armchair in the living room and she gestured for him to come in.

'How are you doing?' he asked, even though he was not particularly eager to hear the answer.

'I can't get up to answer the door,' she said from the corner of her mouth, and that answer was quite sufficient for Sjöberg, who was struggling not to imagine the blackened remnants of lung she had left to breathe with.

He extended his hand in greeting and then sat down in the same armchair as last time. Her breathing was laboured even with the oxygen. The smell of cigarette smoke in the apartment could not be ignored.

'You have a son,' Sjöberg began. 'You didn't mention that yesterday.'

She let go of the mouthpiece for a moment and gave him a surprised smile.

'It never came up . . .'

Sjöberg had to agree with her on that point. When they had spoken the day before, he had not known about the Eriksson and Larsson families' common past. And consequently he had not mentioned Einar's involvement. And that she had had a son after the divorce had hardly had any relevance then.

'He's thirty,' said Sjöberg.

'Yes, soon. His birthday is in April,' said Ingegärd Rydin, still uncomprehending.

'So he was born rather soon after your and Christer's divorce. Who is his father?'

'I don't know. Life was a little turbulent there for a while. After the divorce and everything,' she added with, Sjöberg thought, a slightly embarrassed expression.

'Since we spoke last I've found out what happened,' Sjöberg said seriously.

She did not answer, but he could see how her slender body tensed in the chair. Perhaps she was also breathing a little harder through her mouthpiece. She looked suspiciously at him, but however much he wanted to he could not spare her from this.

'I'm terribly sorry to have to bring this up, but it's necessary. I understand that it's difficult to talk about, but I need to know what it was like after the accident.'

She did not say anything for a while, perhaps wondering what she should say, what could be said. Sjöberg watched her transformation. He saw how, from having been a brittle creature with an oxygen tube in her mouth, she now became a warrior, almost unnaturally straightening up to steel herself against the difficult things. The

Ingegärd Rydin who lost both her children in a dramatic accident many years ago was a strong woman who did not intend to let herself be broken. She was a person who did not allow herself to be pitied and who kept all the terrible things at arm's length. She had not, like Solveig and Christer, been broken down by sorrow and guilt, nor had she fought on like Einar against a constant headwind. Ingegärd Rydin had kept her pain somewhere deep inside her and never let it come out. Reminders of the unmentionable she squashed like vermin. Sjöberg had to force his way through her solid defences.

'Is that why you're here? Do you think that the murders have something to do with the boys?' she asked with doubt in her eyes.

'The story of the accident is a new circumstance that we have to take into account in the investigation,' Sjöberg answered factually, but hurried to return to what really interested him. 'What was it like after the accident?' he repeated.

'It was tough, naturally,' she said severely. 'At that time there were no grief support groups. You had to deal with your problems yourself.'

'And how did you do that?'

'I divorced Christer,' she answered with a crooked smile. 'We couldn't go on together after what happened. There was nothing left. He packed his things and moved to Stockholm and since then we've not been in touch. I moved here. I couldn't stay living in the apartment.'

'Do you blame him for the accident?' Sjöberg asked directly.

She looked searchingly at him before she answered.

'I did then. I have to admit that. I went to work one morning and when the work day was over . . . I no longer had a family. He farmed out the boys, to some people who did not have children themselves. He should have taken care of them. He didn't.'

'And now? Do you still blame him?'

'No, I suppose I don't. I rarely think about him. But when you said that –'

'About his depression?' Sjöberg filled in.

She nodded.

'Then I actually felt sorry for him. It wasn't his fault, of course. It was their fault.'

'Theirs?'

Sjöberg wanted to hear her say their names, but apparently she had no intention of doing that.

'Her fault,' she corrected herself. 'She knew the boys. She knew how they were.'

'Solveig wasn't slow in taking on the guilt either,' Sjöberg attempted.

'All the same, I can't forgive her,' said Ingegärd Rydin, the muscles tensed hard around her mouth. 'Certain things you cannot forgive, however much you want to.'

'It's probably not so much about your forgiveness in her case. She never managed to forgive herself. Do you know what it's like for her?'

Ingegärd Rydin nodded and turned her face towards the window.

'And Einar, have you had any contact with him?' asked Sjöberg.

She turned her eyes on him again and answered without taking the tube from her mouth.

'He was stubborn to begin with. Wouldn't leave us alone. Begged for our forgiveness and wanted to compensate us in every conceivable way. But we didn't want anything to do with him. It wasn't money we needed. Finally he gave up. He hasn't been in touch since I moved from there.'

'Do you still feel bitterness towards him?' asked Sjöberg, well aware that he was out in rather deep waters, but she answered without hesitation.

'They had responsibility for our children and they didn't manage it very well. As I said, things don't go away just because you make an apology.'

'And Mikael?' Sjöberg said provocatively. 'Did he grow up in this spirit of implacability?'

Ingegärd Rydin looked at him with an expression that seemed almost surprised.

'Mikael grew up without any knowledge of these people. He didn't even know what happened to his siblings.'

It was with something like pride in her voice that she answered the question. Sjöberg reacted immediately to her use of the past tense.

'*Didn't* know?'

'Yes, until I told him about the boys and the accident. And I only did that when he was grown up.'

'When was that?'

'A few years ago. Three or four, maybe. That was when I got sick. I thought he had a right to know his family history. I'm not going to survive this, you realize.'

'You mean that he only found out then that the boys had existed?'

She nodded.

'I showed him pictures of them. Yes, of all of us actually. I never look at them myself, but I thought it was time for him to find out . . . how it was.'

'Did you also tell him who his father is?' Sjöberg asked with a look that he hoped was penetrating.

She opened her mouth to say something, but stopped herself and looked searchingly at him until finally she answered.

'No. That will have to wait a little longer. I didn't want to create problems while I'm still alive.'

'You're protecting yourself,' Sjöberg said conciliatorily. 'Can't bear to bring all the old feelings back to life. Are you afraid you would have to see Christer again?'

She sighed and he saw how she shrank a little in the chair.

'More or less,' she said simply.

He had managed to break through the wall. Sjöberg could feel himself relax, but there were more questions that had to be answered before he could leave this sick woman in peace.

'Will you tell me about Mikael?' he said carefully. 'What is he like as a person?'

'He's a good boy. Has never been any trouble. Considerate and loyal.'

'Loyal?'

Sjöberg thought it sounded like a description of a dog.

'Yes, friendly and accommodating. Helpful.'

What had he wanted to hear? Sjöberg could not put his finger on it, but there was something impersonal in Ingegärd Rydin's description of her son. He happened to think of Christer Larsson. His two children with Catherine had not been any trouble either.

'I imagine it might be difficult to bond with a new child when you've just lost two,' he ventured to say.

'I was never a good mother to Mikael,' Ingegärd Rydin admitted straight out. 'I should have had an abortion, but ... that wouldn't have looked particularly good. I couldn't make myself ... He had to manage a lot on his own when he was small. But he has never seemed unhappy about it. On the contrary ... he's almost suffocating in his attention to me. I guess that sounds hard, but as a single mother ... Sometimes you just need to be left alone.'

Sjöberg hastened to smooth things over. He felt that this poor creature did not need any added burden.

'All mothers feel that way sometimes. And fathers too. I'm a dad myself,' he said with a friendly laugh.

Then he quickly became more serious.

'How did Mikael take it when you told him about the accident?'

'He was upset. At first he didn't believe me when I told him about his little brothers. His little older brothers,' she added with a mournful smile. 'Then he got very sad for my sake, wanted to console me, but I can't stand that sort of thing. I don't like it when people feel sorry for me, not even if it's Mikael. He must have noticed that, so instead he started questioning me about the details of the accident. As you can understand, I don't like talking about what happened, but to get it over with, once and for all, I told him.'

'And showed him photographs?'

'And showed him photographs. He wanted so much to create a true picture of everyone involved.'

'By "everyone involved" I assume that you are also referring to Einar and Solveig?'

'Yes, he insisted.'

'Could I look at those pictures?'

'They're in the second drawer from the top.'

She pointed towards the bookcase behind him and he got up and pulled out the drawer.

'Under the tablecloths,' she clarified before he had time to ask.

He hauled out a thick bundle of photographs held together with a rubber band, sat down in the armchair again and scattered the pictures on the coffee table.

'Is he athletic, Mikael?' asked Sjöberg as he studied the photographs.

'Yes, nowadays he is. When he was little he wasn't interested in football and that sort of thing like the other boys were, but in the past few years he has exercised hard.'

'What kind of exercise does he do?'

'He goes to the gym, I think. He has really built himself up. Mikael was always rather small and slight, but recently he has grown into a big strong man.'

'Do you have any pictures of him too?'

'There are a few photos in the drawer here in the coffee table.'

Sjöberg browsed further among the pictures and when he had gone through the whole bundle he pushed it across the table so that she could reach it.

'Did you show Mikael all of these pictures?' he asked.

She nodded, making no effort to reach for the photos.

'Show me the pictures of Einar Eriksson,' he said urgently.

Reluctantly she picked up the pictures from the table and started browsing through them on her lap. After a few minutes she had gone through the whole heap.

'They're not here,' she said with surprise. 'Mikael must have taken them. There are a few pictures of the boys that are missing too.'

Then her expression changed. A suspicious frown appeared between her eyebrows and Sjöberg sensed a flash of worry in her eyes.

'Why are you here actually? Why are you so interested in Mikael?'

'There is one thing I haven't told you,' said Sjöberg. 'After their separation Christer's wife, Catherine, and their children moved into an apartment she could not have afforded by herself. After the murders it has come to light that it was Einar who bought it for them.'

Ingegärd Rydin looked at him with dismay and Sjöberg could tell her breathing was becoming more laboured again. He hoped that what he was now telling her would not shorten her life further.

'To start with we made the assumption that he and Catherine had a relationship, but that did not turn out to be the case at all. Einar met Catherine by chance and when he realized who she was, or more precisely who her husband was, and then that they were going to separate, he decided to help them. A poor Filipino woman with two small children in an inhospitable Stockholm suburb – Einar thought that Christer's children and wife deserved a better fate –'

'But Christer – didn't he do anything to help them?' Ingegärd Rydin interrupted him.

'Christer is mentally worn out and depressed,' Sjöberg explained. 'He never recovered after the catastrophe with your boys. He never managed to live the family life with Catherine that he had hoped for and he never really bonded with the children. When Einar found this out I imagine he saw the chance of his life to do something for Christer. And his children. Even if Christer himself would never find out about it. Einar never revealed his name to Catherine; it was that important for him not to stir up old emotions. His intentions were good. Now he's gone.'

'Gone? What do you mean?'

'Einar disappeared at the same time as Catherine and the children were murdered. I think he has either been murdered too or is being held captive by the perpetrator. We need to get in touch with Mikael.'

Ingegärd Rydin suddenly became defensive.

'How can you know it's not Einar who is the murderer?'

'That's a possibility, naturally,' said Sjöberg matter-of factly. 'But based on what I've told you, I don't think it seems very likely. Einar wished Christer well. To brutally murder his wife and children does not fit in with that.'

Sjöberg paused before he continued.

'On the other hand, as far as Mikael is concerned I can see a motive.'

She looked at him with sudden ice in her gaze and with great control took the tube out of her mouth before she answered.

'Mikael has nothing to do with this. He's a good person. He calls me several times a week, helps me when I need it. He would do anything for me.'

'Perhaps that is exactly the key to all this,' said Sjöberg

in a steady, friendly tone. 'Perhaps he is taking revenge for your sake, avenging his brothers.'

'By murdering his siblings and his father's wife!' she exclaimed before hurriedly stuffing the tube back in her mouth.

'From what you said, I understood he didn't know that,' said Sjöberg with unruffled calm. 'And in that case, if Mikael committed these crimes, he would have seen it purely as revenge against Einar, against the one who had caused his siblings' death and destroyed his mother's life, who blighted his childhood. What could possibly be better revenge than to take the life of the woman and children Einar was now involved with?'

'But it wasn't that way.'

'But that's how it looked.'

'In that case revenge should have been directed at . . . his wife to begin with.'

'As you surely also told Mikael, Solveig has already had her punishment. I beg you, help us find Mikael. In the best case we'll be able to rule him out of the investigation. Otherwise it may be a matter of life or death for Einar.'

Sjöberg had no hope that this plea would strike the right chord in Ingegärd Rydin. He leaned over and pulled out the drawer where the photos that weren't hidden away were stored and pulled out the pictures there, no more than a handful.

'I don't know where he is anyway,' she said sharply. 'If he's not at home he's probably at work.'

'He's off on Fridays,' said Sjöberg, setting two of the photographs on the table.

'Then he's probably working out; I have no idea where.'

'He appears to work out a great deal,' Sjöberg noted, comparing the two pictures he had in front of him.

One depicted a slender adolescent with an unkempt youthful hairstyle, while in the other picture the same man had shaved off all his hair and obviously prided himself on an upper body of a quite different character. From below one sleeve of his tightly fitting T-shirt a tattooed monster's tail was looking out.

'How many years were there between these pictures?' Sjöberg asked, holding up the photographs so that she could see without changing position.

'That one is from last Christmas,' she answered from the corner of her mouth, pointing at the tattooed athlete. 'The other is from my fiftieth birthday three years ago.'

Sjöberg saw no reason to trouble Ingegärd Rydin further with questions about her son's intake of dietary supplements, but he was beginning to get a clear picture of this unwanted son. He tucked both photographs in his notepad and got up out of the chair.

'You'll get them back,' he said, leaving her, his mind weighed down with apprehension.

scorn and degradation was in store. He made no effort to change position when the big man's silhouette showed in the doorway. Nothing could change what was to come and he intended to take his punishment with dignity, without defending himself. But at the sight of his kidnapper he automatically started stretching the rope behind his back. With tiny, tiny movements he tried to get the stiff rope to stretch a little. He must have done it ten thousand times at this point.

'Now we'll have a film showing,' said the man in a smooth but threatening voice. 'And then I thought we should film you a little. You're starting to look weak, Einar. We have to film you before this is over.'

With his functioning eye Einar met his gaze, without turning away. He was no longer afraid of him, had nothing to fear. The man stepped up to where he lay on the floor and put his hands under Einar's arms. Then he dragged him to the far end of the shed and sat him up against the wall. Then he sat beside him and took a small video camera from his jacket pocket. Deftly he opened the display and turned on the power.

'This will make a nice change, right?' the man said softly. 'I thought that maybe you don't believe me, so I brought visual evidence with me. Look closely now, and we'll see if this is familiar.'

Einar was finding it difficult to breathe. He sensed the worst; he had already been informed in graphic detail about what had happened in the apartment on Trålgränd, but he had not allowed himself to believe that it was true. Despite the cold in the shed, the sweat poured down his face. He closed his eyes and took a few deep breaths; he did not want to faint now, had to force himself to see the devastation he was the cause of.

The film began. With his good eye he saw Kate, a vision of loveliness, lying on the bed beside her children. Little Linn was between her mother and her brother, apparently sleeping with her thumb in her mouth, and Tom lay next to her in his Spider-Man pyjamas; he too seemed to be sleeping peacefully. But then Einar noticed the blood, the massive pools of blood around them. The camera approached them slowly, zooming in on their upper bodies until finally the whole screen was occupied by Kate's lifeless face and slit throat. Einar swallowed again and again, he wanted to vomit, faint, cease to exist, but he forced himself to keep looking. The camera wandered over to little Linn. Blood was still running from the gaping wound across her throat, in fine streams down along what remained of her neck. Then Tom. His head was barely attached to his slender body.

He could control himself no longer, his whole body was in revolt. Convulsing violently, he vomited, sweating and shivering at the same time. Then everything went black.

Not knowing whether he had been unconscious for seconds or hours, he became aware of the kicks and blows.

'Don't go to sleep now, you wretch. You're going to have plenty of time to rest.'

When he opened his eye the man was standing astride his legs with the video camera in his hand, kicking him in the stomach and ribcage. With every kick Einar's head struck the wall. The buzzing sound from the camera told him that his suffering was being recorded.

'Tell me now how you killed my brothers.'

Einar moaned feebly.

'I know your voice is gone, but it's okay to whisper. Look into the camera.'

The man crouched down, holding the camera near his face. Einar took a deep breath and with his functioning eye looked right into the lens of the video camera. Then, for the first time in his life, he told the whole story of how one lovely May day long ago he had been planting flowers with his beloved wife on the balcony, how the doorbell had rung, and everything that had happened after that. He spoke straight from the heart, with no evasions or embellishments, omitting no details from that fateful day. Caring nothing about the baleful man behind the camera, he opened wide the door to what was inside him and told only for himself what he had never expressed before. In a hoarse whisper, he described smells and feelings, smiles and caresses. With his broken vocal cords he described all the words, the screams and the great guilt, the guilt that had bounced back and forth between people but which at the same time had settled like a scaffold over them all.

Einar Eriksson then described the day an angel had come to him, an angel in the guise of a lost Filipino woman with two small children who gratefully accepted his help and attentions, and thereby lightened his heavy burden a little. Nor did he shrink away from the new guilt that had been placed on his shoulders, the selfishness that had driven him into the lives of these poor people and the consequence of his actions: the punishment he was now serving.

While he told his tale, the man crouched in front of him and documented his life story with his quietly buzzing camera. When he eventually stood up and in silence gave him a final well-aimed kick in his already mangled face, Einar Eriksson received it with a newfound joy and a feeling of liberation that he had not experienced since the time before the terrible accident so many years ago.

When the man angrily slammed the door and left him bleeding on the floor of the tool shed again, Einar watched him go with a smile.

* * *

After another visit to inspectors Edin and Möller at the police station in Arboga, to scan and email the two photographs of Mikael Rydin to Sandén, Sjöberg got in the car to return to Stockholm. After a few minutes it started snowing. It had been above freezing in the morning, but now the display on the dashboard showed just below zero. With a sigh he said to himself – for the umpteenth time this year – that spring really seemed to be long overdue. He worked his way gradually along the side roads to the motorway, but when he got there he had to drive much slower than he had hoped as a result of the snowfall.

He took his phone from the breast pocket of his shirt and entered Sandén's number.

'Did you see the email I sent you a while ago?' he asked.

'No, I'm completely occupied with trying to hunt down Mikael Rydin,' Sandén answered drily.

'All the more reason to check your email. I attached a couple of pictures of him. Thought that might make it easier. Are you at the office?'

'Just back in the building.'

'One photo is three years old. I included it as a curiosity. The other photo was taken recently. When you compare the two pictures it becomes rather obvious what this chap has been up to the past few years.'

'Has he had a sex-change operation?'

'He's been taking steroids,' Sjöberg answered, not allowing himself this time to laugh at Sandén's joke. 'From nothing to tattooed muscleman in three years. It doesn't happen that quickly without illegal supplements.'

'Oh hell. What did you get out of Ingegärd Rydin?'

'Christer Larsson is his father. Something that neither of them is aware of. Like her ex-husband, she struggled to produce the right parental feeling – the maternal in her case. The kid apparently had to mostly take care of himself. She considers him helpful and loyal. From her description I would more likely define him as a young man who is desperately seeking affirmation of his mother's love. Three years ago she was diagnosed with COPD, and it occurred to her that her days were numbered. Only then did she tell him about his brothers and the accident. He became very agitated and forced her to show him pictures of them. He also saw old photos of Einar. Those pictures are gone now. She said herself that he must have taken them.'

'Which consequently makes you even more convinced that Mikael Rydin is our man?' Sandén said thoughtfully.

'Anabolic steroids have known side effects, such as

mood swings and uncontrolled outbursts of rage,' Sjö-berg continued stubbornly. 'If you want to feel numb and immortal as well, you can enhance that with a little Rohypnol, which you buy from the same pusher. Jens, I'm quite sure of this. Einar is not having a good time right now. If he's alive.'

There was total silence on the other end. Sjöberg felt that now for the first time he had enough meat on the bones to convince Sandén of Einar's innocence.

'Jens?'

Still no response.

'Are you there, Jens?'

After a few more seconds of silence Sandén finally spoke.

'I give up, Conny.'

His tone of voice was now completely different from the sarcastic, bantering tone that normally characterized his happy-go-lucky personality.

'Not a day too soon.'

'And I know how he managed to sniff out Einar.'

Sjöberg noticed that Eriksson had now suddenly become Einar to Sandén. Evidently he finally saw the significance of his disappearance.

'I'm sitting at the computer now, Conny. Mikael Rydin works as a cleaner at the Larsson children's preschool. I saw him when I was there to deliver the news of the deaths.'

'I'll be damned . . .'

Sjöberg was so astonished at this new discovery that he interrupted himself in the middle of overtaking another car and moved back to the inside lane again.

'It may have been a moment's impulse,' Sandén said excitedly. 'Perhaps it's not the case at all that Rydin has chased after Einar for three years like an avenging angel. Perhaps he just happened to catch sight of him with the Larsson children at the preschool. Pumped up with dubious substances he was struck by fury and a sudden longing to pay back that apparently happy father of two children.'

'But after that everything was probably carefully planned,' Sjöberg developed his colleague's line of reasoning. 'He followed Einar, found out where he lived, charted his habits and struck at a suitable moment. What could be better revenge than taking away from Einar the two small children he cared about most in this world?'

'There we also have the explanation for the emotional coldness in the murders,' Sandén interjected. 'He bore no grudge against Catherine Larsson and her children. The whole thing was aimed at Einar, the poor sod. As you said, Conny. What do we do now?'

'Find him,' said Sjöberg. 'Inform Westman and Hamad and find him. Now.'

* * *

In the absence of any other ideas and after careful consideration Hamad sat in front of his computer and tried to summon the energy to look at the damned film one more time. The door to the corridor was closed and he sat weaving the flash drive between his fingers, unable to bring himself to put it into the port. Right now that was the best he could come up with: look at the film again and try to draw some new conclusions from it. He really did not want to see Petra that way, but he worked hard to convince himself that it was not her, that that drugged woman in a rape situation was not the real Petra. The Petra Westman he knew was strong and stubborn, impossible to bully and would never let herself be exploited.

Like in the boxing room, he thought, smiling to himself. Perhaps it was not the most beautiful side of herself she had shown there, but it was genuine. And she had acted based on what she believed was just. Not right, but just. The image came to him of Petra in the corner, how from his position on the mat he had seen her at a slight angle from below, physically fit and good-looking with a cruelly triumphant smile on her lips. Extras like statues all around: the heavy Holgersson leaning over him with a helping hand outstretched, the referee Malmberg hanging over Petra, Brandt in the doorway flourishing his mobile. Even the sounds stayed with him: a kind of ominous silence that was broken so brusquely by the ringtone from a phone; Malmberg's voice when he answered. And then the draught as Petra passed him, completely unmoved. He preferred seeing her that way.

He sighed and, gathering his strength, put the flash drive in the USB port and navigated through the folders until he found the clip of Petra. He decided to turn on the sound, which hitherto he had always turned off, and let the sequence play.

The video camera must be a recent model – the image was high quality, even if the content wasn't. There was a wealth of detail, despite the semi-darkness of the bedroom. The interior was unfamiliar, the male body unfamiliar – well, would he recognize a man's body even if he had seen it before? It didn't matter however; that was not what he was looking for. But nothing he saw or heard told him anything about the person behind the camera. No shadows, no clothes tossed anywhere, no one sneezing or coughing. There was plenty of sound, but no voices.

After two minutes and fifty-eight seconds it was over. The video camera emitted two tones that announced that would have to be enough and was turned off.

At that moment Sandén came barging into his office without warning and put him to work. Hamad was only just able to bring up a different image on to the screen before Sandén was leaning over the desk.

* * *

As the new image of Einar Eriksson began to appear to Sandén, an unfamiliar sense of loyalty to his colleague grew stronger. It produced adrenaline, which in turn resulted in determination. And it was contagious: Westman and Hamad were also finally convinced by the arguments Sjöberg had lined up.

In Sjöberg's absence Sandén had taken command and he was a man of extremes. True, Sjöberg had flatly refused to sanction breaking into Mikael Rydin's home, but that was this morning. During their latest conversation he had clearly stated that the most important thing was to find Rydin, and as soon as possible. In consultation with his two assistants, Sandén decided they should go into the student room after all.

Westman stayed behind at the station and continued the hunt for people who might conceivably have some idea where Rydin was. Sandén and Hamad made their way back to the student housing high-rise on Öregrunds-gatan at Gärdet. Rydin's student room was more like a small apartment, roughly twenty-five metres square with a bathroom and a galley kitchen. That every apartment had its own kitchen made it easier for the two policemen to get in unnoticed. No one had been out in the corridor, and Sandén had picked Rydin's lock in less than thirty seconds.

The bathroom was simple: shower, toilet, sink and a cabinet containing a basic assortment of toiletries. It was reasonably clean, as was the kitchen. No luxury here either: just a chair, a table and an easily tended potted plant that looked like some kind of fairy-tale tree in the window. The most conspicuous thing was a poster on the wall depicting the Swedish national football team circa 1994, and on the kitchen table an empty ice-cream tub which was now full of bottles and blister packs of pills. Vitamins and other healthy things, according to the labels.

In the main room a bed and a desk competed for space with a bookshelf and stereo deck. He had gone to the expense of a flat-screen TV, DVD player and a stereo with a pair of rather good-sized speakers, but they could be considered among the necessities of life these days. Hamad sat down at the desk and turned on Rydin's laptop, while Sandén went through the CDs, DVDs and books on the shelf, without finding anything of interest. If you did not think that rap music, violent films and action thrillers automatically led to acts of violence. Or legal textbooks, for that matter. In the corner by the foot of the bed was a guitar, and on the wall was an old Kiss poster that must surely have come from his teenage room in Arboga.

Hamad found a few documents on the computer, but they were exclusively study-related texts of an older vintage. He went through various email folders – inbox, saved, sent and trash – without finding anything remarkable. Judging by the Internet history, it was mostly tabloids that interested Rydin, as well as various sports sites that mainly seemed to deal with martial arts and strength sports. The Google history pointed in that direction too. Though he didn't seem to be particularly interested in photography, he had saved a hundred or so photos on the computer, and Hamad reviewed each and every one of them in the hope that he might come across something significant.

Sandén continued working his way towards the bed and was about to trip over a pair of dumbbells when he caught sight of a mobile phone charging on the floor under the bed. It could mean that Rydin was nearby and likely to show up at any minute, which might create problems for them. On the other hand it could mean simply that the phone had been out of power when he was about to leave the apartment. Sandén chose to assume the latter, and when he picked up the phone it turned out to be on. He browsed through the lists of incoming, outgoing and missed calls and carefully noted all the numbers. He did the same with the text messages. Then he went through Rydin's contacts, of which there were only a few, but found nothing that stuck out. The calendar was not used, and there were no interesting notes stored in the phone either. However, Rydin did appear to use it as a camera occasionally, because a dozen or so photos were stored in the phone.

Sandén glanced over towards Hamad at the computer and noted that he too was devoting himself to photos.

'Are you finding anything?' Sandén asked.

'Don't think so. He doesn't take that many pictures. A few Ibiza pictures from last summer are probably the most interesting. Christmas at home with Mum. Drinking party with his workout buddies.'

'The Ugly Duckling, do you know what that is?' Sandén asked.

'A fairy tale by Hans Christian Andersen. Aren't you done with the bookshelf yet?'

'It sounds like a preschool or something,' Sandén said thoughtfully.

'Maybe a café,' said Hamad. 'Think someone said that.'

'So you've heard of it?'

'No, I wouldn't say that. It was something that was mentioned in passing the other day.'

'By who?'

'Don't remember. It was someone at work, I think. What about it? What are you doing?'

'I found a picture on the phone of a sign with that on it.'

'Let me see.'

Sandén gave him the phone.

'It's hanging on a gate,' Hamad thought out loud. 'It looks as if it could be an open-air café actually.'

He browsed further among the pictures.

'Doors. Windows. He could have snapped these pictures when he was planning the kidnapping. To improve security. The locks, I mean.'

Suddenly the tension in the room rose, both of them felt it. It was a straw. But perhaps they were on the trail of something.

'Are you finished with the computer?' asked Sandén.

'As good as.'

'Let's go. Make sure everything looks like it did when we came, then let's get out of here. We have to call Petra.'

Hamad turned off the computer; Sandén set the phone back on the floor, made a quick tour of the apartment, checked that the lights were off and listened for sounds in the corridor. It was silent. They quietly opened the door and slipped out.

As soon as they were out on the street Hamad called Westman and asked her to search for The Ugly Duckling on the Internet. A task they realized could be impeded by the fact that, while she was still on the line, she got 45,000 hits with her first search. They filled her in on their café and preschool theories and then texted her the list of numbers from Rydin's phone. Einar Eriksson's absence felt tangible. In more than one way.

'You don't miss the cow until the barn is empty,' Sandén summarized the situation.

* * *

When they came back from their outing, the after-school teachers had set out juice and popcorn in the cosy corner. The children who were left at school on Friday afternoon would get to watch a film before they left for the weekend. The two couches, like the armchairs, were occupied by other third-graders, so Johan and Max were lying on their stomachs next to each other on the floor, each with a pillow under their elbows, waiting for the movie to start. To compensate, they had a bowl of popcorn of their own in front of them. Johan reached his hand into the bowl to grab a fistful of Friday treats when Ivan suddenly appeared in the doorway. He had not been seen for a while, so Johan thought he had gone home. But now here he was, gesturing to Johan that he should come.

Ivan pulled him out into the corridor, eagerly whispering about borrowing something from the woodworking class. At first Johan did not understand what he was talking about, much less when Ivan pulled out what seemed to be a rolled-up towel from his gym bag. But when Ivan revealed the giant pliers inside the towel the pieces started to fall into place.

'It's a bolt cutter,' said Ivan secretively.

Johan already had his suspicions about what Ivan intended they should use it for, and the thought appealed to him in a way but at the same time not at all. Rescuing the pig was one thing, but by breaking apart a lock . . . ? He was quite certain that was illegal. And to top it off, it was that nasty guitar man's lock. Besides, he suspected that Ivan thought the break-in itself was more interesting than releasing the pig.

'I went to the police anyway,' he said in a lame attempt to get Ivan to give up his criminal plans.

'I see, so the pig has been rescued by now?'

Johan shrugged his shoulders.

'Admit that they didn't care,' said Ivan with conviction.

'Yes, they did . . . Or . . . Ah, they did and they didn't.'

He did not want to reveal the thoughts that were going

through his mind. That there had not been a real police report because he had not dared say who he was. That he had been afraid of what his mum and dad would say if they found out what he had been up to.

'Then we'll do it ourselves. Come on now, Johan, what's the problem? Do you have to ask Mummy for permission first?'

Ivan was apparently a mind reader.

'Probably,' Johan answered with a crooked smile.

And so there he was again. In the clutches of Ivan, whom he barely even liked. He went back into the classroom and told the teacher he was going home. Which was okay if, like him, you had a note from your parents to say that you were allowed to walk home by yourself. Shit.

When they got outside it was dark and gloomy and it had started to snow. Perhaps this adventure would have felt less scary if it had been a sunny spring day. Johan had misgivings, but he did not dare back out, did not want to appear cowardly in front of Ivan, who despite the concealed bolt cutter under his jacket was walking along with light, self-confident steps and presumably felt like a bank robber or something, like he was really cool.

'So what will we do with the pig?' Johan asked. 'We can't rescue it and then just let it freeze to death or be run over, can we?'

Ivan had already thought about that and replied that they could call the cops and give an anonymous tip-off that a crazy pig was running loose on the streets and was dangerous.

'And that bloke. What if he kills us?'

Ivan delivered a smile straight out of an American action flick and patted his jacket.

'He won't do that,' he said, dead certain as always.

So they tramped on through the slushy snow, over towards Tantolunden, Johan feeling increasingly uneasy with a lump in his stomach. He felt no enthusiasm for smashing someone's head with a bolt cutter, animal tormentor or not.

* * *

The snow meant that the trip home took longer than he had hoped, but Sjöberg continued driving after the call with Sandén feeling greatly relieved. Finally he had his team on his side, finally they were all striving in the same direction. They were no longer in a state of ignorance either about who had committed the murders. Now it was only a matter of time before they would arrest the killer. On the other hand, concern for Einar was gnawing at him. They must assume that he was still alive and they must find him quickly. For that reason he felt frustrated when he ground to a halt in a queue of cars at the King's Curve. He felt convinced however that Sandén's, Hamad's and Westman's work would sooner or later result in something substantial, and so he called the police commissioner and asked him to put the national SWAT team on alert. Then he could only keep his fingers crossed that the team would be available. He stretched in his seat, longing to get out of the car and shake the stiffness out of his joints.

From Einar and the dead children in his wake Sjöberg's thoughts wandered against his will to the tragic death of his own sister. He felt an urgent need to confront his mother as soon as possible with his new discoveries. No, 'confront' was the wrong word. He would tell her that he had met his paternal grandmother, that he knew the whole story and that he admired his mother for the strength she had shown over all these years. But he would also force her to tell him everything, from beginning to end. I have a right to my own history, thought Sjöberg. Just as Ingegärd Rydin thought her son had. In the end you have to know the truth about your background, but he would express his reaction differently from Mikael Rydin.

What would this weekend look like? If the hunt for Mikael Rydin and the search for Einar were over in the near future, he would take the opportunity to visit his mother. Åsa would not be happy about it, but she would understand. She would also be eager to know the truth about the Sjöberg family. He should have phoned her. She was probably dying of curiosity about his visit to his grandmother that morning. He ought to call her now, but it was the wrong moment. She taught until late on Friday afternoons and then she would be in a hurry to pick up the kids from preschool and after-school care.

He yawned. He was tired as hell after a quiet night at the hotel without noisy kids to wake him. But if it wasn't one thing it was another. He'd had a hard time falling asleep after the call from Jenny. That little nutcase, thought Sjöberg, smiling to himself. Calls in the middle of the night after lying sleepless in bed for hours. She could just as well have waited a couple more hours so that he could sleep. But Jenny was Jenny, and it was probably just as well that everyone was different. She was a newfound supporter of animal rights. Someone should be.

The pig's rights in society. The pig's right to potatoes. Where did that come from? He shook his head, stepped lightly on the accelerator and moved forward another few metres. Sjöberg happened to think of a children's song he used to listen to when he was little, *The Old Man in the Box*. A song by Gullan Bornemark about a little pig. A breath of nostalgia wafted past him, and he started singing to himself: 'Hurry up, little piglet, hurry up, little piglet. Small potatoes you will get, small potatoes you will get.' Yes, perhaps pigs ate potatoes. 'Potato pigs,' Sjöberg mumbled to himself as the phone started vibrating in his pocket.

It was Sandén calling from the metro. He and Hamad were on their way back to the station and he gave an account of their activities on Öregrundsgatan.

'You're absolutely sure you didn't leave any traces? And no one saw you go in, I hope?'

'Don't worry. The Ugly Duckling – do you know what that is?'

'A fairy tale by –'

'Hans Christian Andersen, I know. But Rydin had a picture of a sign with that name on his mobile. It was on a gate. We're thinking cafés or preschools; do you have any better ideas?'

'What type of gate is it?'

'Classic, white, even though the paint has flaked. A good old-fashioned gate, in short.'

'Then perhaps it's sitting outside a good old-fashioned house?' Sjöberg suggested.

'Wait a minute. Looks like Hamad just thought of something here.'

Sjöberg waited; the traffic was moving a little faster now. Was it starting to free up? Sandén came back on the phone.

'He says that Lotten or Jenny mentioned that café. Or whatever it is. The Ugly Duckling. He's calling reception now.'

'I'll hang on. Jenny, yes. She called me last night.'

'Last night?'

'Three-thirty in the morning,' said Sjöberg with a sigh. 'She couldn't sleep. It was something about a pig. And you clearly hadn't been much help.'

'Oh, that. They were both babbling on at the same time, her and Lotten, and I really didn't have time. Or the energy. But now Hamad is saying something . . . Wait a moment.'

That children's song lingered. 'Small potatoes you shall get, you shall get.' Potatoes, thought Sjöberg. Pigs. Police, police, potato pig, like the children's chant. A pig that rolls in its own shit, Jenny had said. It could mean anything at all. Anyone at all. Pig was a term of abuse. A pig could be a dirty person, perhaps a person forced to answer the call of nature where they sat or were lying. Police, police, potato pig. What if it wasn't a pig this was about but a cop? Could it be the mistreatment of a policeman the boy that Jenny talked about had witnessed? Sjöberg stiffened in the driver's seat and then Sandén was back in his ear.

'Lotten says that it refers to a summer house or something like that. According to the boy, it's the address of the place where the pig is being held prisoner. Where exactly it was she and Jenny didn't have time to find out.

He disappeared as fast as your pay packet when they started asking him for personal information.'

'This is no pig,' said Sjöberg, convinced now. 'Jenny was talking about potatoes. A potato pig, Jens. It's Einar this is about.'

'Agreed.'

Sandén was talking faster now. In the starting blocks, raring to do something. The question was simply what.

'And Petra is not finding anything about The Ugly Duckling on the net,' he continued. 'So it's not an address. It must be the name of the house itself. A summer cabin perhaps.'

'How old was that boy?'

'The girls guess about eight to ten years old.'

'Then it's unlikely that he would have made his way out to the countryside on his own,' Sjöberg stated. 'The shack is not that far away. Within walking distance or close to public transport. I'm guessing a house or an allotment garden.'

'So how the hell do we move ahead?'

'Keep calling Rydin's contacts,' said Sjöberg, suddenly struck by a far-fetched thought. 'But first I suggest you call Barbro.'

'Barbro?'

'If it concerns an allotment garden, there is one person who has seen more of those than anyone else. Barbro Dahlström.'

Their paths had crossed about six months earlier, in connection with the discovery of an infant in a serious condition and a dead woman in Vitaberg Park. Barbro

Dahlström was seventy-two years old and if anyone put a face to the expression 'an everyday hero', it was her.

'Of course! I'll track her down.' Sandén ended the call.

Only a short time ago Sjöberg had considered pulling off somewhere and buying himself a sausage, but now circumstances had changed. With his pulse rate considerably higher, he decided to step on it all the way to Stockholm. He turned on the siren, rolled down the side window and put the flashing light on the roof of the car.

* * *

They sneaked the last stretch up to The Ugly Duckling, crouching behind the hedge. The padlock on the gate was in place, but the gate was old and hanging on one hinge.

'Idiot,' whispered Ivan. 'What good is that padlock? A dwarf could climb over that little gate. Or kick it apart,' he added, while trying to do just that.

But Johan took hold of his arm.

'What are you doing?' he hissed. 'Do you want us to get caught before we've even started?'

'Does it look like there's a lot of people here?' Ivan countered, unconcerned.

'You don't know that. Maybe he's inside there,' Johan replied, nodding towards the shed.

'Do you see the padlock on the door? It's locked, so he isn't in there,' Ivan answered with a snort. 'And the lights are off in the house itself. Come on now.'

He set his foot on a crossbar and easily swung himself over the gate and down into the snow on the other side.

Johan stayed where he was for a moment and listened for sounds, but heard none so he too climbed over. Ivan sneaked up to the door of the outbuilding, pulled out the bundle he had been carrying under his jacket and dropped it on to the path with a thud. Johan listened again and looked worriedly around, but there was not a soul to be seen and only a faint hum from the traffic somewhere in the distance could be heard. While Ivan took the bolt cutter from the towel, Johan put his ear to the door, but he could hear nothing from inside.

Ivan started working on the lock, which was hard to cut through, even though the tool was made for the job. It required a certain amount of arm strength, and Johan was about to lend a hand when he suddenly had a mental image of how the yard had looked when they arrived. He interrupted himself mid-motion and looked down at the snow between them. Footprints, that was what he thought. How stupid could you be? With his eyes he followed a set of clear footprints, large ones, in the snow, leading from the shed to the house itself, but only in one direction. So someone had come to the shed before it started snowing – which must have been a couple of hours ago – and then left during the snowfall. And that person was without a doubt now inside the house. He glanced towards the door and noted that it seemed to have been forced open. His heart started beating very fast.

'You've got to stop, Ivan! He's inside the house. Check out the footprints.'

Ivan stopped and looked over towards the house.

'Damn! Do you think he's noticed us?'

'Maybe not, but we've got to get out of here. Quick!'

Johan got up suddenly and started to run in the direction of the gate. Right then the door of the house opened and the guitar man threw himself down the steps and came rushing towards him. Johan took hold of the gate with both hands and jumped up, and he was still straddled over it in an excruciatingly uncomfortable way when the man took hold of his arm, tore him down from the gate and dragged him over towards the tool shed. During all this Ivan stood as if frozen, with big eyes, and the cursed bolt cutters in his hand, witnessing the scene that was playing out before him. He dropped the tool, whereupon his hands with outstretched fingers went up level with his ears.

'It's cool,' he said pitifully, and that was the only thing said during the whole surprising attack.

Johan saw with dismay how a terrifying set of tattooed biceps seemed about to burst out of the guitar man's T-shirt, as with a blank face he dragged the two boys up the stairs and into the house.

'What do you say?' he said, after throwing them down into a sitting position in a dusty corner of the only room in the cottage. 'Who should I get rid of first, the two of you or the fellow over there?'

'We won't say anything to anyone,' said Ivan, trying to sound convincing. 'We'll just forget about that damned pig.'

'Yes, exactly. You're probably here to steal the garden hose?'

'We promise not to say anything,' Johan repeated, embarrassingly close to tears now. 'Please, just let us go; we'll never come back again.'

'I bet you won't. But there's plenty of room for all three of you.'

He smiled in a strange way, not looking the least bit happy. And then he started kicking.

* * *

With Sjöberg, Sandén, Hamad and above all Eriksson gone, Petra Westman was fully occupied going through all of Mikael Rydin's contacts at a furious pace. Long, tedious explanations about what she wanted, embedded in plausible lies about why, were interspersed with unanswered calls to Barbro Dahlström's home phone. Unfortunately she did not have a mobile. And no one that Westman got hold of knew whether Rydin might have access to a house somewhere. Or knew where he was or what plans he had for the immediate future.

The screen still showed, as if to mock her, her most recent failed search. She had searched countless words in combination with The Ugly Duckling: restaurants, cafés, preschools, playgrounds, allotment gardens, libraries, theatres and on and on, but with no pay-off. While she sat and waited out Barbro Dahlström's customary five rings she considered the possibility of calling all the sign makers in the region, but a search on Eniro came up with 228 hits so that was impractical in the short term. Besides, according to Hamad they were looking for an old gate and therefore presumably also an old sign.

Instead she came up with the idea of searching for other fairy-tale titles in combination with businesses she had already tried, in case all the buildings in the neighbourhood were named after fairy tales. This too was without success however. Suddenly it struck her that the basic idea was not so dumb after all. If The Ugly Duckling was in an area where all the houses have fairy-tale names, the street itself ought to have a name that reflects that. After a number of searches, some more wildly imaginative than others, in Eniro's maps she struck gold. She entered Sjöberg's number.

'Fairy-tale Lane,' she said. 'There's a street in the Tantolunden allotment gardens called Fairy-tale Lane. It's a stretch, but it's the best I can come up with right now.'

'Well done, Petra. We'll follow up on it. And I feel that it's urgent now. I'll see about getting armed-response officers there from the national SWAT team and some ambulances. Mikael Rydin may be there and he may be armed. If Einar is there, he's presumably in bad shape.'

'Understood. Where are you now?'

'Just passing Segeltorp. I'm hurrying.'

'When will you be there?'

'In the best-case scenario I can be at Tantolunden in ten or twelve minutes in this weather. If nothing unforeseen happens. Wait for me.'

Sjöberg checked his watch.

'I'll see you there. No sirens, no commotion. If Rydin is there, he must not suspect anything in case he manages to flee. Keep me informed about where you all are.'

'Okay, all systems go,' said Westman with an audible smile.

'I just hope we're on the right track,' said Sjöberg. 'And if we are, that we get there before it's too late.'

* * *

Einar Eriksson felt as if he had finished his life's project. Describing his fate in his own words, putting words to all the emotions and thoughts that had crowded the anthill of his mind, was a marvellous liberation. The frightening man who was Ingegärd's son had unknowingly done him a service in the midst of all the degradation.

While he lay there on his side on the cold plank floor he routinely stretched at the rope behind his back. Tug-tug-tug-rest, tug-tug-tug-rest. The rope stiffly resisted. Occasionally he tried to slip one of his hands through the loop while the other held still, but his hand was too big, the loop too small. A trickle of blood from his nose ran into the corner of his mouth, but that did not worry him. Because, with a jubilant joy in his chest, he gave himself the forgiveness he had coveted for over thirty years. Thirty-one dark years of being grief-stricken, of self-pity and bitterness. And now suddenly, with the very declaration of his heavy guilt, it was as if it had been lifted from him. That a few words from his own mouth could grant him consolation!

It was his hastily made decision to be sincere that had paved the way. To completely and honestly express the unvarnished truth, free from mitigating circumstances and unbalanced self-criticism. That the bloodthirsty butcher who imprisoned him here had had the pleasure of witnessing his oral autobiography did not bother him. This was just about him, not about his self-appointed judge and executioner or anyone else in this world. He had settled accounts with his inner voice and suddenly they understood each other, suddenly they were on speaking terms.

With this new perspective he looked out of the little window opening by the side of the door and while his hands worked he saw the heavy snowfall outside suddenly stop. A ray of sunlight made its way in through the glass and where it cut through the cold air in the tool shed the specks of dust came alive and danced in the narrow beam of light.

With an unfamiliar sense of hope and an energy that came from somewhere deep inside the aching shell that was his body, he prised and tugged at his ropes. And finally, as if someone up there took pity on him – or was it in fact he himself who controlled his own fate in the end? – one hand glided through the loop.

A smile on his lips, he remained lying in the same position for a few minutes, panting after his great exertion. Then he set his free hand on the floor and rose to a sitting position. He fumblingly loosened the knot that had held both his hands together and managed to pull his other hand out of its loop. Greedily he reached for the water bowl and emptied it in one gulp, before giving his stiff fingers a little time to regain their normal mobility. Then he freed his feet from the rope that held them together and also fettered him to the wall behind him.

Where had his terrifying kidnapper gone to? Had he left him for the day? A kick in the face after that self-revealing story and then it was over? That did not seem likely; he did not recognize the pattern. A single kick was never enough. This man needed much more than that to give vent to all the fury he carried inside him. He must be somewhere in the vicinity. He must be lying in wait nearby to give him false hope that the daily quota of hits and kicks was already fulfilled. But why had he left him so quickly? Was there something in his story that had caught him by surprise, something he had not known about?

Suddenly it struck him that perhaps Ingegärd's son had not known who Christer Larsson was at all. His revenge had undoubtedly been aimed only at him. Perhaps it was only now, during the filming, that it had occurred to the murderer that the children he had so cold-bloodedly executed – Tom and Linn – were the children of his own father. That the Larsson children were actually the half-siblings of the children he was avenging, Andreas and Tobias.

Einar Eriksson pictured the small angelic children alongside their beautiful mother in the bed. Enchanting – if the circumstances had not made everything so inconceivably ugly. For the first time since he was very young he allowed himself to weep. A stream of tears ploughed furrows through the dirt on his cheeks.

The perpetrator could come back at any moment to continue to take vengeance, to work off the setbacks of his life. Einar Eriksson got up laboriously from the cold, hard plank floor. Now there was no time to lose.

* * *

When Sjöberg arrived at their agreed meeting place on the outskirts of the allotment gardens, he was only a couple of minutes behind Westman and the others, who as per his orders were waiting for him among the cars. A group of police from the national SWAT team had already set off to search for the house in question, and one of them, Hägglund, now came back to inform the rest.

'It's up there,' she confirmed, to the great relief of Sjöberg and the others. 'The gate is fastened with a padlock
that they're removing now. Straight ahead is a little house
with stairs up to the door, eight steps. The lock has already
been forced. Immediately to the right inside the gate is an
outbuilding, also locked with a padlock, but we'll force the
door when we go in. And someone is in there, at least two
people. In the main building certainly, perhaps in both.
There are plenty of tracks in the snow.'

Sjöberg nodded and divided the assembled police officers into two groups.

'We'll storm the two buildings at the same time. You
take the house, we'll take the shed. No unnecessary shooting. Our highest priority is to get Einar out alive so he can
quickly get medical care. He will presumably be very weak.
All communication equipment off. Now let's go.'

Suddenly it stopped snowing and immediately a gap
in the cloud cover unexpectedly let through the sun's
rays and revealed a patch of clear blue sky. Sjöberg and
Sandén were first in line, half running with Hägglund
between them. She explained that no one had driven on
the little gravel road since it started to snow, but that
they had seen the tracks of two people before they themselves walked on the road. Otherwise the entire allotment
area seemed totally deserted, as expected at this time of
year.

They moved ahead in silence. Sjöberg turned around a
few times to reassure himself that the others were there.
They looked absurd, the police from the SWAT team,
with their helmets and visors among these idyllic little
cottages, surrounded by white snow-covered fences

and well-pruned hedges. He was struck by a sense of unreality.

'Are we close?' he asked Hägglund in a low voice, without revealing the anxiety that was gnawing inside him.

'It's not far now. The plot is over there to the right. Soon we'll be at the hedge by the side of the shed.'

They joined up with the group of police officers who were already on the scene, and Sjöberg slowed his pace. Then, crouching, he slipped along the last stretch of the side wall of the shed to find a suitable gap in the hedge through which he could look into the plot.

The whole place looked decrepit. The garden had not been taken care of for several years, the gate was rotted and hanging on one hinge. In the little yard sure enough there were a large number of tracks in the snow. So there were at least two people here, and the unnecessarily sturdy padlock that locked the door to the garden shed suggested that at least one of them was inside the house itself. And sure enough it looked as if the outside door had been broken open. It would not be particularly difficult to get in. And as far as the shed was concerned it would be easier to force the door itself than the lock.

Sjöberg slipped back to the group.

'Judging by the tracks in the snow Rydin is inside the house,' he explained. 'And he is presumably not alone. The door is broken and should just pull open. There is probably just a single room in the house. I'm guessing that there will be loud creaking when we're going up the steps, so once we're there it's quick response. I'm guessing that Einar is still in the shed, which is locked with a big padlock from the outside. I agree that we should try to break down the door. Everyone with drawn weapons, but no shooting unless necessary. We probably won't need to fire, unless he already knows we are here. Any questions?'

'Should we wait here or back off a little?' asked one of the paramedics.

'Here is fine, but stay down if there's any shooting,' Sjöberg replied. 'If you're needed, we'll let you know.'

He looked around at the serious faces, but no one seemed to have anything to add.

'Good luck. Now let's go.'

Someone from the SWAT team had opened the gate, and one group made their way to the right and positioned themselves outside the tool shed, with a number of heavily armed, helmeted police officers in the lead and Sjöberg and Westman in the rear.

The other group ran quietly up to the steps leading to the ramshackle little house. Hamad and Sandén, who also kept behind their division of the SWAT team, turned towards Sjöberg and awaited his signal. When Sjöberg's raised hand cleaved the air like the stroke of an axe, the tense silence was broken and they rushed with drawn pistols and pounding hearts up the stairs and tumbled into the only room of the house.

At a table next to the wall the sought-after Mikael Rydin was sitting calmly on a wooden chair with a video camera in his hand, in the process of filming something that Sandén couldn't make out at first. But suddenly someone let out a long, heart-rending scream, which prompted Hamad to swing into action. He rushed over to the corner in front of Rydin and threw himself on his knees. There sat the boy that Sandén had encountered at the police station, staring at them wide-eyed. He did not let out a sound, although blood was streaming from his nose. Next to him another boy was lying in a foetal position. Sandén thought at first that he was unconscious, until it occurred to him that he was the one who had screamed.

Showing no visible reaction, Rydin let his gaze wander between the police officers from the SWAT team, who all stood prepared to shoot him if need be. Then he closed up the camera's display with a little click, and turned off the power on the device. While Hamad took care of the terrified boys, Sandén rushed out and summoned the paramedics. Only then did he have an opportunity to make a more or less formal arrest of the apparently unperturbed assailant.

'Mikael Rydin, you are under arrest, suspected of a bloody lot of crimes,' he said in a louder voice than the situation demanded, now that Hamad had at last got the hysterical boy to be quiet. 'What those are you'll find out at the station. Slowly set down the camera and put your hands with your palms upwards in front of you on the table. We will not hesitate to shoot if you put up any resistance.'

Mikael Rydin impassively did as he was told and one of the armed-response officers walked purposefully up to the table and put handcuffs on him. Another stood behind him next to the wall and together they pulled him to his feet and propelled him out on to the steps. Sandén seized the video camera and put it in his jacket pocket.

At Sjöberg's signal two of the policemen from the SWAT team threw themselves against the thin wooden shed door. The door flew into the shed with the police hurtling after it, while the two hinges and padlock stayed behind in the doorframe. Sjöberg was in a hurry to get in, but a number of broad-shouldered police officers stood in front of him in the doorway, blocking the view.

'Oh my God,' he heard one of them moan from inside and he tried to force his way in, but the wall of backs would not let him through.

Actually, they seemed to be backing out of the little shed and Sjöberg was forced to take a few steps backwards too. Then an awful stench of faeces and urine struck him and he hoped that was the only reason the policemen in front of him had complained.

'Let me past!' Sjöberg roared with a fury in his voice he could not really explain.

A few of the police officers rushed in and up to something that Sjöberg still had not managed to identify. With Westman a step behind him he entered the shed, and the sight that met his eyes confirmed his worst fears. Someone switched on the bare light bulb in the ceiling and they could see an empty dog bowl on the floor and a few short ropes lying among the crumbs of a little dry bread. The floor was approximately six metres square, and was completely covered with human excrement. Attached to the far wall was a solid rope that had been hung over a beam in the ceiling, and on the floor below was an overturned little wooden stool. Above it, with a loop of the rope wrapped around the neck, hung the thin, dirty, bloody and almost unrecognizably battered body that had belonged to Einar Eriksson.

Three of the police officers from the SWAT team were

already in the process of taking him down as Sjöberg rushed up. When they had laid the body carefully on the floor he crouched down by Eriksson's side and put two fingers against his carotid artery. The body was still warm but he felt no pulse.

'Ambulance!' he screamed as loud as he was able in his agitation, and Westman rushed out of the shed to meet the paramedics.

Instinctively Sjöberg started artificial respiration, but the ambulance personnel were there right away and took over the resuscitation attempt. Sjöberg stood up and backed a few steps away from the body on the floor. Petra Westman slipped up to his side. He pulled her to him and put his arm around her, more for his own sake than for hers. They stood there like that for several minutes, watching the increasingly resigned paramedics working at their hopeless task.

'How long has he been dead?' Sjöberg ventured to ask in a cracked voice, when they finally gave up.

'Not long. A few minutes I should think,' one of the ambulance personnel replied.

'It's my fault,' said Sjöberg. 'I shouldn't have made you wait. You should have gone in without me.'

'Conny, without you we wouldn't even —'

Sjöberg was not interested in Westman's excuses. His body felt heavy. His grief squeezed his heart as if it were a rag to be wrung out, grief for a colleague he had never been close to but now wished more than anything to get to know. Everything around him seemed to play out in slow motion. His way of relieving his mind from this great misfortune was to focus on the perpetrator.

'That bastard!' he interrupted her. 'Have they arrested him?'

The words echoed in his head, he felt almost ready to faint.

'They're taking him over to the cars now,' replied one of the armed-response officers, who had now taken off his visored helmet and stood with it in his hand.

He suddenly looked quite human, and Sjöberg noticed that the other police officers did too. They were all standing together as if to attention with their helmets in their hands, watching in silence as the ambulance personnel carefully placed Einar Eriksson on a stretcher, covered him with a blanket and started carrying him out.

Sjöberg felt that Westman was seeking his gaze, but he was unable to respond and instead followed the ambulance personnel out of the shed. In the doorway stood Sandén and Hamad, who had also witnessed the resuscitation attempt in distress, but Sjöberg had nothing to say to them. In silence he went back to the cars, needing no one's company.

Johan Bråsjö was sitting in one of the ambulances being looked after by a paramedic when Sandén climbed in and sat down across from him.

'Well done, kid,' he said in a joyless voice. 'But you have no idea how lucky you were.'

'Lucky?' said Johan, looking over at one of the police vans, where a couple of police officers were roughly shoving in the handcuffed man.

'That guy isn't content just to kick. And we lost a man. That was no pig you heard being mistreated, it was a policeman. But that guy is going to get his punishment, thanks to you.'

'But . . .' said Johan, and Sandén saw the tears welling up in his eyes, 'I should have realized . . . I should have made a proper police report.'

'I should have listened to what you said. What you did was completely amazing. You should get a medal.'

Johan lit up, obviously proud to receive the policeman's praise, and Sandén hoped that the guilt that seemed to be transferred like an epidemic from person to person in this story would leave this young chap untainted.

'Now you should go home. They say you're okay, both of you. I'll ask someone to drive you.'

'And you? Can't you come along?'

'I have to go back to the police station and make sure that guy ends up behind lock and key.'

After a lacklustre thank you to the SWAT team, Sjöberg went over to his colleagues, who seemed to be waiting for him, all three with their hands shoved deep in their pockets. Because he could not find the words to describe what they all felt, he skipped that and went directly to the practical.

'Petra and Jamal, thanks for your efforts. Take off for the weekend now and go home and rest up.'

They both looked as if they wanted to say something, but the nod he got in response from Westman was enough for Sjöberg.

'I'll question Mikael Rydin. Jens, if you want to be there, you're welcome. Otherwise you can take off for the weekend too.'

'Of course I'm coming,' said Sandén.

'I'll call Hadar and describe the situation, and inform Kaj Zetterström about the autopsy and Bella about the crime scene investigation. Your reports can wait until Monday. Have a nice weekend.'

The gathering of cars and people dispersed. The Tantolunden allotment garden area was once again empty and deserted. The only evidence of the drama that had just played out in the little idyll was the tracks in the snow, but soon they too would be gone. After its late entrance, the sun had already disappeared behind the small cottages and darkness fell quickly.

Friday Evening

After watching Mikael Rydin's repugnant video on the TV in the conference room together, Sandén and Sjöberg sat for a long time staring at the flickering screen. Neither of them could think of any way to start the conversation that was now unavoidable. Finally Sandén went over and turned the TV off.

'The video is evidence,' he said. 'It has to be archived.'

'What do you think Einar would have thought about us seeing it?'

The question was actually directed mostly at himself, but he did not know what to think. Sandén hesitated a little before answering as he sat down again.

'It was good to get to see Einar as the person he really was,' he replied thoughtfully. 'And I don't mean the degradation or the circumstances, I mean the person behind all that. And behind the bitterness, which was all we got to see here at work. We got explanations for a few things, but above all he suddenly became a real human being, with memories and dreams and feelings. Despite the fact that so often during this . . . confession, or whatever you want to call it, he described himself in negative terms, I think he seems to have been a . . . pretty amazing human being. Damn it, there's a lot of shit I regret!'

His voice broke and for the first time in their lives

Sjöberg saw Sandén cry. He himself had had his handkerchief out during the almost hour-long viewing.

'If I hadn't asked you to wait for me, you would have got there in time,' Sjöberg said in distress.

'We'll never know that,' said Sandén. 'In any event I don't think that would have made it better. He didn't want to go on. What happened was for the best. What was there left for Einar to live for?'

'You can't think that way,' Sjöberg objected. 'He was dehydrated. Physically and mentally broken down. How can we know how he would have felt after a few months? With the right care. And support from those around him, from us, for example.'

'But didn't you see the joy in his revelation there on the floor? Even though he was lying there half broken, he told his story with a drive, a kind of motivation that I had never seen in Einar before. He seemed . . . happy. And I've both seen and heard that you get like that once you've made the decision. He had already decided, Conny. There was nothing we could have done to change that. And to answer your question: I think that Einar both wanted and knew that we would see that video. It was his suicide note. Besides, it contains so much evidence and so many motives that the trial of Mikael Rydin is going to run itself.'

'And how much fun do you think that man's life has been so far? Unwanted, even in the womb. Born as replacement for something irreplaceable.'

'Most of us wouldn't execute innocent people right and left for that,' Sandén pointed out.

'We'll have to see what he says,' said Sjöberg, getting up.

*

Mikael Rydin looked tired now more than anything else. The mask of self-control he had worn at the arrest was gone. Despite his impressive muscle mass he looked small, sitting alone in handcuffs on the other side of the table during the initial questioning. The two police officers studied him for a while in silence before Sjöberg started to speak.

'Mikael Rydin.'

Dully Rydin met his gaze. At a guess, the presumed Rohypnol had stopped working. He no longer seemed to consider himself invincible.

'Son of Ingegärd Rydin and Christer Larsson.'

Rydin suddenly looked panic-stricken. Sandén could not help smiling a little.

'Didn't Mum tell you?' he asked in a silken voice.

Mikael Rydin stared somewhere between them without answering. Sjöberg retook command.

'I saw Ingegärd this morning. She confirmed what I had already worked out with a little simple maths. She probably didn't hop into bed with a strange man so soon after losing her two boys. They probably tried to stay together for a few difficult months after the accident, but for understandable reasons it didn't work out. You were conceived during that time, Mikael.'

'And now you've slaughtered your little siblings and their mother,' Sandén continued. 'You have nearly battered to death and in the end drove to suicide the person who cared for them and helped them have a good life in this country. You have sent your own father to hospital, possibly with incurable brain damage.'

'I just wanted to avenge my brothers. For Mother's sake. All the rest . . . I don't know about.'

Gone now was the fury that must have driven the young man. He looked fearfully at Sandén and nervously pulled on his fingers until the knuckles cracked.

'Do you think that Einar and his wife intentionally let your brothers die?' asked Sjöberg without expecting any response. 'It was an accident. It was not even negligence, it was sheer bad luck. And do you know who managed best after the catastrophe at the Arboga River? Your mother. She is the only one who managed to live a life after this accident without overwhelming guilt and serious mental harm. Something that you, Mikael, will never get to experience. Because what you've done, you have done with the intention of killing and injuring. That's quite a different thing. However angry and embittered you are, and however much revenge you take, you can't change what has already happened. And you don't shake off that guilt easily.'

'I had no fucking idea –'

'You should do your research properly, Mikael,' said Sandén condescendingly. 'That's job number one. But you have a real knack with the hunting knife, I must say. Where do you keep it?'

'In the cottage,' he answered.

'In Tantolunden?'

He nodded dejectedly in response.

'That was a nice video you made,' Sandén continued. 'When they let you out of prison in about twenty years perhaps that's what you should take up. But of course, if you're sent to a secure psychiatric unit, you'll probably never get out.'

Mikael Rydin looked at his hands without saying anything.

Sjöberg suddenly felt that they had nothing to talk about with this man right now. What they were doing was just persecution, exacting revenge for Einar Eriksson and for the Larsson family. What they were doing right now was to carefully make sure that Mikael Rydin would not leave that room without feeling guilt. And suddenly he was convinced that Einar would have wanted to spare him that.

This entire case had been about guilt, age-old guilt, and that was also what a lot of other things in Sjöberg's life were about right now. But Einar, who had lived most of his life with a guilt that knew no bounds, would not have wanted his worst enemy to go through the same. Vehemently Sjöberg shoved his chair back and stood up. Sandén looked at him with surprise, but seeing the determination in his superior's posture he realized that it was best to do the same.

'We'll break off here,' said Sjöberg, already on his way towards the door.

Sandén followed obediently, without really understanding why. Just as they were about to leave the room they suddenly heard Mikael Rydin's voice behind them.

'Forgive me,' he said quietly, but Sandén was not in the mood.

'Soon there will be no one left who can forgive you,' he answered in an ice-cold voice. 'You've killed them all. Mum doesn't have much time left and your old man . . . well, it's doubtful that he'll recover. And if he does, maybe he won't be that eager to hang out with you. But chew that over, my friend.'

By the time he had finished speaking Sjöberg was already far away down the corridor.

* * *

It was with some surprise that Eivor Sjöberg let her son in so late on a Friday evening.

'What in the world do you want, Conny? It's past nine o'clock.'

He gave her a hug and a quick peck on the cheek.

'We need to talk, Mother. And I don't intend to leave until you've told me what I want to hear.'

'Oh dear, that sounds serious,' she said with an innocent little smile, even though Sjöberg was sure she knew what he wanted to talk about. 'Do you want coffee?'

Actually he would have preferred a whisky, but because he would be driving he said yes to the offer. He sat down on a chair at the kitchen table and hung his jacket over the back. While she busied herself making the coffee with her back to him he told her about his visit to his grandmother. When he mentioned her he noticed his mother stiffen at the counter.

'She was openly hostile,' said Sjöberg. 'I only stayed for a short while; it was almost unbearable. I managed to get out of her what I wanted to know anyway. But I think that both you and I would feel better if you, who was there, told me your version.'

His mother rattled the china as if to drown out her thoughts, to defend herself against the unavoidable.

'First, Mother, I want to say that I think you have

been an amazing parent. And you still are. I admire your courage and your persistence. You gave me a very good upbringing and raised me to be a useful and well-balanced person. I'm not accusing you of anything; that's not what this is about. And I understand what you've gone through. Only now do I understand what you've gone through. I'll say it again: I truly think you are an admirable person. I also realize why you haven't told me anything about this before. It was your way of getting through all the difficult things, and you did what you thought was best for me. But now I need to know, Mother. You have to tell me. The whole story about the awful tragedy that happened that night and what happened later.'

His mother's movements had stopped, but she still stood with her back to him. He wondered whether she was crying. He could not remember ever having seen her cry. The coffeemaker emitted a bubbling sound and the comforting smell of coffee permeated the kitchen.

'Come and sit down now, Mother,' Sjöberg said amiably. 'The coffee is almost ready.'

'Would you like a glass of liqueur with your coffee?'

'No, I really shouldn't . . .'

This was the closest to a yes his mother could get in answer to that type of question, so Sjöberg got up and took down a bottle of orange liqueur he himself had bought on some previous occasion from the cupboard above the fridge. He fetched a liqueur glass from the cabinet in the living room.

When he sat down at the table again he poured the glass almost full and waited in silence until the coffee was ready at last. His mother served them each a cup and finally sat

314

down across from him at the kitchen table. He set the glass in front of her and carefully sipped the hot coffee.

'Would you like a sandwich?' she said suddenly, but Sjöberg did not intend to let her off the hook any longer.

'Tell me now, Mother. I know how tough you think it will be and it's hard for me too, but I'm here with you.'

He placed his hand over hers and she made no effort to pull it away.

'Tell me about Alice,' he said gently, looking her right in the eyes.

This time she did not turn her gaze away and he saw the tears welling up in her eyes. He took hold of her hand more firmly.

'I can't talk about Alice,' she said slowly.

'You have to, Mother. I want to get to know my sister.'

His mother took a deep breath and then it burst. The tears ran down her furrowed cheeks and for the first time she let go of what had held her up for so many years – the silence. Sjöberg could not hold back the tears either during his mother's story, which struck a familiar chord inside him.

During the hours that followed they cried together and hugged, while they made their way through the troublesome journey that would come to summarize his mother's entire adult life and Sjöberg's childhood. She told him about *an August night in 1961 when Eivor Sjöberg was woken in the middle of the night by the strong smell of smoke and unmistakable heat in the bedroom on the top floor. Beside her in the bed was her husband, Christian, and she screamed and shook him, but he would not wake up. She tried to pull him up, but he was unresponsive and very heavy.*

'Alice!' she screamed, but her daughter, almost six years old, who was lying furthest away from her, closest to the window, would not wake up either.

She rushed up to Alice and shook her. Her curly red hair was spread out like a fan around her small freckled face. The girl twisted in bed and opened her eyes.

'Alice!' she screamed again. 'There's a fire! You have to run down to the yard! I'll take your little brother!'

From the ground floor the sound of exploding windowpanes was heard. She rushed back over to the double bed, and using all her strength she managed to prise her husband's heavy body on to the floor. Then he finally woke up and grunted something incoherent as he raised himself to a sitting position.

'There's a fire, Christian!' she yelled, as she tore the blanket off the little boy who was sleeping soundly on a mattress on the floor and picked him up in her arms. 'Take Alice and get down to the yard!'

Before she left the room she turned towards her daughter, who had closed her eyes again and rolled over on to her side. But Christian was panting and swearing on his way over to her, crawling on all fours.

'Alice!' she howled again and again, unable to decide what would be the best thing to do, but rather than not do anything at all she made her way down the stairs with her son in her arms.

The lowest part of the stairs, like the entire lower floor, was already on fire, and the flames were licking the dry beams in the ceiling. It could only be a matter of minutes before the fire spread to the top floor. She ran out into the farmyard and set the boy, who had been woken by the noise, down at a safe distance from the burning building. Then she ran back to the house, but the sheet of flames she encountered now was impenetrable. She would have been burned in a few seconds if she had tried to run through the fire in her nightgown with her hair loose. From the door she could see the burning stairs, *and there was no chance she could make her way up them and then down again. Instead she screamed her husband's and her daughter's names again and again, rushed back out to the yard and stood where she could see the bedroom window.*

'Alice! Christian!' she bellowed at the top of her lungs, and then looked around on the ground for something she could throw at the window.

She found a log that she heaved up towards the window, which smashed to pieces.

'Alice!' she screamed again. 'You have to jump through the window! I'll catch you. Alice! Alice!'

A few steps behind her stood the boy, witnessing in silence his mother's impotent struggle against time and fire. And suddenly the little girl actually appeared in the window. Alice was stumbling around behind the broken window and now their eyes met. With a look almost of surprise on her face she looked from her mother to her brother and the scream that was forced up from her mother's throat cut through the air like a knife, her scream at the sight of her daughter's hair suddenly flaring up and the fire standing like broom bristles around her startled face. A face that was twisted in torment before she fell back and disappeared from view, out of their lives and out of her little brother's memory.

The mother took the boy and ran. Their nearest neighbours lived several hundred metres away, but she ran. She ran like she had never run before, with her child in her arms and with bare feet in the darkness on the gravel road. At last she got there and the news spread from house to house that the Sjöbergs' cottage was in flames, and everyone who could went there and helped try to put out the fire. The girl was beyond all help, but the husband, the father, they found lying on the floor and managed to get him out to the farmyard before it was too late.

Eventually, after he had been transported to the big hospital in the capital, he regained consciousness, but with the horrific burns he had incurred it would have been better if he had died. Eivor Sjöberg never let her son see the unrecognizable remnants of his father while he was still alive, and she did not let him attend the funeral either.

The loss of her daughter was too much for Eivor to even mention during the difficult months that followed, with her husband in hospital and her in-laws on the warpath. They could never reconcile themselves to the fact that she had managed to save herself but not her husband – their son. And they were never able to accept her reasoning when she rushed down to the yard without first making sure that everyone in the family was on their feet. They did not leave her in peace with her sorrow until she escaped out of their sight, away from the countryside where she had grown up, taking the painful little likeness of their beloved son with her.

Naturally enough she ended up in Stockholm, where Christian was being treated, and that was the beginning of the life Sjöberg remembered as his childhood. What had brought them there was never spoken of, and what was there really that could have been said?

But many tears, many cups of coffee and many glasses of liqueur later Sjöberg had a feeling that together he and his mother now had a new, better future ahead of them.

* * *

It all felt unreal. Hamad was sitting on the red line of the metro and did not recognize himself. It was as if he was observing himself from outside. He was not in his body, not part of the grey crowd around him either. Hovering above, outside. Nothing hurt, nothing had any significance. He leaned back in the seat with his legs outstretched, with no consideration for the other passengers who were sitting packed together. He said to hell with everything and everyone, taking a much-needed momentary holiday from sense and etiquette.

At Telefonplan he got off the train and was brought back to reality by the chilly evening air. The image of Einar's body just cut down from the ceiling beam came to him again, and with it also came the bad conscience. Weak sense of self, he thought. And then, Peer pressure. Which he immediately rejected as an evasion. He himself bore complete responsibility for his own actions and the way he had treated Einar Eriksson. Likewise his blinkered attitude during the whole investigation.

Instead of following the streets over to Tvingvägen, where Petra lived, he took a short cut in the dark across the deserted athletics field. An idiotic choice for a solitary walker, but he didn't care. Whatever might conceivably happen he would deserve it. Or would he? After all, he had done a few things right. He was the one who had discovered Einar's involvement in the case. And where Petra and Jenny and those videos were concerned, then . . . Well, perhaps he was not a completely awful person.

He quickened his pace and was soon back in the glow of the street lights, on Klensmedsvägen. Now he had to pull himself together a little; he could not descend on Petra unannounced after such a long time and be totally depressed himself. He should support her after this terrible day, and after what had happened that Friday evening at the Clarion almost a year and a half ago. He would show her that he was there for her, whatever happened.

Just as he was about to cross the street and make his

way over to number 24, Petra's building, his attention was caught by a car that was parked right next to him. A dark-red Lexus sedan, more prestigious than you would expect to find on a Friday evening outside an apartment building in Västberga with highway E4 as its nearest neighbour. He knew he recognized it, but at first he could not think whose it was. The wrong person in the wrong place – thoughts were whirling in his head. And then the penny dropped.

And the recollection that had been chafing in the back of his mind ever since the duel with Petra in the boxing hall came out into the light again. There above him stood Holgersson, about to help him to his feet. In the doorway stood Roland Brandt as if frozen in mid-motion, in the process of bringing his mobile to his ear to answer a call. And there over in the corner leaned Petra, glistening with sweat, with her hands still in the boxing gloves and a broad smile on her face. A triumphant smile? Yes, perhaps – then why? Because she had beaten the shit out of him? Or was it because of something else? Where was her gaze directed? Gunnar Malmberg was leaning over her, blocking her into the corner with his hands on either side of her face. As if to hold her back. Don't fight any more now, Petra.

No. That's not how it had been. *She* was looking right into Malmberg's eyes. *He* was marking territory. Petra's smile was not triumphant – well, maybe so, but not because she had knocked out Hamad but because she . . . had knocked out Malmberg. And what had he been whispering to her? 'Take off the gloves and calm down' or 'I'll swing by on Friday evening'?

What was it Petra had said when she told him about her latest conquest? That it would not be anything, *could* not be anything more. And of course that's how it was. Malmberg had a wife and kid and was deputy police commissioner besides. Of course there could never be anything in it. So what was this?

But Hamad was not clear about the boxing hall. He tried to recall that perspective, from below, when he had been lying on the mat, aching and dazed. What was it that happened then? Images, sound. The enchantment was broken, Malmberg's mobile rang. That sound, yes, what was that ringtone? He had only let it ring for a short time before he answered. A single instrument . . . Guitar. Hamad recognized the tune; he had to remember it now. He knew it was important – why was it important? It didn't matter; out with it now. Why did he recognize the song, was it something he liked himself? Apparently. Guitar . . . Could it be Clapton? There it was, it was 'Layla'. Unplugged.

And then he had answered. Hamad had no trouble remembering what was said. 'Talk to Lu– or that new girl. Jenny . . . Sure. No problem.' Was that important too? Perhaps. Who was he talking to? Impossible to figure that out. What did what he had said mean? 'Talk with Lu–'? Lundin, presumably. Lundin and Jenny – what did they have to do with each other? Nothing. Lu-Lu-Lu . . . No, not like in Lundin, the pronunciation had been different. Skåne dialect? No, why should it be that? English? Lu-Lu-Lu . . . Lucy? Lucy in the sky . . . It wasn't possible. Would Malmberg know about that, and Jenny? How? Had he been on amator6.nu? And why that particular one, when there were thousands of sites to choose from?

Back to Petra again. The film of the rape. He knew that he had a fragment of a thought somewhere, a thought that he hadn't yet had the opportunity to follow through. It was close now, he could feel it, achingly close . . . The camera sweeps across the bodies in the bed and then . . . pling-plong, off. No! The sound of the camera being turned off would never be heard on the video. It was another sound that he had heard before the film clip finished. Pling-plong – it was two notes from a guitar. Eric Clapton's guitar. 'Layla'. Unplugged.

Hamad cast a furtive glance up towards Petra's apartment window. A light was shining cosily in there. What were they doing? But that didn't matter, they would never be a couple. They *could* not be a couple. For two reasons. One: Malmberg would never give up his career and his family for her sake. And two: he was not interested in being with Petra. He was a rapist; he was punishing her. Without her even knowing it. Rape was about power, not about sex. Petra had put a spanner in the works for him and he could not tolerate that. After having failed to get her fired he had changed tactics. He had conquered her. She had voluntarily given herself to the man who had once raped her. And that gave him power, triumph.

Hamad did not know at first what he should do. The only thing he was certain of was that under no circumstances whatsoever should he tell Petra. That would kill her. It was not often he agreed that ignorance was bliss, but in this case he was convinced. There would never be anything between Petra and that jerk, and he did not begrudge her living happily not knowing that she had had a short-term relationship with her own rapist.

And what could he do himself? Not much. The Other Man had never left anything behind that could be used as evidence in a prosecution, so it was not possible to put him away for anything. And this was only circumstantial evidence. In an unofficial investigation. But Hamad would keep watching him, would have Malmberg in mind if anything turned up. But first of all he would get the confirmation he needed, for the sake of his own peace of mind.

He turned back towards the metro to go back to the police station. In his mind's eye he saw an empty Ramlösa bottle standing on his desk. And ringing in his ears was a name that Petra had mentioned when she told him about everything that had happened: Håkan Carlberg at the national crime laboratory in Linköping.

* * *

Before Sjöberg could start his weekend there was one more thing he had to do. During the conversation with his mother it had slowly dawned on him what he had been doing over the past six months. He felt both loathing and relief when the revelation came to him that the woman he had seen in Margit Olofsson's lively green eyes and billowing curly red hair was none other than his own sister, Alice.

It was with Alice he had sought consolation when life felt hardest, and it was in Alice's arms he rested when a longing for something unknown, something he could not put into words, got too great. The constantly recurring dream of the woman in the window was simply his final terrifying memory of his sister, and her image had aged with him. Actually it was an almost six-year-old girl who stood up there in the window swaying while the fire consumed her from behind, but in the dream his subconscious had reinterpreted the inconceivable as something more comprehensible. The little girl had assumed a woman's proportions and the woman had gradually taken the form of someone he knew, someone he liked. The patient, warm, nurturing Margit Olofsson had unknowingly filled the almost fifty-year-old vacuum of his big sister, and in a completely wrong way at that. The little boy's boundless love for his older sister had been transformed into the middle-aged man's yearning for the female body. It was time to end what never should have begun.

'I'm going to tell you the truth, Margit. The truth about who I am. It's not flattering for you and even less flattering for me, but I still believe it must be best to know the truth.'

She looked at him with her big, green eyes and he saw that she was frightened by the seriousness in his voice. A slightly worried smile fluttered across her lips and Sjöberg made his own interpretation.

I don't want to hear, I don't want to know. But I must to be able to go on. Satisfy my curiosity.

Sjöberg said, 'You're not going to want to see me any more after this, and that's good. Good for you and good for me. Maybe you'll forgive me some day, but do so in that case for your own sake.'

She put her hand over his and he took hold of it. Now she was just a person to him. A fine, loving person he felt

324

the deepest respect for. Never more would he cry in her arms, never more would he make her dance to his tune.

They sat in his car on the driveway outside her house. Margit's husband was not at home. She had asked Sjöberg to come in, but that would have been wrong. Her house was her home; it should not be their meeting place.

'I've had a dream,' said Sjöberg. 'The same dream, over and over again.'

Then he told her about a woman in a window, about grass wet with dew and bright-red hair. Sweat and desperation.

Margit did not say anything. She looked searchingly at him, but she did not want to interrupt with questions that could not be answered anyway. He squeezed her hand hard and continued talking.

'I didn't know what that dream meant. But I know that when I met you there at the hospital last autumn it was so obvious to me that that woman in the window was you. I could not resist the temptation. It was wrong, but I wanted so much to get to know the woman in the dream.'

Margit still made no effort to pull back her hand. He caressed it gently with his free hand, not to reassure her but as a final sign of the tenderness he nonetheless felt for her.

'I visited my mother today,' he continued.

Then he told her about the fire, about the night when Eivor Sjöberg's life had fallen apart and his own had changed completely, without him knowing it.

'I stood down in the yard and through the window I saw my sister burning inside. How her beautiful red hair caught fire.'

Margit pulled her hand out of his grasp and put both hands in front of her mouth.

'I've mistaken you for my sister, Margit. I'm so sorry. Something in you gave me something that I have longed for all these years. Something . . . I didn't know what it was. But it was not physical love I needed. The whole thing is a terrible misunderstanding. My life is a confused search for a lost sister. I'm a dirty old man who sees a little girl, my own sister no less, in an amazing woman. In you. But I want you to know anyway that I never would have done it if I'd known all this. There are limits for me too.'

She took her hands from her mouth and to his surprise he saw that she was smiling. A friendly, sympathetic smile, and she stroked him carefully across the cheek with the back of her hand.

'I'm sorry,' she said with sincere warmth in her voice. 'Not because it's over, but for what your family has been through. I hope you can stop having that dream. I'll go now.'

She opened the car door and stepped out into the cold night. Her breath came like smoke out of her mouth as she leaned forward and looked at him, her green eyes glistening in the light from inside the car.

'There is nothing to forgive, Conny,' she said with a little frown between her eyebrows, which Sjöberg recognized as a sign of candour. 'And you'll have to work on your own conscience. I was reconciled with mine many years ago.'